THE SILVER MISTRESS

THE SILVER MISTRESS

by

Peter O'Donnell

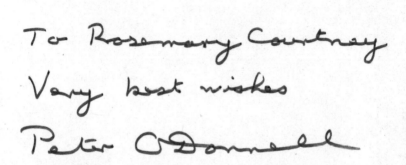

To Rosemary Courtney
Very best wishes
Peter O'Donnell

SOUVENIR PRESS

First published 1973 by
Souvenir Press Ltd, 95 Mortimer Street, London W1N 8HP
and simultaneously in Canada by J. M. Dent & Sons (Canada) Ltd,
Ontario, Canada

ISBN 0 285 62112 2

Printed in Great Britain by
Clarke, Doble & Brendon Ltd
Plymouth

CHAPTER ONE

Quinn wondered vaguely if he was going to die for the miserable reason that he had no particular wish to continue living. The thought produced a spurt of angry contempt in him which cleared his muzzy brain a little, and he muttered, "Gutless bastard."

Slowly he eased his thin wiry body to a sitting position on the broad ledge of rock, and lifted his good hand to push back a lump of hair which had fallen over his eyes.

His head throbbed, and he knew that he was concussed. The period of lucidity would not last long. Soon his mind would drift away from reality, as it had done half a dozen times in the hours since he had fallen, and he would again lie in a stupor, troubled by dreams and memories which made the sweat start from his body.

Six hundred feet below him, the waters of the Tarn whispered in the great gorge as the river wound its way west to join the Garonne. Not far above him was the top of the gorge. It was here that he had stood when the pale March sun was at its height, looking across at the scrub-dotted face of the canyon wall on the far side, looking down at the dark waters which had spent a million years cutting this valley through the French limestone, and trying to feel something, anything other than bleak despair. But the ancient majesty of all that lay before his eyes brought no touch of healing.

He remembered turning away, easing the small pack on

his back. It was then that his foot must have skidded on a mossy piece of rock. He did not remember falling, only coming slowly to consciousness, with nausea tugging at his stomach and a hammer pounding ponderously in his head. That was three hours ago now. He had been able to measure the time by looking at his watch during moments when his head was clear. He had hurt his left wrist in the fall. It was swollen and shiny from the fingertips almost to the elbow. Broken perhaps. He had taken off his wrist-watch because of the swelling.

Carefully he studied the hands of the watch, and absorbed the fact that it was now three-thirty. With an effort he got to his knees and made his eyes focus on the almost sheer stretch of rock which rose above him. Only eighteen feet, and there were a few niches and crevices. Absurd that he could not climb it. But his left hand was useless, and on the two occasions when he had made a fumbling attempt to climb he had been forced by dizziness to abandon it quickly and sit down to avoid another fall.

Quinn looked about him. The ledge was moon-shaped, twenty paces long and six feet wide at the point where he knelt, tapering away to nothing on each side of him. The only way out was up. Apart from the concussion, which made his co-ordination clumsy, he doubted that he could have made the climb without two good hands.

Once more he wondered if he was deceiving himself, if subconsciously he lacked the will to try because he did not really care what happened to him.

His mind clouded again, and there was a time of dream-like confusion, shot through with flashes of the old night-mare. For the hundredth time he saw the grenade rolling along the aisle of the aircraft, bobbling from side to side like a grisly roulette ball choosing its slot. He heard the cries of fear as the passengers shrank away from its passing,

6

huddling in their seats. He saw the white-faced man, sitting with his wife and the little girl, dive forward in what could only have been an attempt to smother the thing under his own body. But the black pineapple lurched under the seat, and was still rolling when it roared its frightful death-cry.

Quinn jerked to wakefulness, shuddering, his hands pressed over his ears. Sweat was dripping from his chin, but he ached with cold. He studied his watch. Four o'clock. Dusk would fall soon, and so would the temperature, close to zero. In his pack was a light showerproof top-coat, a bar of chocolate, and a flask which had held coffee but which had been punctured when he fell. Not much of a survival kit, he thought dully. One night of exposure might not kill him, but a second would do the trick.

It came to him that there would have been little point in climbing to the top, even if he had been able to do it, for he was on the wrong side of the gorge. Here there was no road above him, only a narrow path which dipped and soared as it wound its tortuous way past the ravines slicing the canyon wall, a route to test a fit man. On the far side of this path lay a stretch of broken rock and then the belt of firs he had come through earlier. Beyond the trees stretched the arid region of the Causse de Méjean, a depopulated area so waterless that the few sheep which grazed there had evolved a camel-like ability to go for long periods without drinking. There you could travel a dozen miles and find only an ancient shepherd and his wife living in a crumbling village which had once boasted a population of twenty.

The road which followed the gorge lay a thousand yards away, on the north side of the great gash which contained the Tarn. He could see a short stretch of it from where he sat, a hundred yards of sharply curving bend. He remembered now that during earlier periods of consciousness he

7

had twice waved his handkerchief on seeing a car and a truck pass along that stretch, but they had been in view for no more than ten seconds, and the chances that anyone might spot him in so brief a time were scarcely worth reckoning.

"Up the creek, you are, Quinn," he told himself, and grinned foolishly. "Up a big, big creek without a paddle. Have some chocolate, son. Maybe you can keep it down this time. Full of energy, chocolate. Nearly as good as spinach . . ." It was as he fumbled in his pack that he saw, across the valley, a toy-like van, a Dormobile perhaps, creep slowly into the bend and come to a halt. After a moment, two penguins climbed out of the cab.

Quinn thought about this laboriously, then gave a nod of satisfaction, wincing as his head throbbed. "Nuns," he mumbled. "Can't fool Quinn. No, sir. Sisters of mercy, God bless 'em. The hand of the Lord works a miracle for good old Quinn. Come on now, little sisters, look this way and see me waving."

He could make out the white blobs of their faces surrounded by the black wimples as he began to wave his handkerchief, three short waves, three long. The penguins began to walk slowly round the curve of the bend. They stopped, seemed to speak together, and one of them pointed down the road. They moved on, halted for a few moments, then turned and walked back to the van. There they stood waiting, doing nothing, neither of them so much as glancing across the gorge.

Quinn's arm ached with the effort of waving, and his head was swimming again. He allowed his arm to fall. "Today's miracle will not take place," he thought. Raising his eyes to the sky, he shrugged and said without rancour, "Please yourself, you bloody old tease."

He ate some chocolate and sat watching the distant

figures. His throat was parched and there was a taste of bile in his mouth. When his vision blurred and his mind began to slip stealthily away again he was unaware of it.

*　　*　　*

The younger of the two nuns, the one with the round pretty face, stood by the line of once-white stones which rimmed the outer side of the bend and which had once been a low wall. Beyond them there was nothing, for here the side of the gorge was more than sheer, leaning out over the river a long six-second drop below.

Her companion stood by the Dormobile, a woman in her middle thirties with a fresh complexion and a face in which the strong bones were dominated by a large, proudly-bridged nose. The younger nun looked up the slope of the road, then at the seamed wall of rock which bordered its inner side.

She sniffed and said, "About time we 'ad word from 'is nibs. Don't want to 'ang around 'ere all bleeding day." Her voice held the adenoidal accent of Liverpool, faintly overlaid by an American twang.

The second nun looked at her sharply. "I'll not tell you again, Angel dear." Her voice rose and fell with the sing-song lilt of the Scottish Highlands. "When we're wearing the habit it's as nuns we speak, even with each other. And besides, it's not becoming for a young lady to speak so coarsely."

The girl laughed, her muddy eyes malicious. "I s'pose it's becoming for a lady to run a cat-'ouse in New Orleans?"

"Och, you've a nasty tongue in your head today, Angel. If I once provided a particular service for gentlemen there, it was no more than a professional necessity. It wasn't I

9

who made the world the way it is, and we all just have to do the best we can."

"All right for Madam Clare. You should've tried some of them services they wanted."

"We'll not discuss *that*, dear," the older nun said stiffly. "You were glad enough to take the job at the time, and it's long finished now anyway. You're very lucky that I chose you to bring along with me when I was offered such an excellent new position."

"I was the only one with the guts for it. Can you see Maisie or Jacquie or any of 'em doing a good job with a razor or a bit of piano wire? Besides, sometimes I think you're a bloody old dike, and fancy little Angel a bit." She grinned like a vicious child.

The lips beneath the handsomely hooked nose tightened. "You're a very dirty-minded girl, Angelica. I think a word to Mr. Sexton is called for."

The younger nun's face grew wary. She knew she had gone too far. You could never make Clare lose her temper, she thought, but when the old bitch started calling you Angelica it meant she was angry. And Clare angry was Clare dangerous. The muddy eyes lost their sparkle of malice and became contrite, wheedling.

"No. I'm sorry, Clare, honest. I just get a bit excited when there's a job on, and say daft things. You know. Don't say anything to Mr. Sexton. He put me through it something 'orrible last time——"

She broke off, and together they swung round at a faint sound. A man had dropped to the road from the twenty-foot high cliff which bordered it. He wore dark slacks and blazer, with a pale yellow shirt and a black cravat. Field glasses hung at his chest. Six feet tall, he was broad-shouldered and walked with a quick step of extraordinary lightness, as if his feet scarcely touched the ground. His square face was framed in a neat golden halo by thick curly hair and a beard. The eyes were pale blue. About him there was an air of bounding vitality and the impression of a man from another age, a throw-back. Dressed in armour and with a broadsword in his hand, he would have been the traditional image of Richard the Lionheart.

Clare said, "Ah, there you are, Mr. Sexton." Nobody called him anything other than Mr. Sexton, not even his employer. The man smiled and nodded. He had just covered a mile, moving fast over scrubby broken rock, but his rate of respiration was normal.

"And there you are, dear ladies. The car is on its way and should be here in less than five minutes. Are you ready?"

"Quite ready, Mr. Sexton. There's no change in the arrangements?"

"None, Mrs. McTurk. You and Angel will manage the initial stage. I shall remain out of sight and watch for approaching traffic until it's time for the kill."

"Very well, Mr. Sexton. But I'm sure Angel and I could handle the whole matter without difficulty. The lassie has her wire handy."

"I've every faith in you both, Mrs. McTurk." The eyes glinted with laughter. "But if you allow Angel to use her wire, I'll be very cross with you, and I'm sure you'd have little taste for my corrective treatment."

Angel giggled. Clare's fresh cheeks lost some of their colour. "Och now, there's no need to talk like that, Mr. Sexton. I've never failed in my duty yet. It was a suggestion, just."

"Then forget it, Mrs. McTurk. This is a very important operation and we have precise instructions for it." He moved to the side of the road where the rock wall of the cutting dipped to little more than eight feet, jumped and

11

caught the edge, drew himself up so easily that he appeared to flow over the top, and vanished from their view.

Angel moved to the Dormobile, took out the jack and rested it against a wheel. "I 'ate that bastard," she said idly. "He can make you wish you was dead with no damage to show for it."

A thousand yards away, beyond a dozen of the bends which contorted the serpentine road, the Peugeot 504 kept a steady pace. In the back, Sir Gerald Tarrant yawned. He was tired but happy. Tired because he had spent a wearisome week in Brussels chairing the Co-ordinating Committee for Nato Intelligence, and had now been travelling across France for the past eight hours. Happy because in another twenty minutes or so he would arrive at L'Auberge du Tarn, a small inn perched above the river below La Malène, and there Modesty Blaise would be waiting for him.

He would spend four days in her company, doing nothing except walking, fishing, and probably losing a few pounds to her at bezique of an evening. He could not remember looking forward to anything so much in years. She was the most restful of companions. He half-smiled at the thought, for it was a paradox. Those who knew only what she had done rather than what she was like would never have dreamt of applying the word restful to Modesty Blaise. He wondered if, with sufficient low cunning, he could coax her to talk about one or two of her exploits, but was not optimistic about his chances of success.

Both she and her remarkable friend and retainer, Willie Garvin, seemed to have a fixed aversion to giving any detailed account of their activities, either during the years when she had run the criminal organisation known as *The Network*, with Willie as her right arm, or since their retirement, when Tarrant had been able to make use of them simply because they found that the spice of occasional danger had become an addiction.

A touch of melancholy pressed down on Tarrant. Sooner or later they would go on a job and not come back. It was inevitable, and even in the past year they had come within a whisker of it twice. There was a little comfort, though not much, in reflecting that the last and fatal job would not be one that he had instigated. For some time now he had refused to use them for any further operations. It would not even be a job of their own seeking, he admitted. They seemed born to trouble. It simply came to them.

Tarrant fingered his greying moustache and sighed. With an effort he pushed back the shadow of melancholy and watched the constant movement of the driver's shoulders with the turn of the wheel on the winding road.

"All clear on your instructions after you've dropped me off, Reilly?" he said.

"Yes, sir." Reilly's dark red head nodded. "I carry on to Millau, book into the *Moderne* there, and wait two days for Mr. Clayton to make contact. Further instructions from him. If he hasn't shown up after two days, I ring the office for orders. March code, variation six."

"Good." Tarrant leaned back in his seat. Reilly had been his driver for two years now, and was an efficient man, well able to deal with a routine courier job. It occurred to him that Reilly had been unusually silent during the long drive. Normally he would make a little small-talk—not too much, just an occasional five minutes of casual conversation in that soft Irish voice. Reilly could invariably tell when his master wanted to be quiet.

"Anything wrong?" Tarrant asked.

He saw Reilly give a little start. Then the man shook his head. "No, sir. I'm fine. What makes you ask?"

"Oh, you seem rather quiet."

"I thought you'd be having a lot to think of after the week in Brussels, sir. Didn't want to disturb you."

Tarrant realised now that his own long silence, ever since Nevers, had probably given Reilly the impression that he wished to be left in peace. But he had not been thinking about Brussels, he had been thinking about his coming few days of holiday.

It was Willie Garvin who had suggested it two weeks ago, at Modesty's penthouse overlooking Hyde Park, when she had invited Tarrant to dinner and had remarked that he looked tired.

"Tell you what, Princess," Willie had said in his gravelly voice as he refilled Tarrant's glass. "You're spending a couple of weeks on the Tarn, so why not talk Sir G. into coming down for a few days? Do 'im good."

Tarrant remembered the hopeful pleasure he had felt as she lifted an eyebrow and smiled at him.

She wore a long dress of dark blue silk that matched her eyes. Regrettably it covered her splendid shoulders, but it set off the long column of her throat admirably. Her black hair, piled in a chignon, was in what he always thought of as her grown-up style. When she wore it loose, either in bunches at her ears or tied back behind her neck, she looked far younger than her years. She said, "It's a nice idea, Willie, but Sir Gerald's a VIP. He can't go running off for a long week-end with a woman of doubtful reputation."

"Will you be alone?" said Tarrant. "Willie's not going with you? Or . . . anyone else?"

"Willie's going to be with his titled girl-friend on her farm in Bucks."

"Lady Janet?"

"Yes. His faithful steady, and very nice to come home to. Much better than he deserves. What about it, Sir Gerald?

I'll be staying at a little inn on the Tarn. Would you care to risk your reputation?"

"More to the point, what about your reputation with the patron?"

"Patronne. What will really shock Mme. Martine is giving us separate rooms. She's very romantic."

"She would surely take my advanced age into account?"

"A mature gentleman lover is an established tradition in France."

Tarrant laughed. "I'd better pretend to be your elderly uncle."

"You really mean you'll join me? It won't be exciting. I just walk, and laze, and watch the river go by."

Willie chuckled. "Go careful, Sir G. When the Princess says 'walk', she means she goes roaming out over the causse with nothing to eat or drink, no shoes, no blanket, like a perishing nomad. If you want to learn 'ow to stay alive finding berries and fungi, catching rabbits, milking a ewe, and eating things to make a hyena think twice, you'll 'ave a ball." He looked at Modesty. "You'd better not keep 'im out all night though, Princess. I don't think 'e'd fancy curling up in a gully with dead leaves for a blanket. Oh, and don't give 'im snake to eat, like you gave me that time in New Mexico, remember?"

"I remember the fuss you made. And it was a garter snake, much nicer than the worm snakes I've eaten in the Zagros when I was small."

Tarrant stared from one to the other and said, "I expect you're pulling my leg?"

Modesty gave him an apologetic look. "Not really. I like to revert to my childhood ways now and again. Like an aborigine going walk-about. It stiffens the sinews, and it's nice when I stop and come back to this." Her little gesture took in the spacious dining-room, the gleam of silver and

15

glass on the long table, and the sumptuous silken glow of the Shah Abbas carpet.

Tarrant said doubtfully, "I'm sixty-one, my dear. Such activities might stiffen *my* sinews in a less metaphorical fashion."

"That's where Willie's pulling your leg. He knows I wouldn't go walk-about with you there. You could have a nice rest and we'd just do whatever you happen to feel like doing. There's good fishing to be had, so maybe you could teach me how to handle a rod?"

"It sounds like Paradise," said Tarrant, and meant it. "I'm more than grateful."

Now he was within a quarter of an hour's drive from the Auberge du Tarn, looking forward to a bath, dinner with Modesty, and a leisurely cigar as they talked afterwards, perhaps by a window looking out over the river, with the cruel and devious world of his profession forgotten for a few blissful days.

It was extraordinarily kind of her, he thought, considering the sweat, toil and blood she had expended for him. Scars could be invisibly mended by surgery, but that did not cancel the reality of torn flesh and pain. He was responsible for at least two bad wounds her body had borne. How she could have any affection for a man who had put her at appalling risk on several occasions he could not fathom. But there was no doubt she was fond of him in some very real way. Perhaps he was a kind of father-figure to her, he thought. If so, he was well content with that, and had no inclination to ponder how intriguing it would now be if he were thirty years younger at this moment.

His thoughts were interrupted by a sudden slowing of the car, and he saw that they had entered a downhill bend where a Dormobile stood parked at the widest point, a jack standing by one wheel. There were two nuns, one studying

16

an instruction manual, the other looking hopefully towards them.

Reilly brought the car to a halt ten paces away, switched off the engine and said without looking round, "Shall I give them a hand, sir?"

"Yes, you'd better. They look rather lost."

Reilly got out, then opened the rear door. "Like to stretch your legs, Sir Gerald?"

"No, just carry on. I don't feel like making laboured French conversation with the good sisters if it can be avoided."

"I thought you might fancy a breath of air, sir."

Tarrant looked at the man curiously. His face was pale and there was a film of sweat on his brow.

"If I want to get out I'll make up my own mind, Reilly. Are you all *right*?"

Reilly's hand came into view. Absurdly, there was a revolver in it, pointed at Tarrant, a ·38 Smith and Wesson Bodyguard with a two-inch barrel. Tarrant blinked once, then caught at the slackening muscles of his face to prevent his jaw sagging in a foolish gape.

"Get out," Reilly said in a low voice.

Tarrant looked down the barrel which could drive a piece of lead into his body at a velocity of 855 feet per second. So Reilly had sold out to the opposition. Or to somebody. The opposition did not usually go in for killing or kidnapping Heads of Intelligence these days. The profession had become much more sophisticated since the almost open warfare of the fifties.

Slowly he slid along the seat to the open door, and saw Reilly step back a pace, keeping the gun levelled. Tarrant was getting the first primitive reaction of shock and fear under control now, and said quietly, "You know I'm carrying no documents, Reilly."

"Just get out."

Tarrant obeyed, wondering what he could do. "I'm over sixty," he thought. "Reasonably fit, but the edge is long gone and I've no experience of this." Ironic to remember that he had been responsible for the training of hundreds of men and women for this kind of situation. He had visited the big house in Surrey where they were sent for instruction, and watched them at work, but he had little idea how best to tackle Reilly.

He saw the two nuns moving forward. They were part of it, of course. Glancing along the road towards them he said, "I take it the nuns are all part of the team? And the gendarme?"

Reilly's head twitched round, and in the same instant Tarrant took a pace forward and struck at the forearm with an outward sweeping motion, to carry the gun out of line. His body hit Reilly's chest to chest, and his knee came up hard for the groin. It almost worked, but he was a fraction slow. Reilly had seen in a split-second glance that there was no gendarme, and had turned slightly so that the knee drove into his thigh. Then the gun looped over and hit Tarrant on the side of the head. It was only a glancing blow, but enough.

He staggered, sparks exploding before his eyes as his mind reeled, and would have fallen but for the car at his back. His limbs were rubber, and he half turned, clutching at the car to prevent himself going down. The nuns were there in front of him now. Something jabbed hard against his back, and from behind him Reilly's voice said in a husky whisper, "Keep still!"

Hands gripped his arm, and he felt the sleeve of his jacket being pushed back. He tried to wrench his arm away, but the hands holding it were very strong. For a moment his vision cleared, and he saw the face of the taller nun.

She locked his wrist under her arm-pit and said, "The needle, Angel." The face of the other nun swam into Tarrant's view, a young and pretty face, marred by the eyes. They were muddy brown, and the eyes of an evil child.

There came a sharp prick, followed by the small but longer pain as the injection coursed into him. Then nothing.

Reilly stepped back, lowering the gun, and wiped his brow as he watched the two women ease Tarrant to the ground. The younger one looked across the road, clamped her lower lip between her teeth and gave a sharp whistle. A bearded man in a black blazer appeared on top of the rock wall. He looked down, nodded, then dropped to the ground like a cat and crossed to where Tarrant lay.

"Very good, ladies," he said, and smiled brightly. Bending, he lifted Tarrant's body as if it had been a truss of hay, and carried it down the road to the Dormobile. The older nun followed. The other remained near Reilly, her eyes fixed on him. Neither of them spoke. Reilly's face was haggard as he put the gun in his pocket. He watched as the man and the taller nun put Tarrant on some sort of bunk in the back of the Dormobile, strapped him down, then got out and closed the doors. The nun remained by the van, looking down the road. The man walked back to the Peugeot.

"Very good, Reilly," he said, and took an envelope from inside his jacket. "Five thousand dollars. The balance due."

Reilly opened the envelope, pulled out a slip of blue paper and studied it. His hands were shaking. The younger nun walked a little way up the road to the next bend and stood there.

Reilly said, "All right." He put the envelope away and looked at the man in the black blazer. "We stopped because he wanted to stretch his legs. He was standing by those stones on the bend there, near the edge. I was cleaning the windscreen. I heard him call out, but when I looked round he'd gone. Must have felt dizzy and fallen."

Mr. Sexton nodded, merriment in his pale blue eyes. "Keep it as simple as that," he said. "You'd better find the nearest phone now."

Reilly turned to get into the car. As he did so, Mr. Sexton moved. He glanced up and down the road. Neither of the two nuns gave any sign. He took a quick step forward. His right arm swung up and down with such sudden speed that to the normal eye it would have blurred like the spoke of a turning wheel. The edge of the stiffened hand struck Reilly on the back of the skull, exactly in the centre. There was a soft, deadened sound of impact.

Reilly sprawled forward across the front seat of the car. There was a three inch fracture in his skull, and pieces of shattered bone were embedded in his brain. He was not dead yet, but he was dying fast. Mr. Sexton looked pleased as he transferred the gun and the envelope from Reilly's pocket to his own, took hold of the man's limp legs and pushed him fully into the car. He looked towards Angel, then Clare. They were watching the road as before.

The rear door of the car was still open. Mr. Sexton wound down the window, looked at the set of the hinges, then bent and gripped the bottom of the door with one hand, the upper framework of the window with the other. His eyes half closed and he seemed to relax in this strange position, his hands moving just a little, very gently, as if seeking some esoteric communion with what he held. Then he drew a deep breath, his eyes opened wide, and he straightened up slowly but smoothly.

There came the sound of rending metal as the steel surrounding the riveted hinges gave way beneath the inexorable pressure. The door broke away from the lower hinge. Mr. Sexton continued lifting and twisting. The metal round the upper hinge tore. He stepped back, hoisted the door on to the roof of the car, dusted his hands, pushed Reilly's body into a crumpled ball on the nearside of the front seat, and climbed in behind the wheel.

The engine came to life and the Peugeot moved forward. Mr. Sexton slipped into third gear, then steered with one hand, holding the door open. The car gathered speed. The line of stones protecting the outer curve of the bend made a frail barrier. One second before the wheels struck, Mr. Sexton dived. He hit the road, rolling in a perfect break-fall, and came lightly to his feet, watching as the Peugeot reared up over the stones, hesitated, hovered, then lurched forward to plunge over the edge. It did not once touch the inward-leaning side of the great gorge. The first thing it struck was the river, six hundred feet below.

Angel and Clare walked to the Dormobile. Mr. Sexton brushed dust from his jacket and said, "One last look round, ladies." He moved to the wall of the cutting and drew himself up.

Angel muttered, "Bloody show-off."

"Now, Angel."

"Well, 'e is. Smashing the mick's 'ead when it just needed a tap on the neck. And ripping that door off so they won't be surprised when they don't find the old bloke's body in the car. It'll be split open like a sardine can any-way, after that drop——" She broke off as Mr. Sexton jumped down to the road again and walked towards them. He carried the field glasses and wore a thoughtful look.

"There's a man across the gorge," he said. "On a ledge a little way from the top. He was waving an SOS, but then he stopped and toppled over sideways. Passed out, I imagine."

Clare gave him a startled look. "D'you think he saw anything, Mr. Sexton?"

The broad shoulders shrugged. "He wouldn't be able to make out much detail without glasses. Anyway, he must be too badly hurt to climb up, so he's stuck there. A night in the open might well finish him off."

"All the same, if he did see something, and if he's found before he dies of exposure . . ." Clare peered across the valley. "Perhaps we should see to him, Mr. Sexton?"

"We'd have to get across to the other side, then back up-river from the bridge. And there's no road that side. It might take four or five hours to find him, Mrs. McTurk, especially after dark." He glanced at the Dormobile. "And we can't roam around with that cargo aboard."

"You'll just leave him, then?"

"He'll keep for tonight." Mr. Sexton looked at his wrist-watch. "We'll be back at base in four hours, then Colonel Jim can decide. He might send me back, or put in one of the odd-job teams to fix it."

"Well . . . it's your decision, Mr. Sexton."

"Always remember that, Mrs. McTurk. Colonel Jim is very hot on chain-of-command. We don't want him sending you along to me for disciplinary measures." His eyes twinkled. He reached out suddenly and pinched Angel's buttock, saying, "Or do you think she might enjoy it, Angel?"

The girl bit off a scream of pain and jumped back, teeth set in her lip, face screwed up in agony. Foul abuse was on her tongue, but with an effort she held it back. "No," she said, panting. "I don't reckon she'd enjoy it much, Mr. Sexton."

"There's the voice of experience." Mr. Sexton opened the back doors of the Dormobile. "We'll get started, then." He climbed in and sat down beside Tarrant's unconscious form. "Drive carefully, Mrs. McTurk. We want no trouble. That's more important than speed." He closed the doors.

Clare and Angel moved to the cab, Angel limping a little and rubbing her buttock. "Bastard!" she hissed. "I'd like to get be'ind him one night with a bit of wire. Make 'is eyes pop clean out of 'is rotten 'ead, I would. He's just about made a bloody 'ole right through my bum."

"You're being *coarse* again, Angel."

CHAPTER TWO

Four hours later, in the Auberge du Tarn, Modesty Blaise stood by the big window which looked out over the river and tried not to let her mind picture Tarrant's broken body.

Mme. Martine stood with hands clasped beneath her large bosom and said, moist-eyed, "I am so sorry, mam'selle. So very sorry. Milord was an old friend?" Since she had known that Modesty's guest was called Sir Gerald Tarrant she had insisted on referring to him as milord.

Modesty said, "Yes. I was very fond of him." She wore slacks and a sweater, both damp with the same heavy night dew that lay on her hair. It was now three hours since a boatman passing down the Tarn had seen, in the last of the dying light, the wreckage of a car protruding from the shallows. On his report, two men from the Poste de Police at La Malène had taken a motorboat up-river to investigate. One of them had braved the chill waters to find a body in the car and two torn suitcases in the broken boot.

It was two hours since they had sent another man up to the heights from which the car had fallen; and there, even by torch-light, he had found evidence of the car's plunge to destruction in the metal-scrapes on the rocks bordering the curve. On his way back he had called at the auberge to drink a pastis and tell of the accident. It appeared that there had been two in the car, he said, and they were foreigners, English. A search would be made for the other body down-river by daylight. The clothes in one of the suit-cases had tailor's name-tabs. The name was different from that in the passport found on the dead man. Presumably it was the name of the other unfortunate, whose body was missing. A M'sieu Tarrant.

Mme. Martine had clasped hands to her head in shock, and run to tell Modesty. In the past two hours Modesty had been down to the Poste de Police to look at the body. She knew Reilly as Tarrant's driver, and had identified him. She had taken a large flash-lamp, driven up the road to the point where the car had gone over the edge, and spent twenty minutes there. A strange thing to do, Mme. Martine thought, but then Mam'selle Blaise was an unusual young woman. Even now, as she stood looking down from the window upon the river where her milord friend had died, there were no tears. Except for her stillness and the quiet emptiness in her eyes, one would not have known that she grieved. The English were strange people.

The telephone rang. Mme. Martine ran into the hall to answer it, and returned a few moments later. "It is your call to London, mam'selle."

"Thank you, madame."

Modesty went through to the phone, flinching from what she now had to do. This was going to hit Jack Fraser badly. He had spent fifteen years as an intelligence agent in the field before taking a desk job as Tarrant's number two, a man who had walked with death and dealt it out himself when occasion called. Under Tarrant he had sent men on missions from which they had not returned, and he had the case-hardened attitude his job demanded; but this would hurt him deeply. Fraser held no more than a handful of people in any esteem, but Tarrant was one of them.

She picked up the phone and said, "Jack?"

"Fraser speaking, Miss Blaise." The voice was humble and ingratiating, Fraser's habitual pose.

She said, "I'm sorry to hit you with this, Jack, but it's bad news. About Tarrant."

A pause, then: "How bad?" The voice had changed.

"There's been an accident, and he's dead."

Fraser said softly, "Oh, God."

She gave him the facts briefly, and ended, "They don't seem too certain about finding his body. Apparently it could get sucked into one of the under-surface caves before it reaches the Garonne, and then just . . . stay there. I've given them your number to call—not this one, the official one."

Fraser said, "Thank you." After a long silence he went on, "You don't think this might have been arranged?"

"I wondered, and I've had a quick look round, but it seems like a straight accident. Would any of the various oppositions make him a target today?"

"I doubt it." Fraser's voice was flat. "That's gone out, like gunboat diplomacy. It was only a thought." Another long silence. "This probably won't be published for a day or two, until the Minister's had a full report from the French. Do you want me to call Willie and tell him?"

"No, I'll call him myself tomorrow. There's nothing he can do, so I don't want to hand him this as a night-cap. I'm sorry, Jack. So damn sorry."

*   *   *

Quinn lay huddled against the rock, teeth chattering, his thin coat wound tightly about him, and watched the early-morning sun lift over the canyon edge of the river bend. His head was clearer now, and did not throb so painfully, but the night had been a confused eternity of misery, and there seemed no strength left in his chilled, aching body.

26

Sometime during the night, between periods of sleep, half-sleep and stupor, he had eaten the last of his chocolate. He was desperately thirsty, and sucked dew from his coat to ease his parched throat. Perhaps the sun would begin to warm him soon. He ought to get up and stamp about, to stir his sluggish circulation. Wearily he pushed himself to a sitting position and sat nursing his hurt arm. A movement drew his eye, something on this side of the gorge, where the cliff-top jutted out in a point, only a hundred yards away. He screwed up his eyes and opened them again.

A woman. Gleam of brown legs below a dark green skirt. Black hair. Something like a small sack hanging from one shoulder. She stood on the edge, looking across the valley.

Quinn's heart pounded. He drew in a breath and called, but only a croaking sound came from his lips. He seized the coat in his good hand and began to flap it about wildly as he scrambled to his knees. She turned towards him . . . but continued turning. Christ, she was going away! Her head came back, and he saw the white of her face under the black hair. For a moment she was still, then one arm lifted in a wave, and she moved away from the cliff-edge at a run, vanishing from his sight.

Quinn found that he was panting, trembling. He did not dare stand up for fear of falling. An age seemed to pass, and then he saw her above him, on one knee on the cliff edge, looking down. Surprise tinged the wave of relief that swept him, for the face above the charcoal sweater was not a peasant-girl's face. Wide mouth, broad forehead, handsome bone-structure under the firm tanned flesh, raven hair tied back at the neck, large calm eyes.

"Vous êtes blessé?" Her voice was pleasantly mellow. Quinn groped for words from his meagre stock of French. "Oui. Je tombe. Mon bras." He held up his swollen wrist.

She said, "You sound English. Is it just the arm?"

27

"God, you're English too!" He shook his head to clear it. "That's a help. No, on top of the arm I gave my head a hell of a crack. Been here since yesterday afternoon. Can you go and get somebody to haul me up? I'm a bit groggy."

She nodded and stood up. He saw that a small duffle-bag hung from her shoulder, and that simple monk sandals were hooked to the draw-string of the bag. She said, "I won't be long. You'd better lie down and rest, your colour's battleship grey." Then she was gone.

Quinn sank back on his haunches, bemused. What the hell was an English girl doing, wandering about on the edge of nowhere? Any girl other than a peasant, in fact, and she wasn't that. No weird hippie, either. Quinn had an eye for quality, and was certain her sweater had been of fine cashmere. A thirty guinea job at least.

She hadn't wasted time on questions. He liked that. But if she thought she wouldn't be gone long, then she wasn't too bright. Quinn visualised what he knew of the causse. No inhabited village for miles. She would have to follow the tortuous river track all the way to La Malène. He would be lucky to see a rescue party in under four hours. He shivered. God, he was cold. He had not felt so cold since that long trip through Lancaster Hole two years ago. He sat down with his back to the wall and began to exercise, bending and stretching one leg, then the other, then his sound arm, trying to drive the blood through his veins a little faster.

Ten minutes later a sound made him look up. The girl was climbing down. She wore the sandals now, and carried a coil of rope like a bandolier. The duffle-bag hanging from her shoulder bulged squatly. She moved with certainty, finding toe and finger-holds with little groping. He saw the full length of one down-reaching leg, right up to the black pants, and noted the smooth play of lean muscle in the elegant curves.

"A dancer," he thought. "With those legs, a quid says she's a dancer. But why the hell———?" Anger exploded in him as she dropped the last few feet to the ledge and turned to face him. "Very clever, ducky," he said spitefully. "And now what? If you think you can haul me up on your own, you're out of your tiny mind."

She showed no sign of resentment, but put down the coil of rope, pushed back a wisp of hair, and began to open the duffle-bag. She said, "My car's in the woods only a quarter of a mile away. I just went back to collect some stuff from it. Don't worry about climbing up, we'll manage." She took a first-aid box from the duffle-bag and knelt beside him. Her hand rested on his brow for a few seconds, then she picked up his wrist, her long fingers on the pulse. "Did you hit your head very hard?"

The anger drained out of him. Her quietness made him confused. He muttered, "Hard enough. Knocked myself out. And afterwards I kept fainting or something. It's all a bit muddled now."

She took his head in her hands, turned it to look in each of his ears, tilted it back to look into his nostrils, then pulled down his lower lip and examined his teeth.

He said sourly, "What's all that in aid of?"

"No bleeding from your ears, nose or mouth. That's good. With any luck you haven't cracked your skull. Now turn round a little and lie back. No, so your head's on my lap. That's right, now just lie still."

He felt her fingers exploring his scalp. They found the lump above his right ear and rested there for a while, probing gently, then moved on. It was an extraordinarily pleasant sensation. Quinn felt the knots within him loosening. There was something about the touch of her hands that gave him a foolish sense of well-being.

"All right, sit up now." She helped him, then knelt in

29

front of him and held up one finger. "Look at my fingertip as I move it from side to side." She watched his eyes follow her moving finger. After a few seconds she reached out her other hand to cover his left eye. "Good. Now again. No, don't look at *me*, watch the finger. That's better. Let's try the other eye." Her hand moved slowly from right to left and back again. "Good."

She sat back on her haunches and drew the duffle-bag towards her. "You'll need an X-ray, but I don't think there's much damage apart from concussion. I expect your arm took the main fall and your head hit the rock afterwards." She took out a long section of French loaf wrapped in greaseproof paper, a packet of raisins and a quarter-bottle of brandy. The loaf had been split and buttered, with slices of ham between.

She said, "You're lucky I'm travelling first-class today. Start eating while I see to your arm, and then you can take a little brandy."

Quinn bit hungrily into the bread, watching her as she poured a colourless liquid on to a piece of lint. She rested his hand on her knee, wrapped the lint about his swollen wrist and forearm, and began to bandage.

He swallowed and said, "Are you a doctor or something?"

"No. I've done some casualty work." She spoke almost absently, and he felt a little nettled by her manner.

"My name's Quinn," he said.

"Hallo, Mr. Quinn."

"Christ, is this going to be formal?"

"What do your friends call you?"

"My enemies call me Henry. My friends just call me Quinn."

"Hallo, Quinn. I'm called Modesty Blaise. What are you doing here?"

"I was just walking. Misjudged time and distance, so instead of heading back to the hotel at St. Chély I thought I'd carry on to La Malène for the night." He glanced up. "Took a look at the river and bloody well slipped."

She knotted the bandage and looked across the gorge. "You must have been here when the car went over the edge yesterday. A grey Peugeot. Did you see it happen?"

He stared. "Went over the edge? God, no, I didn't see it go over." He wolfed the last of the bread and ham, and picked up the packet of raisins. "I kept passing out then coming round again. Must have missed that bit." He looked across the gorge, and grimaced. "How many?"

"In the car? Two."

Quinn shook his head. "Poor devils," he said soberly. "You'd have a long time to think on a drop that deep. I mean, it would seem a long time. You get through a lot in a few seconds when you can see your number coming up."

"Yes." She picked up the bottle and poured a measure of brandy into the cap. "You can get this down you, now there's something in your stomach. Then we'll see about moving."

His hand was shaking so much that she had to hold the cap to his lips for him to sip the brandy. He could feel it spreading warmth through his chest. Between sips he said, "You came in a car? How did you get it up here?"

"If you cut south from La Malène there's a rough track that loops round into the causse. You can make seven or eight miles an hour on it. The last mile's rough going, when you turn off the track to reach the woods. You have to move at a slow walk, but it means you can tuck the car away in the trees, out of sight."

He looked at her, puzzled. "And then what?"

"I go for a walk. Usually over the causse. Today I came

to have a look at the river first. I was just going when I saw you."

"You walk over the causse?" He looked at her light clothing and the sandals which were no more than soles and leather thongs. "You're mad, ducky."

She gave a little shrug, evidently not interested in his opinion. He realised now that almost from the first moment it had been as if her thoughts were elsewhere, even while she talked and tended his hurts. And she had not smiled. Not once. He had a sudden urgent wish to see her smile.

He chewed on another handful of raisins, and swallowed. "Modesty Blaise, you said?"

"Yes."

"Nice name. I like it. What happens now?"

"I'll fix a sling for your arm, then walk you up and down a bit to get the stiffness out of your muscles." She glanced up the eighteen-foot stretch of wall. "It's not far, and there are some fair holds. I brought a cross-peen hammer from the car, so I can chip them deeper for you before we start. I'll be at the top, holding you on the rope."

"You're competent, ducky. I'll give you that. But I don't fancy another fall."

She looked at him from eyes of midnight blue, and there was no morsel of doubt in them as she said, "You needn't worry, Quinn. I won't let you fall."

Ten minutes later, with the rope looped in a bowline about his chest, Quinn began the short climb. His one-handedness unbalanced him, but the rope helped to counteract this. She stood braced on the crest above him, the rope belayed round her body, not merely keeping it taut but taking a good part of his weight as he hung on the rock face and groped for one of the foot-holds she had chipped for him.

Halfway up, one of his legs began to shake uncontrollably. He gasped and swore as he felt himself sag to one side, but the rope held him. He looked up. He could see only the line of the rope and then the line of one arm with her face looking down over the point of her shoulder as she took almost the whole of his weight. The eyes seemed black now, and coldly ferocious, but her voice was quite neutral as she said, "Take your time, Quinn. I've got you."

He set his teeth, flexed the treacherous leg several times to gain control of it, then moved another few inches higher. Two minutes later he heaved his trunk over the edge. She helped him crawl clear, and he lay panting as she slipped the rope from his body and began to coil it. He saw that there was blood on one of her hands. She was breathing deeply and sweat shone on her face, but she did not seem distressed. She glanced across to the far side of the valley and her brow creased in a small frown, as if something was puzzling her.

Quinn said breathlessly. "I'm . . . giving you . . . quite a bit of trouble."

"Don't worry about it. Do you want to rest before we make for the car?"

He shook his head, and managed a grin. "The old blood's crawling around a bit faster now, and the Quinn body begins to feel as if it might belong to Quinn again. Sorry if I've been a bit terse."

"That was nothing. You've done well."

"There's no need to be bloody patronising, ducky."

She almost smiled then, and said, "Are you Irish?"

He glared indignantly. "Do you *mind*?"

"No offence."

"Just because the name's Quinn, I don't have to be bloody Irish, do I?"

"I was thinking more of the temperament. Never mind. Let's get moving. You'll have to lean on me."

"I can manage."

But he could not manage, and after fifty unsteady paces he was glad when she looped his sound arm over her shoulders, and held him at the waist. Now he could feel the sinewy power in her as she moved, steadying him and acting as a prop to ease the burden of his weight.

"Look," he panted when she made him sit and rest for a few minutes in the belt of firs, "I forgot to say thanks, right? Sorry about that. The fact is, I don't often get my life saved by a beautiful girl, so I'm not used to the routine, but you've been a cracker, ducky, a real de luxe cracker, and I'm bloody grateful. I really am."

"Good. You don't think you could stop calling me ducky?"

Quinn's teeth showed and he made a sweeping gesture. "Consider it done. Nice to get a reaction at last. Tell me, what were you wearing on your feet *before* you put those sandals on?"

"On my feet? Nothing."

He stared at them. They were not small feet, but shapely and strong. "Are you crazy, or doing some kind of penance?"

"No. I've got peasant feet. Soles like leather. But the sandals help on broken rock if I'm moving fast."

"I *see*. Yes, I see now. Some people might think you an unusual lady, Miss Blaise—oh, is that right?" His eyelids fell shut and he jerked them open again with a little start. "I mean, Miss?"

"Yes. Come on, Quinn, before you fall asleep. Last lap."

As she helped him up he said vaguely, "A spinster . . . saved by a spinster."

The Renault stood in a clearing amid the trees, a dozen paces from the open causse. Quinn was leaning on her heavily by the time they reached it. She eased him into the passenger seat and fastened the seat-belt. He slumped back with a sigh of relief. Her hand rested on his brow as she said, "How's your head?"

"Muzzy, but not too bad. Better than last night. I thought it was going to come apart then. I'm just tired now, I think."

"I'm not surprised. Last night could have killed you."

"I'm very thirsty."

"All right, but you'd better not drink too much." She gave him water from a bottle, put the first-aid box on the floor in the back, and moved away to put the rope and duffle-bag in the boot. When she returned Quinn sat leaning back with his eyes closed. As she took off the sandals for driving she found herself studying him for the first time.

Until now he had been an anonymous character who needed help, a man of no particular interest to her, with a few quirks which might have been either amusing or annoying at any other time, when her mind was not troubled by sorrow. His face was drawn and haggard now, but she placed him at twenty-five or six. No older. His hair was dark brown, long but not too long, brushed back and reaching to the middle of his neck in a few tousled curls. His eyes were grey-green, she remembered, set nicely wide above a rather large mouth and a longish nose. The chin was good, and he had excellent teeth.

As she got behind the wheel she frowned again, trying to think what he could have said or done that was itching somewhere in the back of her mind. There had been something not quite right in a word or phrase or look, but she could not pin it down. She put the nagging question from her mind as she eased the car slowly out of the trees and began to crawl across the just-possible route she had found leading from the track which wound through the causse.

35

The bad stretch took twenty minutes, but once on the track she was sometimes able to push the speed up to eight miles an hour. The track looped away from the Tarn, through undulating terrain, eventually joining a small road which led west to La Malène. She wondered what to do about Quinn. She could take him straight to Millau, to the hospital there. That was only an hour's drive once she was on the N.107. Alternatively she could go on to Toulouse, where Dr. Georges Durand's very excellent and expensive clinic stood in its own splendid grounds two miles out of town.

She had financed the setting up of the Durand Clinic several years ago. Georges Durand was brilliant and discreet, and could call on the finest specialists. In the old days her men of *The Network* had been mended there when need arose. So had Willie Garvin, and so had she, both more recently than *The Network* days. Plastic surgery had eliminated scars from her body on two occasions, and dental surgery replaced broken teeth after she had been brutalised during the *Sabre-Tooth* business in Afghanistan.

Quinn needed no discreet treatment—at least as far as she knew. But if she took him to Durand he would get the best, and on the house. She spared a glance at him. He was very young, and would probably find the costs of a stay in a French hospital alarming. Better make it Toulouse, then. She felt a flicker of irritation with herself for weakly taking on a three-hour drive when she had no responsibility for the boy beside her, but then shrugged mentally. What the hell did it cost her to drive a few extra miles anyway? She had nothing else in particular to do.

She wondered why she had thought of Quinn as a boy. He was probably no more than two years younger than she was. That was if you counted in calendar years, of course. She glanced at him again, half-smiling as she remembered his flashes of petulance and the youthful male arrogance, and she thought wryly: I was nearly as old as God when you were first starting to shave, Quinn.

She first saw the car a mile away, moving slowly along the track to nowhere. It was a big black car, a Citroen perhaps, and they would meet in less than five minutes, down in the long shallow basin which lay between them, where a stand of straggly trees bordered the track.

She braked to a gentle halt, took field glasses from under the dashboard, and focused them. The black car was a Citroen, and it had stopped. One man in a dark suit had got out and was looking towards her, also through glasses. She thought she could make out two others in the car.

A small early-warning light flashed on in her head. Thoughtfully she put the glasses back and shook Quinn gently by the shoulder. His eyes opened at once, and she realised that he had not been asleep, only dozing.

She said, "Have you got any friends in the district, Quinn?"

"Eh? No. I'm on my own here."

"Any enemies?"

He stared. "For God's sake, what are you talking about?"

She pointed. The black car was moving again. "There are some men in that car, and I fancy they're looking for you. I can't think of any other reason for them to be up here."

"There could be a dozen reasons. You were here."

"And you said I was crazy. Never mind, we'll soon find out." She let in the clutch and drove on. The gap between the two cars grew smaller. When the Citroen reached the stand of trees and halted she was still two hundred yards away. The trees squeezed the track at that point, the one

37

place where she could not pass the other car. The warning light in her head grew stronger.

Three men got out and stood looking towards the Renault. They all wore dark suits, and two of them wore hats. She could not see their faces yet, but she knew these men were trouble, knew it without knowing or caring how she knew. Perhaps it was something in their stance, or in the leisurely way they had positioned themselves, one beside the bonnet of the Citroen, the other two well forward and on each side of the track.

She slowed a little, but kept going and said, "Listen Quinn, and don't argue. Those men mean trouble. Maybe you know what it's about, maybe not, but that doesn't matter now. You're in no shape for trouble, so whatever happens you sit tight and do nothing. Understand?"

He gave a huff of incredulous laughter. "Look, ducky, have you suddenly developed a feverish imagination? Do you think they've driven up here to find someone they can roll for a wallet?"

"No. I'd put it a bit higher than that. The one with folded arms has got his hand on a gun under his jacket." She reached under the dash and put something in the pocket of her skirt. He glimpsed a spindle of wood with a rounded knob at each end, like a miniature dumbell. "Sit tight, Quinn," she said. "Just sit tight, that's all."

She had not raised her voice, and her expression had not changed, but there was a new quality about her which made the derisive protest die on Quinn's lips. This was no nervous female, he had proof enough of that. He looked ahead at the figures of the waiting men, and a cold finger touched his spine. There *was* something about them . . .

The track improved slightly and she pushed the speed up to ten miles an hour. Reaching across him, she unlatched the door, then unlatched her own offside door. They rattled, but the forward speed prevented them from swinging open.

"Just hold your door to, with your fingertips, very lightly," she said, and as he obeyed he saw that she was using her left hand to keep the offside door pulled to. His tired, muddled brain tried to imagine what her purpose could be.

Fifty yards now. Another ten seconds and they would have to stop, nose-to-nose against the Citroen. Quinn saw the men's faces clearly. They were impassive, almost bored. His mind still could not accept her certain conviction, but some deep instinct brought a cold sweat to his face.

"Look," he muttered, "for Christ's sake stop and make a run for it."

"Shut up. Keep still. Hold that door lightly."

The two nearer men stood one on each side of the track, so that she would pass between them with half an arm's length to spare on each side. The third man, the only one without a hat, leaned against the side of the Citroen's bonnet and seemed to be cleaning his nails with a knife. He looked up, and waved a languid hand in a signal to halt.

Modesty began to slow down, and then, as the bonnet of the Renault passed between the two men, she stamped hard on the brake. The wheels locked in a short straight skid. Quinn was flung forward against his seat-belt. Both doors swung open hard, with the stored energy of their forward motion suddenly released by the abrupt halt.

The man with folded arms, on Quinn's side, had turned a little. The impact of the swinging door took him on his left arm and shoulder, the metal corner of its top edge gashing the side of his face as he stumbled and went down. Quinn heard him cry out. The other man had taken the blow partly on one hand, and had probably broken a finger or two, for he was clutching at his hand as he staggered, struggling to hold his balance.

Modesty Blaise was out of the car. Dazedly Quinn realised that she must have virtually gone out with the swinging door. He groped for the clasp of his seat-belt, heart pounding, but could not tear his eyes from her as he watched her take one stride and swing a long brown leg. The ball of her bare foot made precise and explosive contact with the man's jaw. Before he hit the ground she had swung round, but a hand on the bonnet and vaulted across it with a fluency which made the preceding kick-and-turn an integral preliminary of the whole movement.

The man with the gashed face had rolled away from the car and come to his knees. There was a gun in his hand now, but before he could lift it she had kicked again. He squealed as her foot smashed against his elbow, and the gun flew up in a loop to land five paces away. Her right hand swung smoothly, not very hard, and again the flowing movement seemed all of one piece with the rest.

In her fist was the little wooden dumb-bell. One knob of it rapped sharply against the side of the man's head, below and behind the ear. He fell limply sideways and lay still. Her head came round instantly to sight the third man. His reactions were quick, for already he had covered half the distance towards her, running hard, the short-bladed knife held low and angled upwards.

To Quinn it seemed that she relaxed a fraction, almost with relief. Then she raised the little dumb-bell as if in readiness to strike, took two running paces forward, and dived. It was totally unexpected and impeccably timed. She hit the ground in a long rolling somersault which brought her in under the oncoming man's knife-hand, and her legs flashed up in a two-footed kick which drove into his middle just below the rib-cage.

Even in the car, Quinn heard the agonised whoop of the breath being driven from his body. His feet came clear of the ground as he was flung back, a boneless puppet tossed through the air to land in a crumpled, unmoving sprawl.

She was on her feet again, her head moving quickly to sight the first two men. They both lay still.

Quinn called in a croaking voice, "Hey . . . !" He did not know what he would have said next, but if she heard him she ignored it, knelt over the hatless man and fumbled under his jacket, then at his hip. When she stood up there was a wallet in her hands. She flicked quickly through the contents, dropped the wallet and moved to the man who had drawn a gun.

Quinn watched dazedly. She repeated the procedure, picked up the gun and moved to the unconscious man on the off-side. Her quick search produced another gun, a revolver. She walked to the Citroen, got in behind the wheel, started the engine and backed the car quickly to where the track widened. Quinn saw her get out, lift the bonnet and reach down into the engine.

She straightened, walked back to the Renault, put the Citroen's distributor-arm and the revolver into the cubby-hole under the dash, slipped the magazine from the automatic, worked the slide to eject a cartridge from the breech, clipped the magazine into the butt again, and put it in the cubby-hole as she got in behind the wheel.

Quinn saw that she was frowning, in annoyance now rather than puzzlement. He found that his heart was still thumping, and made a great effort to keep his voice cool and steady as he said, "Well . . . congratulations."

She gave a small angry shake of her head, started the engine and let in the clutch. "I kicked that gun too damn far. Out of reach. If the last man had pulled a gun I might have been in trouble."

After a long silence Quinn said, "Never mind. We all make mistakes." He was furious to find that he was shaking and had difficulty in speaking without a stammer. Irrationally, his fury focused on the girl beside him. Drawing a deep breath he said savagely, "I do hope they weren't cops of some kind."

She shook her head. "They weren't cops."

"You can tell these things, of course?"

She nodded absently, and his restraint broke. "Jesus Christ, who *are* you?"

"What do you mean?"

He jerked a thumb over his shoulder. "That! It was——" He rubbed a hand along his brow angrily. "It reeked of long practice, and you didn't bloody well learn it in the Girl Guides."

She said, "Gaston Bourget, Jacques Garat, and the third one had no identification on him. You know the names?"

He stared blankly. "Why the hell should I know them?"

"If they came up here to do you some mischief there's a connection somewhere."

"If they did, I haven't the faintest idea why. After what I've just seen it seems a lot more likely they came after *you*. Are you a Mafia chief or a secret agent or something?"

She almost smiled. "I run a hat-shop in Kensington, Quinn. I'm sure they weren't looking for me."

His red-rimmed eyes glared with exasperation. "All right then, they must have been after a spot of rape. Not me. You. They saw you come up here and thought, 'That's a nice rapable bit of crumpet, let's follow her up on the lonely causse and—wham, bang, thank you ma'am'."

She said slowly, "Could be, I suppose, but I doubt it."

He began to laugh, feebly and rather painfully in his weakness. "Jesus, they picked the wrong bird today," he stuttered, hiccuping. "Wh-wham, bang, th-thank *you*

42

ma'am for that kick in the gut . . ." The laughter went wrong, and tears ran down his cheeks. He felt shame and rage, but could not stop the shaking and the tears. She brought the car to a halt, and he felt her cool hand on his neck. He tried to push her away, croaking, "I'm all right! I'm *fine*, ducky—just for God's sake leave me alone."

But the comforting hand remained, and her voice held a warmth and gentleness he had not heard in it till now as she said, "Poor old Quinn with his rotten head. Come on now, stop being tough and just let go. You're going to swallow a couple of tablets, and go to sleep, and when you wake up you'll be in a nice comfortable bed and you'll feel a new man."

With an enormous effort Quinn took hold of himself. Through bleary eyes he saw that she had lifted the first-aid box from the back and was taking a bottle of tablets from it. When she turned towards him she smiled. It was a friendly smile, and a wave of self-loathing rose within him.

"Sorry . . . about calling you ducky," he said shakily. "Trouble with me, I'm a nasty bastard."

CHAPTER THREE

There was a congregation of fifty in the small Norman church of St. Mary's, Wixford, two miles south of the Thames, in the county of Berkshire.

Lady Janet Gillam sat at the end of the third pew, hymn-book resting on her trousered knees, her jaws aching with the long strain of suppressing the explosive giggles which kept threatening to burst from her. The stern Presbyterian upbringing of her childhood in the Scottish Highlands was proving a feeble barrier against irreverence as the tall young vicar announced the last hymn.

At the organ, his brown and weatherbeaten face emerging from a white surplice, his thick fair hair well-greased to make it less unruly than usual, Willie Garvin turned his head towards her and rolled up his eyes. Then with grave dignity he began to play the introductory bars of the hymn.

This was the fourth time he had played the same tune during the morning service. Lady Janet's chest hurt, and her eyes brimmed with tears. She ducked her head of short chestnut hair low over the hymn-book and moved her lips slightly, but did not dare to relax her control sufficiently to sing.

She could still conjure up the look on Willie's face two days earlier, in his pub, *The Treadmill*, when she had asked him to help.

"*Me?* Ah, come off it, Janet. You're putting me on."

"No, Willie. The organist's sick and they have a man

coming for the evening service, but Mr. Peake can't find anyone to play for the morning service, so I said I was sure you'd do it. He's an awful nice man, the vicar, and with such a wee congregation it'll be just pathetic without music for the hymns. I didn't like to say no when he asked if I could find somebody."

"Why ask you? You're not exactly a regular member of 'is flock."

"No, but I'm the nearest thing he can find to a Lady of the Manor, and I knew you could play."

"Play? That was at the orphanage, Jan. I never learnt any music, all I did was learn what notes to press for one 'ymn. Just one."

"I know, but you told me it was a tune you could sing several different hymns to. What tune was it?"

"St. Flavian. But——"

"How does it go, Willie?"

"Oh, blimey. Dee-dee-dah-dee-dah . . . *With weary feet and saddened 'eart from toil and care we flee*——"

"Just right for Mr. Peake's congregation. I told him he'd have to find four hymns to fit whatever your tune was."

Willie looked at the earl's daughter dazedly. "You crazy Scotch nit!"

"That's no way for a man to talk to his mistress, is it now?"

"I 'aven't been to a church since I was seventeen," Willie said reminiscently. "And then it was to pinch some lead off the roof."

"You must have been a very nasty boy."

"I was, Jan. 'Orrible. And I got caught, so I was stupid, too."

"Well now's your chance to make up for it a little bit. And think what a good story it'll give you to tell Her Highness."

That was how Lady Janet usually referred to Modesty Blaise. There had once been a hostile undercurrent in it, but no longer. She had learned that the strange, dark-haired girl did nothing to bind Willie Garvin to her. The fact that a part of him would always belong to her was something neither she nor Willie could help, for it derived from the years past, when Willie had worked for her and become another man through her; when shared danger forged bonds woven from a thousand threads of steel.

Lady Janet had come to terms with this. She knew she possessed a part of Willie which would never belong to Modesty. It was not so much that he and Modesty denied themselves the ultimate physical union but that neither of them had ever seemed to regard it as a possible part of their relationship. The pattern had been set from the beginning, and it would not change now.

Lady Janet did not know if her mention of the good story it would make for Her Highness had swayed Willie's decision about playing the organ. If so, she did not care. It was enough that he had agreed. The hymn ended. Willie played the Amen, sat back with a smug, pontifical air and folded his hands. When the final blessing had been given and the congregation began to shuffle slowly along the aisles to the door, he played them out with the same tune. Some of them were looking a little bewildered.

In Willie's car, driving back to her farm which lay a mile from *The Treadmill*, Lady Janet let her laughter have free rein at last, dabbing at her eyes, choking. "Lord, Willie, you—you looked such a clown in the s-surplice. I thought I'd never get through."

"I could see you were moved, Jan. I got a lovely ecclesiastical touch, eh? And I'll tell you something else. I nearly got paid for it. Seventy-five pence, 'e said was the rate.'

"Willie! What did you do?"

"Told 'im it was all fixed and you were going to pay me in kind."

"You——? Oh, you liar!"

He turned a hurt face towards her. "You mean you're not?"

She laughed and slipped a hand through his arm. "That depends. I don't do short-times. Can you stay the night?"

"Got me nightshirt and toothbrush packed."

"There's a clever little organist."

* * *

At one o'clock the next morning Lady Janet lay with her head on Willie's shoulder, her good leg resting across his thighs. It was an hour since they had gone to bed, but they had not made love. The phone-call from Modesty, from her flat in Montmartre, had cast a shadow over the day.

A man called Tarrant, a friend of Modesty's and Willie's, had been killed in a car accident. Sir Gerald Tarrant. Lady Janet had met him once at The Treadmill, a courteous man with a rather Edwardian style of dress and manner. She had liked him.

Willie said softly, "You awake, Jan?"

"M'mm. My damn leg's itching."

"Want me to give it a massage?"

"Maybe, if it doesn't stop soon. Tarrant was a big Intelligence chief, wasn't he?"

"Yes, but you're not supposed to know that."

"Lord, Willie, I've eyes and ears, and I've learned a few things about you and Modesty these past two or three years." Her fingers found the puckered scar on his thigh. "Sometimes I've guessed when you were going on a job, or whatever you call it. Was that for Tarrant?"

"Once or twice."

47

"I know you don't have to, so what makes you do it? Why look for trouble?"

"We don't look for it, Jan. Something comes along, and you just can't turn round and walk away from it."

"Why not?"

"There's always some reason."

She was silent, remembering. Here she lay, Lady Janet Gillam, daughter of an earl, with her head on the shoulder of a Cockney who had walked into her life three years ago. That was after her jet-set, hell-raising days; after her stupid, defiant marriage to Walter Gillam, the drunken playboy who had killed himself in the same car-crash which had deprived her of her left leg from just below the knee.

She had limped out of hospital months later on a steel half-leg, a different person. Rejecting all help from her father, she had set to work running the farm Walter had bought on a whim and in which he had lost almost all his money. After four years of ferocious work the corner was turned. By then she was twenty-eight, and it was then that the three cold-eyed men had appeared on the scene, offering protection against all the disasters which could so easily ruin a farm. Protection at a price.

She had never known how Willie Garvin, the mainly absentee landlord of *The Treadmill*, found out what was happening. But he appeared at the farm one day, told her he knew of her difficulties, and smilingly assured her that she need worry about them no longer. She would not be troubled again.

His promise was good. Later she learned something of how he had dealt with the problem, and realised that he had put himself into considerable danger for her, though he seemed to think quite genuinely that it had been a very minor exercise. She did not take him to her bed from grati-

48

tude, but simply because she wanted to. And that was strange, for she had thought she could never again bring herself to lie freely with a man, exposing the ugliness of her injury. But some deep-seated instinct had told her that this, her missing half-leg, would make no difference to Willie Garvin, and her instinct had been sound.

With Willie she felt no shame or embarrassment at her deformity. He did not ignore it, but accepted it. And the quality of his acceptance was so complete that she could now let him strap the steel leg on for her, or massage the itching stump, without a moment's fear that he would feel any distaste.

By unspoken agreement there were no strings to their relationship. Willie was often away. She knew there were sometimes other girls. When he came back, she was always glad. By the same token, he did not take her for granted. There was always the tacit but unmistakable agreement that if ever she wanted to be finished with him he would accept it without question or rancour.

Her thoughts shifted suddenly to the nagging worry she had been tempted to speak of several times over the past two months. She was not quite sure what had held her back. Pride, perhaps. Reluctance to break a confidence. Even an element of fear as to what the outcome might be if Willie decided to involve himself.

In the darkness he said, "What is it, Jan?"

"What do you mean?"

"Something's been bugging you. I don't want to be nosey. I thought for a bit that maybe you wanted to call time on me, but it doesn't seem like that now. So if it's anything I can 'elp with, just say."

She propped herself on an elbow, turned on the bedside lamp and looked down at him, trying to make up her mind. He touched her hair and said, "Just up to you, love."

49

Without making any conscious decision she said, "What does a person do about blackmail, Willie?"

He stared. "You?"

"No." She hesitated, then went on, "Fiona, my young sister. She's married to a tycoon in New York, and she was over here on a flying visit a few weeks ago. You weren't around at the time."

"Someone putting the screws on her?"

"For two years now. She broke down and told me, but I think she was sorry afterwards."

"What's the lever?"

"She had an affair with some man three years ago. It's long finished and I don't know the details, but somebody does."

"Best thing she can do is tell 'er tycoon and say sorry."

"You don't know Tommy Langford. He'd be for crucifying her. And there are the two children."

"Does she know who's doing it?"

Lady Janet shook her head. "It's not the ex-boyfriend. He died of a coronary."

"Does the blackmailer 'ave proof?"

"She doesn't think so. But it's not really needed. They know. Where and when and who. She could never outface Tommy on it if they gave him the word."

"They?"

"The one who put the squeeze on her was a nun. A Scottish nun. But Fiona's sure there's somebody behind her."

"A nun? You mean a phoney one?"

"I suppose so. You'd not be likely to find a real one mixed up in it."

"No blackmail note? They just sent in the nun?"

"I couldn't say about a note, Willie. I didn't really know what questions to ask."

He took her hand. " 'Course you wouldn't. Did Fiona tell you 'ow much she's paid so far?"

"I'm not sure of the total, but it's one thousand dollars a month."

"*What?* Just that? Regular? How's it handed over?"

"By transfer from her account to the account of some charity relief fund at a bank in Macao."

"D'you know the name of the bank?"

"Fiona did tell me, but all I remember is that it started with *novo* and a word like provident came into it."

"*The Novo Banco Previdente e Comercial de Macau?*"

She stared down at him. "Yes, I'm sure that's what she said. Willie, how did you know?"

"We used to do business in Macao and Hong Kong." He spoke absently, busy with his thoughts. "The New Provident, eh? Well there's a thing. And the charity angle means it's done all nice and legal through Exchange Control." He thought for a few moments, then frowned. "But it's too small, Jan. A thousand dollars a month doesn't fit."

"Doesn't fit what?"

"The caper. The organisation's too fancy for the turn-over."

"What do you know about any organisation?"

"I know something about The Provident."

"Well, I can only tell you what Fiona told me. I asked why she didn't get on to this bank and try to find out who was behind the charity account, and she almost flew into a panic. She said there wasn't any point in finding out, because it wouldn't make any difference. She'd rather go on paying than risk Tommy being told."

"It'll come to that in the end, Jan. They'll bleed 'er till she cracks."

There was a silence, then Lady Janet said slowly, "It

doesn't seem like that, Willie. I mean, they haven't demanded any increase, and she can *afford* twelve thousand dollars a year. She has an income of her own. She said it bites hard, but it's not a back-breaker."

"She'll just go on paying, then?"

"I think so. I believe she only told me about it because she had to tell someone. It wasn't that she thought I could do anything." She gave a little shrug. "But it seems an awful thing, Willie. I thought maybe you could . . . well, advise me. They say the police in this country are very discreet in dealing with blackmail, but I don't know about America and I don't know about Interpol. Maybe that's silly. Do Interpol deal with such things?"

Willie shook his head. "They'd only work on requests from member police forces, and it doesn't sound as if Fiona would play ball on that." He was silent for a full minute, eyes thoughtful, idly stroking the crisp chestnut curls above her ear. "This is a funny one, Jan. Very off-beat. Mind if I talk to The Princess about it?"

She smiled. "That was nice, Willie. I didn't think you had any secrets from Modesty."

"None of me own, I suppose. But this is yours. I won't speak if you say so, but this caper makes no sense, and she's red 'ot at working out that kind of thing."

"And if she works it out?"

"There might be something we could do. Privately."

She put her head down on his chest and said gently, "Willie, I wouldn't want to be under any sort of obligation to her."

"You wouldn't be, Jan. It's the other way round."

"You mean because I took my father's plane and flew you up to Glasgow that night when those men had her in Castle Glencroft?"

"She was a goner if we 'adn't got there in time. It was you commandeering Daddy Earl's plane that turned the trick. She's not the sort to fall on your neck, Jan, but any time you've got trouble she'll come running."

"All right. If you think it might help, speak to her, Willie."

He nodded. "She'll be back in a few days."

*   *   *

At nine o'clock in the morning, Dr. Georges Durand telephoned Modesty at her flat in Montmartre. He said, "Your Mr. Quinn is not what I would call an ideal patient, Modesty."

She was standing by an easel, oils and brushes set out, trying to put on the small canvas an arrangement of fruit in a bowl. She had no talent whatsoever for painting, and always destroyed a picture as soon as she had gone as far as she could go with it, but she found the constant striving and constant failure oddly therapeutic.

She said, "I'm not going to bleed for you, Georges. Most of your patients are rich and cantankerous. Quinn's poor and cantankerous, that's all. Have the tests shown any damage?"

"No. The wrist is unbroken and we are giving it intensive treatment. The young man is fortunate to have a thick skull, but the concussion was quite severe, and I have said he must stay here and rest for three more days."

"He knows he won't have to pay?"

"Yes. And he keeps demanding to be told where you have gone and how he can get in touch with you."

"Don't tell him, Georges. Hide his clothes if need be, to keep him there for three days, then just let him go."

"As you wish, Modesty. I think a little sedation will help. Your Mr. Quinn seems to have—what is it you say in English? A monkey on his back?"

"So I noticed. There's a lot of it about these days, Georges."

"Truly. My psychiatric section thrives increasingly. A great success."

"For the patients?"

He laughed. "Well . . . occasionally. How is the good Willie Garvin?"

"He's all right. We're both a little down at the moment."

"Ah, your friend who was killed. Again I express my sympathy."

"Thank you, Georges. And thank you for ringing."

She put down the phone and eyed the canvas with wry contempt. A mess. A ludicrous mess. She squeezed more paint on to the palette and began to mix it thoughtfully. She still could not pinpoint the thing about Quinn which had left a smudgy question-mark in her mind. The fact that it continued to irritate her, like a piece of grit in a shoe, was in itself irritating, for she knew it could be of no importance to her. No importance whatever.

Deep beneath the layers of conscious thought, in the dark wells where memories lie dormant and logic has no meaning, some tiny threadworm of instinct struggled doggedly to reach the light of her awareness and tell her that she was wrong.

*　　*　　*

Mr. Sexton said, "It was unfortunate, of course. If we'd known Modesty Blaise of all people would stumble on him at such an early hour, I'd have dealt with the matter myself. These sub-contractors are only to be trusted for run-of-the-mill work."

On the other side of the long dining table Angel shifted her weight to favour the left buttock, where the bruise made by Mr. Sexton's finger and thumb still hurt. She pulled up her short skirt a little more, so that da Cruz, beside her, could get a better view of her legs. Da Cruz was the only one in this godforsaken old castle she fancied at all. He wasn't exactly chatty, but there was something a bit exciting about him. Maybe it was being a mixture of three-quarters Portuguese and a quarter Chinese.

Mellish, on the other side of the table, with the light gleaming on his balding head through the fuzz of sandy hair, was a miserable sort of bugger, and she hated his posh drawling accent. The three Japs or Chinks or whatever they were who did the work and the cooking didn't appeal. Too foreign. As for Mr. Sexton . . . she winced inwardly. Gawd, not him!

Her review did not include the man who sat at the top of the table, wearing a bright yellow woollen shirt with a red neckerchief held in a gold ring, chewing ponderously on a piece of cheese as he considered Mr. Sexton's remark. You didn't even begin to think about Colonel Jim like that. He was a heavy man, over fifty, pear-shaped, with a big chest sloping out to a bigger belly, massive chin set under a wide loose mouth, crew-cut grey hair and shaggy eyebrows. Sometimes Angel thought she was even more afraid of Colonel Jim than of Mr. Sexton.

You wouldn't flash your legs at Colonel Jim anyway, but especially you wouldn't do it with his wife sitting there on his right, between you. Pop-eyed Lucy with the blonde curls, curvy figure and wheedling voice.

Colonel Jim. Angel gave a mental snort of contempt.

Everybody had to call him that. Except Lucy of course. Anyone would think he was running an old soldiers' club or something. Still, he was clever. Christ he was clever to have worked up this lark. He'd got it running good in the States, and now he was breaking new ground. Angel hoped he'd send her out on plenty of work. Sticking around in the chateau was enough to send you up the wall, and he'd taken this place for a year.

She hitched her skirt another fraction higher and shot a sideways glance at da Cruz.

Clare, wearing a sensible jumper and skirt with a single row of pearls, sat between Mellish and Mr. Sexton, finishing her crème caramel, transferring small portions on the tip of her spoon to her prim mouth. She put down the spoon and was on the verge of speaking, but stopped short. Lucy Straik was about to utter words, once she could formulate whatever vague concept was drifting in the wide empty reaches of her mind, and Lucy Straik did not like to be interrupted. Neither did Colonel Jim Straik like Lucy to be interrupted.

She put a hand on her husband's forearm and said, "Poppa, I been *thinking.*" Her voice had the heavy twang of the Deep South.

Colonel Jim nodded fondly. "Good girl. What you been thinking, Momma?"

She pursed short fat lips and absently smoothed the white sweater over her large bosoms. Her complexion was smooth, creamy and natural. The bright brown eyes, whose protuberance hinted at thyroid imbalance and sexual appetite, were thoughtful. "We-e-e-ll, I been thinking we don't *know* if this man saw anything across that gorge place. But we oughta find him and find out——"

"Sure, Momma. But its counter-productive to worry about finding out *if* he saw anything. Wastes time.

56

Efficiency-wise, the right answer is you just find him and make him redundant."

"I hadn't *finished*, Poppa,"

"Aw, sorry, honey." He chuckled and patted her cheek. "You go right ahead."

"We-e-ell, if this woman Mr. Sexton said about, if she took care of them *stupid* men, and took this man away, the one across that gorge place, so they didn't get to kill him after all, then sure as hell she'd take him to a doctor or a hospital, wouldn't she? So there can't be *many* doctors and hospitals just around there, can there? So why not have Clare and Angel put on them nuns' clothes and go look?"

Mellish blinked once then looked away, his face completely neutral. Clare smiled and nodded, and only Angel knew her well enough to detect the flicker of contempt in her eyes. Da Cruz drank some wine. Mr. Sexton, eating fresh fruit, nuts and honey, drinking water, was the only one who made no attempt to hide his reaction. With open amusement he said, "But Mrs. Straik, that's exactly what the dear girls were doing from noon till midnight yesterday. Colonel Jim sent them out as soon as Bourget phoned in to report their miserable failure."

Lucy Straik's eyebrows rose in two high curves. "Aw, gee. Is that right, Poppa?"

"Sure, Momma. You were here when I sent 'em."

"I was? I musta been thinking about something else."

He leaned towards her with a loose-lipped grin and rested a large hand on her thigh. "I know the kinda things Momma thinks about mostly."

"Poppa! You'll *embarrass* me." She wriggled shyly.

"Don't you worry your beautiful head about business, honey. I'll take care of that." He turned to Mr. Sexton, still smiling, but there was suddenly a new quality in the smile, a million miles removed from the maudlin fondness of a moment before. "You know this Blaise girl, Mr. Sexton?"

"By reputation. It must have been her. We know Tarrant was joining her at the Auberge du Tarn. Reilly told us so, and Bourget's description fits. I don't know of any other woman who could have walked over Bourget and his colleagues like that. Not even Angel and Clare together."

"Does Blaise know you by reputation?"

"I think not. I only came into the business a couple of years ago. As you know."

"I think maybe we'd better take out a little insurance, Mr. Sexton."

"I'll put it in hand tonight." Sexton paused, then added politely, "How long will you let Tarrant sweat before we go to work on him?"

"I'm going to give it another twenty-four hours. Then a general chat, so I can lay it out for him. Then you rough him up. Then Mellish makes with the pentothal." Colonel Jim stripped the band from a cigar. "Clare treats him nice but talks ugly to make him sweat. Angel gives him a lay to loosen him up. Another civilised chat . . ." He shrugged. "Maybe we'll switch it around a little. I like to play these deals ear-wise." He looked up from the cigar, smiling, but the eyes were slits of grey granite. "Don't overdo the hard treatment, Mr. Sexton. He's no chicken, and a stiff's no good to me."

Mr. Sexton nodded. "I'll exercise careful judgement, you can be sure of that."

Lucy Straik said, "You're sure as hell right Poppa can be sure of that, if he says so."

Mr. Sexton grinned and inclined his head. "His wish is my command, Mrs. Straik."

"His wish is . . .? Hey, that's *cute*!"

Colonel Jim chuckled and put away his unlit cigar. "So

are you, honey. So are you." He got to his feet, taking her by the arm. "C'mon now, let's go bye-byes."

She giggled. "You're a tiger, Poppa."

He walked her to the door, an arm about her waist, his gait rather lumbering. The belly did not sag when he stood. The heaviness was of muscle rather than fat. He said, " 'Night, boys and girls," without looking back, and the door closed on a murmur of polite response from the company.

Clare got up briskly and said, "Would anyone care for a rubber of bridge?" She knew da Cruz was usually willing. Angel would have preferred poker, but she would play bridge, badly of course, if the Portuguese did. Mr. Sexton never played. Clare looked at the thin sandy Englishman beside her and said hopefully, "Mr. Mellish?"

He shrugged agreement, but still sat holding his brandy, watching the door. After a moment he shook his head and said softly, "Extraordinary. I'll never get it."

Mr. Sexton said, "Get what?"

"Colonel Jim and her. Little Lucy."

Mr. Sexton put down his napkin and stood up, his bright clear eyes amused. "It's simple enough." Moving round the table he tapped Mellish on the shoulder with a finger, and the sandy man jumped nervously. "You're the technical expert, Mellish, so you ought to be able to figure out the pattern. She fills a need in him. Colonel Jim dotes on that idiot lump of forked meat—mainly because she is an idiot. She's nicely put together, of course, but that's a secondary attraction. You can add that she's spiteful and selfish, and he enjoys indulging her."

Angel said, "Sounds bloody kinky to me."

"Aren't we all, Angel?" Mr. Sexton turned his smile upon her. "You ought to know." The smile lost its amusement and became empty. "But I hope none of you will

59

ever mistake Colonel Jim's indulgence of Lucy for weakness. If it became a necessary business requirement, he'd tell me to snap her pretty neck and wouldn't feel a qualm. He can easily find another just like her."

Setting chairs round a card-table, Clare said, "Och, that's not a nice thing to say, Mr. Sexton. You've no romance in you."

"We're not in a romantic business, Mrs. McTurk."

"Business is something else, Mr. Sexton. It shouldn't mean there can be no romance in our *personal* lives."

"Ah, you have a tender heart, dear lady. Do you still carry a torch for the good sailor McTurk, who wedded and bedded and left you?"

Angel giggled and said, "She carried a razor for 'im. Followed 'im all the way to Santiago and cut 'is rotten throat while 'e was asleep."

"It's no matter for humour, Angel," Clare said stiffly. "We reap as we have sown. McTurk should have remembered that."

"Christ, you're a corker, Clare. A right corker."

Da Cruz said slowly, in accented English. "May I ask you a question, Mr. Sexton?"

"Yes?"

"Are you . . . afraid of Colonel Jim?" There was a sudden silence. Mellish plucked at his lower lip. Angel froze in the act of rising, eyes flickering with alarm.

Mr. Sexton said calmly, "No. I'm not afraid of him, da Cruz. The rest of you are, and should be. But it's my unique satisfaction and delight to be afraid of nobody in this world."

Da Cruz hesitated, then said, "I work for him for money, but mostly because I would be afraid not to. I think that is so with the others here. But I do not know your reason, Mr. Sexton."

He threw back his golden head and laughed. Angel, Clare and Mellish relaxed. "My reason? That's very simple. He provides clients for me, da Cruz. Or perhaps patients would be a better word." Mr. Sexton rested his hands on the end of the table, looking down the length of it and far beyond the faces turned towards him, the blue eyes focused on some point immeasurably distant. With no hint of vanity, and like a man uttering an article of faith, he said lightly, "I am the greatest combat-man in the world. You know that, all of you. You've watched me at practice with Tokuda and his friends downstairs. Those three are among the best. And I handle them like a man stropping a razor. I've devoted my life to it, studied under the greatest masters of Japan, Korea, Thailand . . . and the west, for what that's worth. And I've gone far beyond them all."

He paused. His eyes focused and he straightened up, smiling again. "But it wasn't enough, dear friends. When a man spends his life acquiring a huge skill, he must find means to exercise that skill in its ultimate function. And Colonel Jim provides that for me."

He stood with hands in the pockets of his blazer, and gave da Cruz a measured look. "There. You're answered, da Cruz. But do think twice about asking personal questions in future, won't you? I might not be in so expansive a mood next time." With an amiable nod he turned and went from the room, walking with the lazy, feline walk of a strolling leopard.

Angel let out a sigh of relief and hungrily lit a cigarette. Except for Colonel Jim, nobody smoked at meals until Mr. Sexton had left the room. He did not like tobacco smoke. She rested a hand on da Cruz's shoulder so that her knuckles touched his neck, and said, "You want to watch it a bit, Ramon. You never know with 'im. Mind you, I still don't see why 'e plumped for coming in with Colonel

Jim. I mean, if 'e likes a bit of killing now and then there's much more of it about in the States with the Mafia, say, or some of the new darkie mobs."

"I sometimes wonder if you've any sense at all, Angel," Clare said impatiently, opening two packs of cards. "Mr. Sexton's a gentleman, and a Colonial gentleman too, so naturally he'd not wish to work for any riff-raff. Our turn to be partners, I think, Mr. Mellish?"

As they settled at the card-table and cut for deal Mellish looked at his watch. "I've only time for a quick rubber. I want to run over my notes on Tarrant for an hour before I go to bed." He stroked his thin nose. "If I were Colonel Jim I'd try the degradation technique first. Stick him in the oubliette and let him stew in his own muck for a few days, till he hates himself."

Angel grinned. "It's not all that sweet in the cell. Besides, you'd disappoint Mr. Sexton. He likes to do 'is little bit." She picked up her cards and began to sort them, shifting uncomfortably on her chair. "Honest to God, my arse is killing me. And you ought to see this lot of bus-tickets. No bid."

CHAPTER FOUR

Sir Gerald Tarrant finished reciting to himself as much of Mark Antony's part as he could remember from the long-ago University days when he had belonged to an amateur dramatic society, and opened his eyes.

He supposed another hour had passed. He threw off the blanket, rose a little stiffly from the hard wooden bunk, and began to walk up and down. The cell was dry but cold. He could move only four paces each way. The bunk was set against the wall opposite the door, which was of solid oak and had no peep-hole that he had been able to discover. At one end of the cell stood a small table, bearing the remains of a loaf of stale bread and a half-empty flask of water. At the other end was a large bucket with a wooden lid. Light came from a low-wattage bulb hanging by two inches of flex from an ancient beam in the ceiling. There was nothing in his pockets, not even a handerchief, and his wrist-watch had been taken away.

This was where he had woken from a drugged sleep . . . twenty hours ago? Thirty? Forty? It was hard to judge. No window allowed him to tell night from day. He had seen nobody, heard no sound. Rasping a grimy hand across his cheek and chin, he judged that he had a two-day stubble of beard, and decided that they would probably show themselves within the next twelve hours.

Who were They? One of the official opposition groups, or one of the independents, like Salamander Four, who had taken on the job under contract? Not important. The ultimate aim would be the same—to scoop out the information in his brain like the yolk from an egg. A surprising move, this kidnapping. It broke a pattern of international Intelligence which had been established for a good many years. But that, too, was of no importance now. It had happened.

This was the softening-up period, of course, designed to work on his nerves. Interrogation would come later. It might be crude, but would more probably follow a slower but surer technique, the hard-soft play, the man of brutal menace alternating with the sympathetic type who offered cigarettes and coffee. And they would probably use drugs, thiopental combined with methamphetamine. He decided that later it would pass some time usefully if he set about recalling all the reports he had read on that procedure.

He looked at the bread and water. He was a little hungry and very dry, but it might be unwise to drink again for a while yet. Impossible to be sure how long this first stage would last. Tarrant continued pacing. He felt the crawling of nerves in his stomach, and acknowledged to himself that he was afraid. This was natural and reasonable, and did not matter, he told himself. The only thing that mattered was his degree of resistance to interrogation when the time came. His own agents were trained to withstand a considerable level of mental and physical torture. Some had known the grim need to call upon that training. Of those, some had died before talking, others perhaps had talked before dying. He would never know who had done which.

He wondered which category he would be in, and very soberly considered whether or not it was his proper duty now to destroy himself. If he left it until the moment when he could endure no longer, he might well lack the will to do it. Perhaps it would be premature now, he knew too little of the situation to be able to judge. But it would be wise to give thought to the matter early on, for it would not be easy to find the means, here in the cell, if and when the time came. The flask was soft plastic. No hope of cutting an artery with that. Hang himself with strips torn from the blanket? There was nowhere to secure the blasted rope high enough above the stone floor. A head-first dive against the wall? Or from the bunk to the floor? Not promising. Unless you did the trick at first attempt you'd simply knock yourself silly.

He felt exasperated by his own inadequacy, and found himself wondering what Modesty Blaise or Willie Garvin would have done. Immediately he knew that self-destruction would not have entered their minds. Their entire energy would have focused upon finding a way out. Tarrant's shoulders moved in a rueful shrug. It was different for them. They did not carry in their heads the same mass of information. They were a generation younger, had rare skills, and would probably have been prepared for trouble to some extent—a hidden pick-lock or other ingenious small devices.

All the same, it was worth thinking about Modesty. At best it might bring a useful idea, and at worst it helped pass the long hours. So what would she do now, assuming she could find no way past the cell door? Tarrant concentrated, drawing on snippets of memory from the rare occasions when she or Willie had let slip a few words about their philosophy of response when a caper went sour.

It came down to opportunism. Sooner or later the opposition must make some sort of move, and her mind would be tuned to recognise opportunity, or the chance of creating it. This might come in a dozen different ways, and would usually be unexpected, easy to miss. But it would come.

Tarrant sighed. It would come for her, perhaps. Willie had told him of the time when Mike Delgado, the mercenary killer, had held a gun on her at point-blank range. He had relaxed for no more than a mocking word, and in that instant she had drawn and fired across the small of her back, a trick shot, killing him with the smile still on his lips. She had been armed then, of course, but she had not been armed that day in Kalimba when . . .

He shrugged irritably. All well and good, but you needed the capacity for such opportunism, and Tarrant knew that he did not possess it. Another thing. While waiting for the next move she would have put herself to sleep, for days if need be, husbanding her resources. This was a faculty verging on the mystical, acquired in the harsh days of her childhood and later brought to a higher pitch of control under the guidance of an impossibly ancient *yogarudha* in the Thar desert north of Jodphur.

Willie Garvin also possessed it to a lesser degree. Soon after she had taken him into *The Network* she had sent him to spend two months with Sivaji. It was, according to Willie, an eerie experience. The skeletal old man said little and explained nothing. He just sat. And you sat with him, living on a few dates. After a while you didn't need to lie down to sleep, you weren't even sure of the difference between sleeping and waking. You simply sat. But at the end of it all, something had been imparted. You couldn't name or describe it.

Tarrant sat down on the bunk and rubbed his eyes wearily. No use wishing that he had the abilities of Modesty Blaise. Whatever was coming to him, he would have to meet it from his own meagre resources.

Play for time, he thought. Resist up to a point, then feed them a little false information. Make it hard stuff to check, mix in a little truth where it's unimportant. Plan your role and get into the skin of it. Stiff upper-lip type, high resistance to pain (oh, God!), but susceptible to dialectic argument. Fascist leanings—always good material for conversion to the other extreme.

All right. Now, what do you hang on to when it gets bad? You're playing for time. Time for what? There has to be a spark of hope. Modesty. She was there at the Auberge du Tarn, no distance from where Reilly held a gun on you while the nuns gave you the needle. Did they fake an accident? Presumably. So Reilly will have a prepared story to tell. And Modesty won't swallow it. She won't. She'll talk to Reilly, that's certain. She'll spot something. Hunch. Instinct. She won't swallow it. She'll come looking for you. That's right. Just give her time. Play for time . . .

In a small part of his mind he knew that he was deceiving himself. The opposition would have covered his disappearance in a way that was water-tight, and there was no real hope at all. But a false hope was better than nothing.

*   *   *

"I once knew a girl who was a dactyliomancist," said Willie Garvin. He sat on a high stool in the big kitchen of the penthouse, eating raisins from a jar at his elbow.

Modesty, in a white blouse and tartan skirt, was making a batch of quiche lorraine for the deep-freeze, with constant reference to a cookery book. Her moderate-to-good culinary results were gained more by application than flair.

It was nine of a March evening, two days after her phone-call from Montmartre to tell of Tarrant's death. Willie had picked her up at London Airport a few hours ago. Little had been said between them about Tarrant. His passing had saddened them, but it did not lie in their natures to mourn.

Modesty looked up from the book and said, "A what?"

"A dactyliomancist. This girl I knew."

She gave a casual nod. "Oh, was she?"

"M'mm." Willie ate some more raisins. "She used a ring about two inches across, made of iron, with a little 'ole on one edge and a spike opposite."

"Not a bad idea." She returned to the cookery book. "Willie, why tell me that mixed grill snack we had was enough, and then sit eating all my raisins?"

"Oh, I'm not 'ungry, Princess. I just like eating raisins."

"I know. I seem to keep that jar filled just for you."

"Saves 'em going stale. You 'ardly ever use 'em for cooking."

"I'll be lucky to get the chance. Just a minute."

She went out of the kitchen. Willie pricked up his ears, listening for her footsteps and the opening and closing of doors. Yes, she had gone into the little study adjoining her lapidary work-shop, to have a quick look at the dictionary. He grinned. She wouldn't find the word in the Concise Oxford Dictionary there.

He ate a few more raisins. It was good to see her back. He never felt quite complete without her—not necessarily there with him in the same room or house or even county, but in the same country at least. She came back into the kitchen, frowning a little, and began measuring flour on the scales. Willie chuckled inwardly. He'd got her with dactyliomancist all right.

She said idly, "How did this girl make out with her predictions? I wouldn't have thought a suspended ring could tell you much."

He stared indignantly. "You've got a new dictionary!"

She turned her head and grinned at him with urchin triumph. "The complete O.E.D. You'll have to sweat for obscure words now, Willie love. How does this suspended ring work for fortune-telling, or were you just making it up?"

"I never make it up, Princess. It was when I was a kid, on the run from Borstal, and Doreen was an Irish scrubber I shacked up with in Liverpool for a few weeks. Thick as a brick, she was, but quite a looker, and like a demented anaconda in bed."

"That's good?"

"No. But at seventeen you're not all that discriminating, so it seems not bad. Trouble was, it was murder *getting* 'er to bed. Full of guilt and doubt, Doreen was. Spent hours arguing aloud with 'erself about whether she would or wouldn't. I'd sometimes drop off to sleep on the couch listening to 'er."

"What about the ring?"

"She used to 'ang it on a fine wire, 'old it up over a little table with a cross chalked on the top, so the spike on the ring nearly touched the cross, and ask it questions. It swung one way for yes, and the other way for no."

"That's not prediction."

"I know, but Doreen thought it was. She'd ask it about 'er job and 'er love-life and which stuff to use for dry 'air, and what picture to go and see. Everything."

"And trusted the answers?"

"Like 'oly writ. After the first week I rigged a big magnet on a swivel bar under the table, and I'd sit opposite 'er, working the answers with the magnet."

She gave a splutter of laughter. "You mean the should-she shouldn't-she answers?"

"Especially that. Saved 'er a lot of agonising and guilt."

"Golden-hearted Willie."

"They don't make 'em like me any more."

"Look, let me finish this, then I want to talk about Janet. Why don't you make yourself comfortable in the sitting room while you're waiting? There's a new Frank Zappa album on the stereo."

"I'd rather stay and watch, Princess."

"All right, but shut up while I concentrate, or I'll make a mess of this."

He sat contentedly, watching her move, think, frown, turn, bend, straighten, pour and mix. Her legs were a marvel, he thought without any shred of longing. But most of all he liked looking at the column of her throat. Even after so many years there were still moments when he felt amazed that it should be Willie Garvin, gutter-bred rough-neck, to whom she had given her total trust and friendship.

Half an hour later she sat with her legs tucked beneath her at one end of the big chesterfield, holding a cup of coffee. Willie, in a deep armchair on the other side of the coffee-table, said thoughtfully, "I still can't make much sense of it. The New Provident and Commercial Bank of Macao means Mr. Wu Smith, and 'e's the biggest villain in South-East Asia."

"Too big to bother with the handling percentage on a thousand dollars a month, that's certain. So it has to be more."

" 'ow can it be more, Princess?"

She stirred her coffee. "I don't know. But we do know Wu Smith, so there's more in it somewhere along the line."

They were silent for a while, thinking about the man in Macao. Wu Smith did not initiate crime. He was a backer and a handler, and he dealt in any commodity, no matter how dirty. His bank would finance any project Wu Smith deemed sound, and he was a skilled judge. He financed those who operated in drugs, vice, gold-smuggling, currency coups, and whatever else he thought sufficiently profitable. His backing was expensive but reliable. He also handled stolen goods on a huge scale, and his bank was available to those who needed absolute secrecy concerning whatever passed through their accounts. The New Provident was even more secure than a Swiss bank, for it had the advantage of being immune to official inquiry on the grounds of suspected criminal activities by its clients.

Macao made this possible because it was small, a miniature Hong Kong, six square miles of Portuguese territory lying eight thousand miles from Lisbon, hemmed against the South China Sea by the great brooding mass of the Chinese mainland. In this colonial speck of ground the law had always been flexible, yielding to the corrupt systems of the old China. Here Mr. Wu Smith was too big to be touched as long as he did not directly provoke Lisbon.

Five minutes after she had last spoken Modesty said, "You don't go into the plastic gnome business with only one plastic gnome to sell. So Janet's sister can't be the only one on the hook. Wu Smith's handling the take for somebody with a lot of clients to squeeze."

Willie looked mildly surprised. "A blackmail job's usually a one-off thing. Mr. X knows Mr. Y did something nasty to Mrs. Z in the woodshed, and puts the screws on. I mean, you can't exactly advertise for customers, so where do you pick up the dirt on a whole block of 'em?"

"I've never thought about it before, but I fancy someone has now, so let's do the same. Go on Willie, where do you dig dirt by the shovel-load?"

Another five minutes passed, and Willie said slowly, "The Americans use psychiatrists like we use dentists. Regular sessions. A shrink would collect dirt wholesale, wouldn't 'e?"

She gave him the rare smile that lit her face from within and always brought him a special pleasure. "Willie the Wonderboy does it again. Yours may not be the right answer, but that doesn't matter a damn. It's an answer.

Anyone with access to the tapes and records of the right kind of shrink could get himself a list of clients. You might ask Janet if her sister has a psychiatrist."

"I'll do that. It's somewhere to start from."

After another long silence she said, "It's beginning to take a little shape, Willie. Suppose they've given a switcheroo to the old technique. You don't squeeze your clients dry, you make a careful assessment of what they can afford to pay on a regular basis, without becoming so desperate that they cut their throats or break down and blow the whole thing."

"A steady income and all risks cut to minmum?" He blinked. "Jesus. If it's a phoney charity account, like Janet said, they probably get tax relief on what they pay."

She half laughed. "It's smooth. But it's still blackmail. We'd better go out to Macao and see Wu Smith."

Willie rubbed his chin uneasily. "Look, you don't 'ave to mix in on this, Princess. Janet said——"

"I can guess what she said, Willie love. Did you put her right?"

"I said you'd jump at a chance to square things a bit."

"Good."

"What do we do about Wu Smith, though? We put a load of stolen bullion through 'im once, back in *The Network* days, but we're not exactly dear old mates. We want whoever's be'ind the blackmail account. Wu Smith won't give it away and won't sell it, that's for sure. Maybe we could snatch 'im, but it'd be quite a trick." He frowned. "Even then you'd need a blow-lamp to make 'im talk, and that's not our form."

"We'll just have to think of something."

Her Indo-Chinese houseboy, Weng, came into the sitting room and said, "Have you finished with the coffee, Miss Blaise?"

"No more for me. Willie? All right, you can clear away, Weng. And when you've done that, get on the phone and book three seats on the earliest flight you can get to Hong Kong."

"Three seats, Miss Blaise?"

"Yes. You'll be coming with us."

Weng's dark face above the white jacket broke into a smile. "It will be very enjoyable for me to see Hong Kong again." Modesty had put him through University there, and it had been his home for four years.

She said, "You're still in contact with your old friends?"

"Yes. I am an industrious correspondent, Miss Blaise."

"Good. When you've fixed the flight, book two calls to Hong Kong. The first to Li Feng. Do you think he'll rent us that house he owns on Lantau for a few days?"

"For the right price, certainly. Better to let me negotiate for you, Miss Blaise."

"All right. Then I want to speak to Charlie Wan. Or Susie if he's not in." She looked at her watch. "He should be, it's three a.m. there now, and it'll probably only be six when you get the call through."

Willie said, "Charlie Wan?"

She gave a small shrug. "Nothing specific yet. I just think he might be helpful."

"You could 'ave Charlie's right arm after what you did for 'is wife."

When Weng had picked up the tray and gone, Willie said, "Look, are you sure you want to dive into this right away, Princess?"

"I'm glad of something to do." She got up, went to the sideboard, and returned with a board and chess set. "Let's play for a while, Willie."

"Sure. You got any ideas?"

"It's my turn for white, and if you play your usual

Indian Defence against a Queen's Pawn opening I've thought of a variation on the seventh move that's going to devastate you."

He smiled. "I meant about Mr. Wu Smith."

She began to set out the pieces. "I've got a germ, Willie. A very small germ. It'll grow better if I leave it alone and don't keep prodding it about." She moved her queen's pawn forward two squares. "Come on, take your thrashing like a man."

At noon the next day Lady Janet Gillam received a phone call from Willie Garvin. He said, " 'Allo, Jan. Just thought I'd let you know I've talked to Modesty and we'll be away for a bit. Maybe a week, maybe less. It depends 'ow things go."

She felt sudden anxiety. "You mean about my sister?"

"That's right. It's only the first step, but if it comes off we'll know who's be'ind that account, and we can take it from there."

"Willie, I want to come with you."

"Eh?" His voice was incredulous. "Don't talk wet, Jan. There's nothing you could do."

"I know. I won't get in the way, but I want to . . . to be somewhere near, anyway."

"But there's no point, love."

He heard her impatient exhalation. "Willie, this isn't easy to explain, but there's a big piece of you that's just— oh, I don't know—a sort of blank to me. For God's sake, I don't want to *own* you, I only want to get a wee glimpse inside that blank."

"Better not, Jan," he said gently. "It gets a bit dark in there sometimes."

"Ah, you stupid . . . *man!* Let me speak to Modesty, she'll know what I mean."

"I expect she would, but it's just not on, Jan. Not this

time. We're flying out to Hong Kong in a couple of hours." There was a long silence. "You still there, Janet?"

"Aye, I'm here. And you'll be going on from Hong Kong to Macao? Is that it?"

"Something like that."

"All right, Willie. I'm too late this time, but I wish . . . well, tell her what I said, anyway." She gave a dry little laugh. "And please take care. We one-legged girls find fellows hard to come by."

"I'll probably 'ave to carve me way through a seething 'orde of 'em by the time I get back."

"Please call me as soon as you do, Willie. My best to Modesty, and thank her."

"I'll do that. 'Bye, Jan."

*　　*　　*

Mr. Sexton said in French, "So you believe she checked your wallets for identity?"

Gaston Bourget fingered the plaster on his jaw, and thought that this man's accent was even more horribly English than that of the English Prime Minister, Mr. Heet, whom he had once heard speaking in French on television. He said, "She checked for identity, yes." Hunching his shoulders he pushed his hands deeper into the pockets of his top-coat. "Why bring us to this godforsaken hole to talk?"

The four men stood within the thick walls of a dry-stone hut set on the slope of a thinly grassed valley amid the foothills of the Pyrenees. The floor was of beaten earth, the roof timbers had rotted at the ends and fallen in years ago. The heavy door had survived its hinges and lay on the ground. There had never been a window.

Mr. Sexton eased the rucksack from his back and set it

down. It gave the sound of iron clanking on iron as he did so. He said, "It is a convenient place. You took a taxi from the station to Miellet, then walked over the hills as instructed?"

The biggest of the three Frenchmen, the leader, said sourly, "Eight kilometres. It was unnecessary."

"I think not. This woman Blaise has important friends in high places here in France. They could well be looking for you."

Jacques Garat, who had two fingers in a splint, said, "They will not find us. And if they did we would tell them nothing, you can rest assured."

Mr. Sexton smiled. "I shall do that."

The leader said, "There remains the question of payment. That is why we have made the journey today, m'sieu."

"Payment, Servalle? But you failed to carry out the work. You fumbled the job, and now you must disappear. I don't want you questioned by the police."

"*You* failed to warn us that Modesty Blaise was involved."

"That was a chance matter. Such contingencies are your affair."

"We do not agree with you, M'sieu Sexton. You expect us to disappear without payment?"

The three men moved a little, making a half-circle about the Englishman, and abruptly the atmosphere was ugly. Mr. Sexton gave a genial chuckle. "I certainly expect you to disappear," he said, and on the last word, with no apparent preliminary movement, he rose clear of the ground in a twisting jump, his left foot driving forward like a piston. It took Gaston Bourget in the throat, smashing his larynx.

Mr. Sexton landed on his right foot, lightly poised and

76

spinning, the heel of the left striking the back of Servalle's knee as he lunged at the place where Mr. Sexton had been an instant before. Servalle cried out in pain as his legs were swept from under him, the cry changing to a gasp as his back hit the ground.

Garat had a gun half-drawn when his arm was paralysed by the grasp of fingers which felt like rods of iron driving into flesh and muscle. The scream was still in his throat when Mr. Sexton, with a sharp exhalation of breath, struck a hand-edge blow which stove in a section of Garat's skull above one ear.

Servalle was coming unsteadily to his feet. Mr. Sexton turned briskly, drove a stiff thumb into his midriff, took him in a curious grip of the head, turned again and flipped him almost casually over in a somersault, retaining the grip on the head so that the neck snapped abruptly in mid-throw.

When the dead body hit the ground, Mr. Sexton looked about him, white teeth showing in a grin of delight. With sprightly enthusiasm he moved to his rucksack and opened it. Inside was a considerable length of steel chain. Five minutes later he had passed an end of the chain through a small gap in the wall opposite the doorway, and secured it round the door which he had carried out and propped against the outside of the wall at that point.

He put on thick gloves, took the other end of the chain, moved back through the doorway, found a projecting ridge of rock against which to set his feet, passed the chain round his waist, took a grip on it like the anchor-man in a tug-of-war team, and braced himself.

For half a minute he breathed deeply, concentrating, then suddenly poured his strength into a steadily increasing pull. The ancient door pressed hard against the outside of the wall, its timbers groaning. The chain quivered, then grew still, rigid as a bar. A big stone fell from the top of the wall, then another. The wall itself teetered, leaned slowly inwards, and fell.

Mr. Sexton straightened up and nodded approval, then moved to release the chain and draw it from under the pile of stones. The two end walls, unsupported by the rear wall now, offered less resistance when he came to topple them inwards by the same method. And the front wall, pierced by the doorway, came down easily in two sections.

At the end of ten minutes there was nothing to be seen but a great mound of rough-hewn grey stones. The three bodies lay buried beneath it. Mr. Sexton surveyed his handiwork, packed the chain into his rucksack, put the heavy rucksack on his back, and set off cheerfully on the fifteen kilometre walk to the small village where he had left his car that morning.

It was satisfying to feel he could now report to Colonel Jim that he had taken out a little insurance, as instructed.

CHAPTER FIVE

Mr. Wu Smith yawned contentedly as he made his way up the gangway of the hundred-ton motor cruiser, *Dama Infeliz*, anchored at his private mooring in Taipa harbour, the green and red flag of Portugal fluttering at the mast in the moonlight.

He had just won a thousand dollars at the one form of gambling he permitted himself. His cricket, Silver Dragon, had defeated the much-favoured cricket of his old friend Chung in a twenty-minute battle. Wu Smith leaned on the gleaming brass rail with no fear of soiling his beautifully tailored white suit, and recalled the event with pleasure.

Victory had involved careful training. Silver Dragon came from a graveyard, as did all the best fighting crickets. But Silver Dragon had come from an English graveyard in Hong Kong, perhaps where the dust of one of Wu Smith's own ancestors lay. He had fed it a special diet of lotus seed with rice which had been soaked in milk before being cooked with frogs' legs. And he had allowed it union with a female cricket once a week, to maintain the Essential Harmony of yin and yang. Tonight Silver Dragon had won, despite old Chung's brushing at his cricket's antennae with a hair before the fight to make it angry.

Yes, it had been a good evening, thought Mr. Wu Smith. In fact it had been a good year, with his various enterprises prospering handsomely. Not for the first time, he reflected how fortunate it was that a Chinese ɯandarin had granted this scrap of land to the Portuguese more than four centuries ago, in recognition of their work in suppressing piracy.

It was good to be a citizen of this tiny European province which clung to the great bulk of China like a flea on an elephant, to be one of the quarter-million human beings packed into the mainland peninsular and the two islands of Taipa and Coloane, which together made up the colony. The whole area was smaller than Kennedy Airport, which he had once passed through, but there were advantages in smallness.

Because Macao was small, Red China did not covet her. Like Hong Kong, little more than an hour's run eastward on the hydrofoil, she provided a commercial pore through which the giant could breathe. Mr. Wu Smith approved the government of the colony. Those responsible to Lisbon did not allow Macao to degenerate into a cess-pit of vice and crime, though this was a myth that died hard in the West. At the same time, they were prudent and understanding men in a commercial sense, who knew the value and necessity of invisible exports. Free trade in gold. Twenty-two tons imported annually. None officially exported. It went out all over the Far East in small packets, to people who would never trust in paper, and who paid a high premium for the yellow metal to store away in secret places.

The New Provident and Commercial Bank of Macao prospered. The network of various agency operations prospered. Through Mr. Wu Smith you could buy a woman in Aleppo and sell her in Monte Video. There were packets of heroin passing through Marseilles now which had originated as raw opium in the Golden Triangle where Burma met Thailand and Laos; on this Wu Smith had received commission, though the produce of the poppy had never come within five hundred miles of Macao.

Even the cross-border commerce with the Communists was thriving. There were commodities Mao's children needed which Wu Smith could supply. His relationship with General Ching Po, the authority in the Kwangtung area beyond the Barrier Gate, was excellent according to the agents who handled these matters. Mr. Wu Smith himself would not have dreamed of crossing the border, even if the Chinese permitted it. He considered them too unpredictable. In a business sense you could trust them, but their political suspicions were so violent and illogical as to make them dangerous. Never mind. He could deal with them without exposing himself to personal risk.

Mr. Wu Smith was a man who had spent most of his life being careful not to expose himself to personal risk. He was well aware that he had enemies, both within the law and within its opposite extreme, the underworld. He moved nowhere without his personal bodyguard, the silent Thailander who stood two paces away now. His house was a stronghold, and when he slept on the motor cruiser, which he much preferred when the weather was fair, it always lay at anchor half a mile off-shore. There were five other guards aboard, all armed, and two of them took shifts in watching the radar screen once the vessel had anchored for the night, to give warning of any approach.

Wu Smith wondered whether to send for a girl to round off the evening, and decided against it. The pleasure of the cricket fight was enough. Only a foolish man made the mistake of crowding one pleasure upon another.

He turned to the Thailander and said in Chinese, "Cast off and move out to the anchorage. I shall sleep now."

As he entered his cabin he felt the engines murmur gently, easing *Dama Infeliz* away from her mooring.

81

Under the hull, where the keel knifed down, two scuba-suited figures clung to magnetic limpets clamped to the steel plates. They were large limpets. If the cruiser accelerated suddenly it would be the grasp of human hands that broke before the grip of the limpets. But *Dama Infeliz* was merely moving out to anchor for the night, and idled gently on her way, as expected.

Ten minutes later the guard on radar-duty switched on the screen and settled down to his four-hour vigil. Close under the rake of the stern, Modesty Blaise and Willie Garvin surfaced quietly. They had already unstrapped their aqualungs and weight-belts, allowing them to sink. A waterproof bag was attached to Willie's leg. He inflated a rubber ring, so that they could float easily without treading water, and attached it to the stern by a large rubber suction disc on the end of a cord. Together they waited in the darkness. The water was cool but not cold, and their wet-suits provided insulation, but at intervals they exercised for five minutes, hand against hand in a session of controlled and silent Indian wrestling, to forestall stiffness.

One hour after midnight the guard on the radar screen in the wheelhouse felt a current of cool air, though he had not heard the door open. As he turned, the light went out. That was the last thing he remembered for some hours. The two patrolling deck-guards had each suffered a comparable experience already. One had a stiff neck and the other a lump over one ear as mementoes, but neither remembered when the blow had been struck. Soon the three off-duty men, including Wu Smith's personal bodyguard, passed from sleep to deeper unconsciousness as a result of inhaling ether sprayed from an aerosol container. So did Mr. Wu Smith, lying asleep in his luxurious cabin.

Ten minutes later the beam of a flash-lamp flickered twice from the deck, and in response two men in a dinghy with an outboard motor began to row steadily towards the *Dama Infeliz* from the point half a mile away, where they had been waiting. Weng was at the tiller.

The dinghy came alongside the motor cruiser, and left almost at once with three extra passengers, one of them unconscious and wrapped in a blanket.

*   *   *

Mr. Wu Smith woke to find himself lying on a canvas bed in a room with peeling white-washed walls. The shock was considerable. A single naked electric lamp of high wattage hung from the ceiling, its dazzle making him wince. One large window was heavily curtained with blanket material.

Wu Smith lifted himself on one elbow. How could this be? he wondered dazedly. He had gone to sleep in his cabin on *Dama Infeliz*, securely guarded, and woken here in this . . . this place. Bare boards, trestle-table, filing cabinets against the wall, cheap wooden chairs. It was like a room in army barracks.

His stomach turned over as he brought the figure sitting behind the table into focus. Chinese. Forty or fifty years old. Black cropped hair. Drab greenish-brown uniform with red tabs on the collar. Cap with a five-pointed red star resting on the table at his elbow as he sat with head bent over an open file, one of several stacked in a neat pile.

Wu Smith sat up slowly, feeling sick. A soldier stood at the door. Slung on his shoulder was a Type 56 assault rifle, the Chinese Communist version of the Russian 7·62 mm. AK-47. Another soldier sat at a radio in the corner, earphones on his head, writing on a message-pad. Wu Smith looked again at the man behind the table. There would be no insignia of rank, he knew. The Party had abolished such bourgeois displays of class since 1965, dividing the People's Liberation Army into two groups only, commanders and fighters. The man's uniform was of better quality cloth than the uniforms of the other two soldiers, but Wu Smith did not need this to tell him who was in which category.

The man looked up. "So you are awake," he said in Chinese, and lit a cigarette. Wu Smith recognised the packet. The cigarettes were manufactured in Canton.

Wu Smith said shakily, "What has happened?"

The man behind the table exhaled smoke and studied Wu Smith with cold, uninterested eyes. "I am General Wang Shi-Chen. You have entered the People's Republic secretly, without permission, and will now be interrogated."

Wu Smith gulped and waggled a protesting hand. His head throbbed and his mind was fuzzy. "I did not enter secretly——I mean, of my own wish I did not enter at all!"

General Wang Shi-Chen closed the file and said to the soldier at the door. "Take him away and bring him back one week from today in a more co-operative frame of mind."

Wu Smith said frantically. "No! If you please, General, I simply wished to say that I am here by . . . by mischance. That my offence was not——was not deliberate. I should be greatly obliged if you would call General Ching Po on the telephone. He will vouch for my . . . my goodwill towards the People's Republic."

"Ching Po has been arrested," the man at the table said, his cold eyes flaring with sudden anger. "It was Chairman Mao himself who discovered that Ching Po was no true comrade but a capitalist spy and an enemy of the party."

Wu Smith felt as if he had been hit with a hammer. After a long silence he said with a ghastly attempt to smile,

"Thank heaven for Chairman Mao's infallible perception. I was completely deceived."

"Chairman Mao's abilities are not to be attributed to a non-existent heaven."

"Of course, of course. A thoughtless phrase, General." Wu Smith ransacked his mind for safe words, and said hopefully, "I shall be very glad to answer whatever you wish to ask me."

General Wang Shi-Chen drew a pad towards him and stubbed out his cigarette. "You will bear in mind that we know a great deal concerning your operations, Wu Smith. If what you tell me fails to conform with what we know, you will have cause to regret it."

Sweat broke out on Wu Smith's face. "There is no question of that, General."

"Sit there." The pencil pointed to a chair facing the table. Wu Smith got unsteadily to his feet and almost fell into the chair. The man behind the table looked at the watch on his wrist and said, "Let us begin with an account of your commerce with the traitor Ching Po."

An hour later Mr. Wu Smith's throat, already dry from fear, was becoming sore from talking. It was a horrible thing to find himself pouring out secrets of professional contacts and activities he had nursed to himself for so many years, but he no longer cared. Given total co-operation, these maniacs might, just might decide to set him free. For Wu Smith at this moment nothing else counted. He had always made the protection of his clients a firm principle, even at financial expense to himself, but he saw no virtue in doing so with his own well-loved skin at the mercy of fanatics.

He talked of gold and drugs, diamonds and wheat shipments, foreign exchange manipulation and casino operations. He named officials amenable to bribery, and men who aided the flow of escapees across the channel from Lapa Island. He was able to deny indignantly and truthfully that he gave any aid to traitors escaping from the happy paradise of The People's Republic, or that he passed secrets of the peace-loving army and navy to the imperialist powers.

It was somewhere towards the end of the first hour that General Wang Shi-Chen turned a page of the pad and said, "Your bank, The New Provident and Commercial Bank of Macao, has the account of . . ." He referred to a thick notebook. "The South-East Asia Refugee Childrens' Relief Fund?"

Mr. Wu Smith shook his head dully. "No."

The black eyes hardened, and the pencil tapped warningly on the table. "Think carefully, Wu Smith. We know what we know."

Anxiety pierced the lethargy which had settled upon Wu Smith. His hands fluttered. "I assure you, General. I handle no account of that name."

"Think again. It is a cover account. A false charity."

"Ah!" Relief spread through Wu Smith. "We have only one such account. You must mean The Orient Society for the Disabled."

"Possibly." There was suspicion in Wang Shi-Chen's look. "Who is the principal?"

"I have not met him. My dealings have been with a man called da Cruz, a white Portuguese. Almost white."

"I ask again, who is the principal?" Wang Shi-Chen glanced at his notebook, then looked up again with the manner of a man awaiting confirmation.

Wu Smith said, "All cheques, drafts and authorities must bear the signature J. Straik."

"The spelling?" Wang Shi-Chen jotted the name down. Then, "A foreign name. English perhaps. In Hong Kong?"

"No. Until a few weeks ago the address for correspondence was in New York. I—I cannot remember the details. Since then the bank has been given a new address. In France." Wu Smith rubbed his forehead in an effort to concentrate. "A castle. Chateau Lancieux. I do not remember the town or village, but it lies in the department of Ariège. I can of course look it up in our records, and would be very glad to send you all details——"

"It is quite unimportant, Wu Smith." The man at the table tore the page from his pad and crumpled it. "A number of my questions are designed to ascertain whether or or not you are telling the truth."

"I assure you——"

"I am assuring myself, Wu Smith. Now let us move to another matter. You have a financial interest in a group which distributes dirty films."

"*Dirty*, General?" Wu Smith was horrified. "I understood they were instructional. I have not seen any myself, of course . . ."

Wu Smith did not know how much later it was when his tormentor at last put down the pencil, sat back and made a curt gesture towards the soldier at the door, who came forward with a glass of water. Wu Smith took the glass in unsteady hands and drank greedily.

"Thank you, General," he croaked, bobbing his head and trying to smile. "Most kind of you. I trust I have been of some assistance . . ." The glass was taken from him. "And that my—my mischance in entering The People's Republic without permission will be excused?"

General Wang Shi-Chen permitted himself a shrug which seemed to hold some degree of approval. "That is yet to be decided. But it lies in your favour that you have behaved wisely throughout this interrogation."

Wu Smith barely heard the last words. A great darkness was engulfing his mind. He felt himself toppling sideways, and then there was no more. The soldier caught him and nodded to the radio operator, who got to his feet. Together they carried Wu Smith to the bunk.

General Wang Shi-Chen blew out a long breath and stood up. In excellent but slightly accented English he said, "My God, I'm a damn sight more tired than when I last played Hamlet."

The door opened. Modesty Blaise and Willie Garvin came in. They both wore slacks and sweaters. Behind them came Weng, grinning. Modesty went to General Wang Shi-Chen, put her arms round his neck and pressed her cheek against his. "You should win an Oscar for that, Charlie. We got everything on tape. I couldn't follow it all, but enough to know you were marvellous. And you had only twenty-four hours to rehearse."

Charlie Wan, who had graduated from Pembroke College, Cambridge, sixteen years ago, smiled and said, "It was a good brief you gave me, and I've always liked improvising."

"You're sure he'll never recognise you again?"

"Not without the cheek-pads, and when my hair's grown again. He rarely comes to Hong Kong anyway, and I'm too busy directing for the University to appear on-stage myself. You got the main thing? Straik?"

"Yes. Chateau Lancieux. You buried it beautifully in a mass of other stuff."

"Susie says I'm to bring you and Willie home for dinner. Young Weng and his friends too, of course."

"We might just make it before we fly out tonight. I'll call you at home, Charlie. Can you and Weng's boys get this studio of Li Feng's back in shape?"

"No trouble." Charlie Wan, President of the Drama Society at Hong Kong University, looked across at the unconscious form of Wu Smith. "What about that?"

"He'll wake up soon after dark in a boat tied up near the Hydrofoil Pier on Macao."

Willie Garvin said speculatively, "Wonder what 'e'll make of it all?"

"He'll probably think it was real, until he finds that General Ching Po still runs Kwangtung." Laughter sparkled in her eyes. "After that . . . well, I suppose it'll give him something to sweat about for the next few months, wondering who made him sing and why."

Willie grinned. " 'For they that led us away captive required of us then a song.' Psalm 'undred and thirty-seven, verse three."

*　　*　　*

Tarrant sank down on to the bunk and stretched out his legs. His mouth felt coated with bile, and throughout his body the nerves twitched and shrilled their message of pain. His clothes were rumpled and grubby, the jacket ripped. He felt like a living scarecrow.

His mind was a little clearer than it had been since the session with Mellish and Colonel Jim earlier. No doubt the more recent treatment from Mr. Sexton had helped to clear some of the drug-induced sluggishness.

Tarrant looked at the tiny marks made by his thumb-nail on the wooden head of the bunk. Six days now, if his calculations were correct. They were taking things slowly and carefully, thank God. It made sense, of course. You could break a man in hours with violent torture, but you were almost certain to produce severe mental confusion in him. This could reduce the output of his memory by as much as fifty percent, and rendered what he did tell you unreliable.

They weren't using large doses of the barbiturate/

stimulant, he thought. That could be self-defeating, too. The so-called truth drugs didn't make anybody tell the truth. They relaxed tension and made you expansive, then put you very quickly to sleep. So the trick was to blend in a stimulant like methamphetamine, which produced a sense of alertness and well-being. So you talked, and garrulously. But with great effort you could just keep ahead of your words and steer them into half-truths or lies or non-sense.

He closed his eyes and made a conscious effort to relax his weary body. Six days now. It might soon be time to pretend collapse and start feeding out a little of the false information he had spent so many hours concocting. That might give him a few days respite.

It wasn't the kind of information he had expected them to squeeze out of him. This much had emerged at that extraordinary first interview, after the bearded man had come to take him from the cell. Mr. Sexton. Tarrant knew all their names now, even knew that this was the Chateau Lancieux, a small and lonely castle standing amid the foot-hills of the Pyrenees. Only one part of it was in use, but from what he had seen he judged it to be of the sixteenth century, restored in the nineteenth. Today it would be a white elephant, of interest only to a recluse . . . or to some-body like Colonel Jim.

Tarrant remembered his first sight of Colonel Jim, sitting at the desk in what had probably once been a sewing room and was now a study. The brainless blonde woman, astonishingly his wife, was lolling in an armchair to one side of the big desk, painting her nails, when Mr. Sexton ushered him in. The hook-nosed Scotswoman, called Clare by everyone except Mr. Sexton, who called her Mrs. McTurk, was about to leave.

Colonel Jim was watching his wife fondly, but swivelled

his chair to face them as the two men entered. Mr. Sexton said, "Sir Gerald Tarrant, Colonel Jim."

The big head nodded and a big hand gestured ponderously. "Sit down, Mr. Tarrant. I guess we don't worry too much about titles here. Okay, Clare, you run along."

Tarrant sat down in a chair facing the desk, weighing up the American and coming to the unhappy conclusion that he was formidable. Mr. Sexton moved away and leaned against the wall. Colonel Jim smiled a toothy, saurian smile and said, "Let's get down to the nitty-gritty, Mr. Tarrant. You're in charge of the Special Intelligence Section of the British Foreign Office. You've had quite a lot of time to think about things the last day or so, and you're pretty damn sure that you're in the hands of somebody who's going to dig a lot of important secrets out of you."

The blonde giggled. "Like secret formulas, Poppa, and the plans of the new carburettor for a submarine, I bet that's what he thinks."

"Now hush up, Momma," Colonel Jim said amiably. "I'm talking business with this guy." He looked at Tarrant. "Well, you can stop sweating, Mister. We don't want your crummy secrets. Just lemme tell you about my kind of business." He opened a humidor on the desk. "Cigar?"

Tarrant said crisply, "No, thank you."

Colonel Jim lit one for himself and leaned back, looking at the glowing end. "I'm in blackmail. You could say I'm doing for blackmail what Ford did for automobiles. Lemme ask you a question, Mr. Tarrant. Where's the big dough these days? The big tax-free dough?"

Tarrant said, "I'd rather you told me."

"It's in crime, Mister. But there's a hell of a lotta competition, on the trading side and the service side both. Drugs, flesh, heists, gambling, whatever you do you gotta fight cops and competitors. Blackmail's different." He leaned forward and jabbed the air impressively with his cigar. "Blackmail's the *only* crime where the losers co-operate with you. Right? And they're more scared of the cops coming in than you are. Right?"

His wife said, "Right, Poppa." She waved her hand in the air, fingers spread. "You like this colour?"

"Suits you fine, Momma. Just fine. I like 'em good and red. You know anything about business, Mr. Tarrant?"

Tarrant fought down a sense of unreality and said, "Not a great deal. But more than you, if you seriously imagine I'm likely to be a profitable blackmail client."

Colonel Jim chuckled, and the slatey eyes gleamed. "You're not a client, Mr. Tarrant. You're more like virgin ground where there's raw material waiting to be dug out. In a business like this we need material to work on. Now over in the States I got a big stake in six very ritzy private nursing homes. All legitimate. Right? The only thing is, I get to see the records. A lotta folk have breakdowns, a lotta folk have sex problems, drink problems, kink problems. So we help 'em. We use deep analysis, hypnosis, modern drugs, all ways to crack 'em wide open and get at what's screwing 'em up. You beginning to see the shape of the picture, Mr. Tarrant?"

With carefully judged distaste Tarrant said, "I assume a proportion of the material you extract in this way is suitable for blackmail."

"Right on the nose. So now I'm moving into Europe and I need raw material here, but we can't work the same set-up. They won't have me start any nursing-homes here. Same in Germany, Spain, Italy and the goddam U.K."

His wife looked up. "They said *we* were foreigners! Imagine it. Who do they think they are, calling you an' me foreign, Poppa? They're crazy."

"I guess the way they look at it, we could be kinda

foreign to *them*, Momma," Colonel Jim said reasonably. Then, to Tarrant, "So you can see where we're at, Mister. You're our starter for raw material. I figured we'd cover U.K. first."

Tarrant frowned. "I don't follow you," he lied.

Colonel Jim spread a hand. "Security. Screening. I had a real expert assessment made on the number of files that pass through your hands in a year. Some of 'em have to carry a lotta dirt. I figure if you really got down to remembering hard, you could come up with maybe fifty or sixty names to make suitable clients for this operation."

"Absurd."

"Man in your position, right at the top, he needs a real good memory, Mr. Tarrant. He's the one with the overall picture. You see a little thing here and a little thing there, and they click with a little thing you read in a file last year someplace. Then you set your boys to check up. Right? So we can use that kinda memory. You know the dirt and the names that go with it, so all you got to do is tell us." Colonel Jim smiled the toothy smile that formed a horizontally curving slit almost to his back teeth. "And you don't even have any trouble conscience-wise. Right? Like I said, I don't want to know about bombs or torpedos and all that crud. Just the dirt."

He lifted a hand as Tarrant started to speak. "One more thing. A real rich client's fine. But revenue-wise we're very happy to service the little guys. Lemme put you in the picture. We run an inquiry on a client, and we *don't* squeeze him till the pips squeak." He curled his big, spatulate fingers gently, as if holding an imaginary orange. "We just pressure him to twenty-five percent below the safety line, and that's where we fix the retainer he pays for our goodwill. You get me?"

"A retainer? You mean they keep paying?"

93

"Ninety-eight percent, so far. We've had only three clients who got dissatisfied and went to the cops. Only line of inquiry they got is through our receiving agency. Soon as that happens, we get word. Then Mr. Sexton here takes over."

"He reveals the dirt?"

"Hell no. Never that. He kills 'em, Mister. Makes it look accidental. He's the greatest at that. You should know."

"But meanwhile your receiving agency has been pinpointed."

"Foreign-based institution. No easy way of bringing action against it. Besides, we got a nice routine. Say the F.B.I. or Interpol make enquiries. Our agent says what the hell is this all about? He says he's had payments from the client totalling so much over a period so long, for a charity relief fund that this agent operates. So the guy wants it *back* now? He's telling some crazy *story*? So here's a draft for the dough. All of it. And we want no further subscriptions from this person."

Colonel Jim waved a hand in a conclusive gesture, then smiled again. "By this time he's dead. Or she is. Right? So the cops think they been taken for a ride by some kinda nut. What blackmailer gives the dough back? What blackmailer doesn't spill the dirt when a guy turns stubborn?" He drew on his cigar and shook his head sagely. "Cops get confused easy. Mind you, if it happened ten, fifteen times, maybe they'd get to wondering a little. But it won't, Mr. Tarrant. I'm a good marketing man, and I fix just the price the market can carry."

Tarrant hoped he was hiding what he felt. Danger lay in this sense of relief welling from the knowledge that if secrets were torn from him they would be secrets of little importance to security. The danger was that once you began to talk it was hard to stop, and he had no way of knowing whether Colonel Jim's plausible account of his business activities was true. This might be a subtle psychological move, to open him up readily in one area so that it would then be easy to probe him in other areas. There was the more positive personal danger that when he had been sucked dry, regardless of the purpose, he would be killed. That was obvious.

He said stiffly, "I have no information to give."

Colonel Jim nodded. "I figured you'd feel that way. Well, we're not gonna hurry you, Mr. Tarrant. You just think it over for a few days." He heaved his bulk from the chair and moved to where his wife sat. "Get your pretty li'l butt off there and sit on Poppa's lap, Momma."

She giggled, and Tarrant watched them settle themselves in the armchair. An arm round the woman, Colonel Jim said, "Make it just two minutes, Mr. Sexton."

The man in the black blazer, who looked like a Viking or a Crusader, stepped forward briskly and took Tarrant's arm. Next moment Tarrant gasped with shock as he was plucked from his chair. He had never dreamt that such strength could exist in a man. He was on his feet for no more than a second, then a finger jabbed at him twice, in the shoulder and thigh-joint. It was like being jabbed by a steel bar, and each finger-blow hit precisely upon a nerve-centre. Paralysing pain exploded through his arm and left leg. He crumpled to the floor, and Mr. Sexton flicked a foot at the side of his knee, striking with the toe.

Somehow Tarrant prevented himself from screaming, and the sound he uttered was a quivering grunt of agony. He was lifted to his feet like a child, felt his arm seized and wrenched sharply, and reeled back against the chair as he was released. New pain swept him like a wave, and he thought his arm was broken.

The rest was a blurred nightmare of agony and

humiliation. Mr. Sexton worked briskly and clinically, like a man operating a machine he understood perfectly, probing the nerve-centres, knowing the precise degree of stress that sinew and bone could take without permanent damage.

Sometimes Tarrant was on the floor, sometimes on his knees, and sometimes, when he was lifted by those terrible hands, on his feet briefly. Once, as he swayed on all fours, his vision cleared for a few seconds when Mr. Sexton stepped back to consider his next move, and then he saw the stupid, excited face of Colonel Jim's wife as she sat on his lap in the armchair, eyes sparkling, body wriggling with pleasure.

The humiliation of being so helplessly punished before her was as bitter in its way as the pain was searing. When it ended, when he lay curled on the floor and Mr. Sexton stepped back for the last time, Tarrant could hear his own sobbing grunts, could feel tears running from his eyes, and knew a shame more crushing than anything his imagination could have conceived.

Later, in his cell, he lay making a conscious effort to repair the breaches that shock had made in his defences, enlisting pride, anger, hope, hatred, any emotion to help seal the cracks.

"Now you know," he told himself contemptuously. "Now you know, to just a small extent. This is what lies at the end of it for some of the men and women you've sent out. Remember Pirie? Remember him when you got him back by swapping the Hungarian? They'd broken Pirie, but it took them six weeks. There's a target for you to hang on to . . . Stiffen the sinews, you chairborne bastard, summon up the blood. Are you going to sing for creatures like these? Dear God, that ghastly woman . . . wriggling on that fat-bellied ape's lap, watching. And Mr. Universe

Sexton with his clever tricks. Modesty would take the smile off his face. Or Willie. But it's going to take time for them to find you, so you're on your own for a while. Like Pirie. Six-weeks Pirie. Relax . . . it's only pain. Let it wash through you. Don't fight it. Watch yourself, watch your reactions, keep a mental initiative . . ."

It was then that the Scottish woman, Clare, came into the cell. He thought fleetingly of trying to knock her unconscious, but abandoned the idea almost at once. His limbs were like lead, and she looked very strong. Also, he was quite certain that somebody, probably Mr. Sexton, was outside the door.

Clare sat down on a folding chair she had brought with her and began to work on a piece of crochet she carried, fingers flashing nimbly. As she worked she talked in her ladylike, sing-song accent. The content of what she said was all the more horrible by contrast with her manner, for she spoke of torture as if discussing cake-making at a vicarage tea-party.

"I'm sure I hope it won't come to the worst, not for a gentleman like yourself, Sir Gerald. You'll not mind me calling you Sir Gerald? Oh, whatever am I thinking of—— that's quite formal, isn't it now? What else should a body call you? And speaking of bodies, I remember another man Mr. Sexton had to deal with a few months back. In September, I think it was——och, no, it must have been late October, for I mind it was turning a wee bit chilly. Some sort of electrical thing it was that Mr. Sexton used in the end. A transformer, would it be? I've no head for such mechanical things, I'm afraid. I always say men have a more *natural* grasp of mechanics and suchlike, wouldn't you agree with me now, Sir Gerald? Well, whatever it was, it did awful severe damage to the poor wee man. His genitals, you know. I well mind saying to Angel at the time——but you've not really met Angel yet, have you? A nice girl, though maybe too kind-hearted for her own good in some ways, I often think. Well, I said to Angel at the time, 'That's one poor man who'll not be copulating again, mark my words,' I said. Of course that didn't arise in the end, for he completely lost his reason. I felt it was a happy release when Mr. Sexton finally did that bone-breaking-by-numbers performance of his, to put him to rest . . ."

And so it went on, the obscene menace clothed in tones of conversational gossip. Tarrant knew the purpose was carefully calculated, as everything that lay ahead of him would be calculated. This was to weaken him by anticipatory fear, and the fact that he realised the intention did very little to diminish its effect, for there was small cause to believe that the threat was a bluff.

The following day he was taken to the study again where a sandy man with sparse hair injected a drug into his arm and began to question him. Colonel Jim and his wife, Lucy, sat watching. The woman was eating chocolates fed her by Colonel Jim, who kept popping one between her full pouting lips every few minutes.

Tarrant was cautiously pleased with his control throughout this session. He could not help talking under the power of the drug, but he found himself able to anticipate the flow of what he was about to say, and to modify the truth so that it became either meaningless or harmless. Later, sitting in his cell with a mind still clouded, he warned himself against giving into a feeling of euphoric confidence. That would be a classic symptom presaging breakdown.

The same evening he suffered another session of pain and humiliation at Mr. Sexton's hands. It took place this time in a large room with a gallery round it. The room had been converted into something of a gymnasium, and reminded him a little of the long windowless building behind Willie Garvin's pub, which enclosed the work-out room where he and Modesty Blaise practised their skills.

There was no questioning, either before or after this beating by Sexton. It seemed to be more of a demonstration for the audience looking on from the gallery, Colonel Jim and his company. With them was a man Tarrant had not seen before, a dark man with a touch of Chinese in him, whose name he had since learnt was da Cruz. The session went on longer than before, to the accompaniment of excited little whoops and cries from Lucy Straik. "Hey, go man, go! Give him the finger job, Mr. Sexton! Wow! Hear that squeal!" But strangely, Tarrant found himself better able to endure this time. Perhaps anticipation had reduced the shock of the assault, he thought later. Perhaps one adapted to humiliation, and even to pain. Certainly he had not cared about the beastliness of the gloating Straik woman this time. He had simply let himself go limp, knowing that any attempt at protection would be useless, and tried to withdraw mind from body, not attempting to quell the sounds of agony that burst from him.

That night Angel came to him in the cell, whispering sympathy, glancing fearfully at the door, telling him what bastards they all were, and in the end trying to edge on to the bunk with him and offer the use of her body in consolation. He knew that this was their angle for the soft play; but even knowing it, he found to his horror that for a moment or two he was roused to crude desire. It was primitive reaction following the fear and the beating, the subconscious urge of the aching body and shaken mind for any form of reassurance, and he killed it quickly, with self-disgust, turning away from the half-naked girl with the muddy, evil-child eyes.

Next day he was provided with bread and cold soup, and left completely alone. Today, the sixth day he believed, there had been another session with Mellish and the needle. Some hours later Sexton had taken him to a well-appointed bathroom suite, provided him with an electric razor, and allowed him to make a complete toilet. Tarrant tried to remain impassive and avoid showing how thankfully he seized the opportunity to be clean and shaven. It was with distaste that he put on his grubby and rumpled clothes again.

When he was dressed he was taken to the dining-room, where Colonel Jim and his companions were being served dinner by two silent Japanese, broad-shouldered men, above average height for their race, who moved lightly on their feet. Noting their hands, the flesh thickened to hard corn along the edges, Tarrant knew them for karate men.

Dinner was a curious experience. The conversation was dull, dominated mainly by Lucy Straik, who rambled on with aimless enthusiasm and almost complete inconsequence about any subject that her husband or Mr. Sexton brought up. Tarrant was neither excluded from the conversation nor brought into it. He sat at the table with a sense of disassociation, accepting everything offered him to eat, but restricting himself to two glasses of the rather poor wine.

When dinner ended, the company moved to the gymnasium as if adjourning for entertainment in a drawing-room, and Tarrant was beaten again. This time, because of the sudden contrast, the shock hit deeply before he could brace himself against it.

He lay in his cell now, struggling to recover his mental balance. It would be Mellish with the hypodermic again tomorrow in all probability. Or a soft-sell interview in the study with Colonel Jim. Or one of Clare's talks followed by sympathy from Angel. Or something new. If he was going to feed out a little false information, better not to do it under the drug; he might too easily slip up. Squeeze out something reluctantly under Colonel Jim's questioning, perhaps. A show of wavering to begin with.

Tarrant considered his body for a moment. One eye half-closed. Plenty of bruises, and a swollen knee and elbow. Any number of minor twinges. But no broken bones yet, and no permanent damage. Sexton knew his job. They wanted him left with memory unimpaired when finally they broke him. A tricky business, to destroy the will without damaging other areas of the mind.

Six days now. Well, he could keep going for a while yet, Until Modesty came. (She won't and you know it——*stop thinking like that, fool.*) He could keep going till Modesty came. A few days? A week? Best not to look too far ahead.

Tarrant turned painfully on to his side. Like an alcoholic withstanding his devil in measures of twenty-four hours, he told himself that he would not break in the coming day.

CHAPTER SIX

Willie Garvin said, "No, I'll do it."

He took Modesty's empty plate and fork from her, and put them on top of his own. "A nice dish of spaghetti that was, Princess. Lovely sauce."

"It's all in the way I open the tin, Willie."

As he carried the plates out to the kitchen, Modesty refilled their glasses with red wine. Willie returned, sat down in the armchair by the coffee-table and picked up his glass. They had come into Heathrow that morning, and slept for most of the day. This would not prevent them going to bed in another two or three hours and sleeping the night through. Both possessed the knack of storing sleep or of going without for long periods. Modesty had put on a dark blue shirt and a grey skirt with a gold mesh belt. Willie wore a black sweater in fine jersey.

He said, "What's next then, Princess?"

"Well, it looks as if we've found the baddies." She thought for a few moments. "I suppose we ought to check with Janet before we make another move. Have you rung her?"

"I phoned from the airport while you were in the loo, but just to say we were back safe. I'd promised."

"We could go down and see her tomorrow."

"That's the day she usually comes up to town. I'll give 'er a ring and ask 'er to look in sometime during the afternoon, if that's all right."

"Fine." Modesty looked down into her glass. "She's going to want to come on this jaunt, if we go ahead."

"I only told you what she said about that because she asked me to. But she can't, Princess. I mean, taking Janet on a caper with us is crazy."

"Not exactly on it. But she'll want to be around. We could make a base twenty miles away, where she'd be all right. We'll get the map out again later."

Willie looked baffled. "I thought you'd just reckon it was a nonsense. We can't take 'er on a conducted tour up the sharp end of a caper, and she won't get much out of sitting around in the middle distance."

"It's something. She'll get a peek into the area of Willie Garvin that's a blank to her."

"Well . . . if you say so, Princess. I don't really get it."

"That's because you're male and dense, Willie love." The phone at her elbow rang. She picked it up, listened, and said, "Thank you, Albert, ask him to come up." Then, to Willie, "Jack Fraser's here."

A private lift from the reception area served the penthouse. When the gates slid open and Fraser stepped out on to the tiled floor of the wide foyer, Modesty was waiting to greet him. He was a rather small and very unimportant-looking man in a dark suit, carrying a bowler hat and a rolled umbrella. To the world in general he presented a nervous and humble aspect. This was as deceptive as his appearance. Before his promotion to a desk job, Fraser had fought in the great underground spy-war that erupted in Berlin during the fifties. He was clever, ruthless and experienced.

Tonight he did not wear his ingratiating manner, but put down his hat and umbrella on the drum table and said, "Hallo Modesty. Where the hell have you been hiding? Got any of that brandy left?"

"Large and neat?"

"That would be fine. Hallo, Willie." He moved down the three steps which pierced the low wrought-iron balustrade separating the foyer from the long sitting room with its ivory tiles, golden cedar-strip walls and Isfahan rugs.

Willie was at the small bar set in an alcove. He said, "Hallo, Jack. I'm sorry about Tarrant."

Fraser took the glass of brandy, murmured his thanks, and moved to the chesterfield, waiting for Modesty to seat herself before he sat down at the other end. "Something pretty rum came up," he said. "I'm buggered if I know whether it means anything or not, but I just want to throw it at you." He sipped the brandy, exhaled a little sigh of wonder and raised the glass to Modesty. "You must have robbed Olympus for this."

"Not Olympus. A German steel tycoon, some years back now. It came with the sundries, and I've only six bottles left."

"You're mad to offer it. Look, this morning I found out that Reilly had gone bent."

"Tarrant's driver?"

"That Reilly. I had a routine report from F. Section and there was a bit in it about Reilly."

"F. Section's the Far East?"

"Yes. We sent Reilly out to Hong Kong six weeks ago."

"That's odd. We're just back from there. Why did you send him?"

"Partly for experience. I've had in mind to recommend him for promotion to regular courier work, so I found a few small jobs for him to do. I was also testing him, so I had him covered."

"What happened?"

"A woman happened."

"Couriers go to bed with women like other people, Jack."

"This woman is suspect. A free-lance go-between. We've made use of her ourselves."

"If somebody paid her to pick up Reilly, how would they identify him for her?"

Fraser grimaced. "Look, I know Tarrant's position was supposed to be secret in this country, but half the Press knew and all the foreign opposition. Hundreds of people could have fingered Reilly as Tarrant's driver."

"All right, she picked him up. Then what happened?"

"We've no idea. But about two weeks later somebody paid three thousand pounds into an account Reilly had opened a few days before at a bank in Dublin. Transferred from The New Provident and Commercial Bank of Macao. That's Mr. Wu Smith, so we've no hope of tracing the payment to source."

He saw the glance exchanged by Willie and Modesty. "What's wrong?"

Willie said, "Nothing. It's just the flux."

"The what?"

"Willie calls it the flux," said Modesty. "He doesn't believe that coincidences are coincidences. He says there's a magnetic flux about the earth which causes like events to occur simultaneously or in sequence. Open *The Times Literary Supplement* and you find three different people have written books about Queen Victoria's third cousin twice removed who was Governor of Honduras or somewhere. All published in the same month. And nobody ever heard of him before. It's the flux."

"What the hell's it got to do with this?"

"We were talking about Wu Smith's bank half an hour ago. Something quite different. But go on. How did you pick up the Dublin account?"

"Just luck. The Treasury undercover boys have been twisting a few arms for us, to find out about I.R.A. money coming in from abroad. Reilly's name popped up under the heading of New Deposits. The Hong Kong report came in the same day. Some fool had held over the thing about Reilly and this woman for the monthly summary, instead of sending through a special. When we checked back hard, we found Reilly broke his journey home to spend two days somewhere in France. Falsified his time of departure from Hong Kong to cover it in his report."

Fraser rolled some brandy round his mouth. Modesty said slowly, "You think Reilly was paid to arrange an accident for Tarrant?"

"No. That doesn't quite fit with the fact that Reilly died too. I think he was paid to set Tarrant up for somebody else to do the job, or paid half in advance more probably, and that whoever did it knocked Reilly off at the same time, as a safety-play." Fraser paused, looking down into his glass. Then he looked up, his thin features suddenly haggard. "I'm not so sure Tarrant's dead. There's still no body."

Willie Garvin sat up straight. "A snatch? With the car accident to cover it?"

Fraser shrugged. "It makes more sense. Action against Intelligence top brass hasn't been trendy for a while now. But if somebody's coming back with it, they'd do themselves more good by snatching Tarrant and scraping information out of him than by a straight killing."

Both men looked at Modesty. She sat with her hands folded in her lap, eyes blank, looking at nothing. After a few moments she said very softly, "Oh, my God. That's what I've been trying to remember." She stood up and began to pace slowly, holding her elbows, eyes half closed in concentration.

Fraser said, "Remember what?"

"Tell him about Quinn, Willie. I want to play it back in my mind, just what he said."

In a few short sentences Willie gave Fraser the story Modesty had told him of the injured man she had found on the heights above the Tarn, and of their way-laying by the three men on the deserted causse.

Fraser said, "Christ, you mean he could have *seen* something?"

Modesty stopped pacing, took a cigarette from an ivory box and lit it. She said, "He was concussed, and he'd been passing out on and off, so he was pretty confused. I said to him——and these are the exact words: 'You must have been here when the car went over the edge yesterday. A grey Peugeot. Did you see it happen?' Now listen carefully. He said, *'Went over the edge? God, no, I didn't see it go over.'*"

Willie frowned. "There's something . . . a bit wrong with it."

"I know, and it's been nagging me. But I've got it now. If he'd said, 'God, no, I didn't see it,' full-stop——that's fine. But the last two words make all the difference. There's an implication. He saw the car, but didn't see it go over."

Fraser said doubtfully, "It's a bit subtle."

"I heard the words, the intonation, Jack. And if he saw the car but didn't see it go over, then it *must* have been parked there for a while, on that bend."

Fraser rubbed the heel of his hand across a damp brow. Willie said, "Suppose Reilly set it up at that spot for the opposition, by arrangement. And suppose some'ow they spotted Quinn across the gorge. Then you've got a good reason why them three villains turned up. They were sent to do Quinn." He looked at Modesty. "We'd better get 'old of him, Princess. Quinn maybe doesn't realise it, but 'e knows something."

She bit her lip. "That's the hell of it. He'll have left Georges Durand's clinic now, and he could be anywhere. God, I'm a fool."

Willie grinned faintly. "I often wonder 'ow you get by." He looked at Fraser. "You can trace 'im, Jack. The Princess got the names of two of the villains she clobbered. Réné Vaubois of SDECE will 'elp."

Fraser nodded. He looked very tired. "He'll help quicker if Modesty asks him. He owes you for that Montmartre business. His life."

Willie leaned forward. "Look, all of a sudden we think Tarrant's alive, right? So why sit there looking like an undertaker's mute with the belly-ache?"

Fraser drained his glass and put it down. "Because I like the old bastard," he said bleakly. "Because if we're right, he could be in a mental home in Moscow now, or somewhere similar. Because they're going to pull him to pieces very slowly, and then kill him."

Modesty said, "Then we must get him back in a hurry." Her face was calm, her voice mellow, but about her there was an emanation so intense that Fraser felt he could almost see it as a luminosity. He had known this experience with her once before, and remembered comparing the impact of it with the tingling frisson of apprehension he had felt when de-fusing a booby-trap with a three-way detonator.

He suppressed a flare of hope and said dourly, "Get him back? From Moscow?"

She looked at him. "From anywhere, Jack. If it came to that, I've still got two lines into The Centre from the old days. Besides, it may not be Moscow. And in spite of Hong Kong, I don't think it's Peking. They don't work that way.

This could be an independent group, in which case Tarrant might still be in Europe. Who's running your section at the moment?"

"I am. With limited authority, pending the appointment in a few days of whoever replaces Tarrant. If you're wondering whether I can mount a big operation to find him, the answer's no. I'm just minding the shop, and it's no use going to the Minister with nothing more than a hunch drawn from a few shreds of information."

"You must have some idea who the new man will be."

"Yes. Corder. The Minister's pet."

"What's he like?"

"A brontosaurus."

"What?"

"That prehistoric monster with a brain the size of a walnut located somwhere in its arse."

She half smiled. "I thought it was in the tail, and that it was a myth anyway."

"Corder hasn't got a tail." Fraser shrugged. "I could be flattering him there, maybe he just keeps it hidden."

Willie said, "I don't reckon a big operation, Princess. It's bound to leak."

She nodded. "I was only worried that a new man looking at what Jack's dug up about Reilly might make the same kind of guess and start something."

"He won't get to see what I dug up if that's how you want to play it," Fraser said.

Willie stood up and took Fraser's glass. "Finding Quinn's the first move. Let's 'ope it doesn't take long."

"We can try phoning Georges Durand," Modesty said. "He might have some idea where Quinn was going when he left the clinic."

Fraser lifted a hand reluctantly. "No refill, Willie. I

want to make those six bottles last." He looked at Modesty. "What do you hope Quinn can give you?"

"A lead, perhaps."

"He wouldn't have seen much detail at that distance."

"If the opposition sent a party to sign him off, they must have been worried about whatever he might have seen."

Fraser's eyes narrowed and a hard smile touched his lips. "Maybe they're still worried. Still looking for him. He might be useful bait if we can get hold of him."

"I'd thought of that too." She moved to the huge floor-to-ceiling window that looked out over Hyde Park. "See if you can raise Georges now, please Willie."

The phone rang a second before Willie picked it up. He said, "Yes, Albert?" His eyebrows lifted suddenly. "Who?" He shot a startled glance at Modesty. Then, "All right, can you pour 'im into the lift or shall I come down?" A pause. "Fine."

He put down the phone and ran a hand through his hair. "It's the flux," he said. "There's a bloke down in reception wants to see you, Princess. Albert says he's stoned to the eyeballs. And 'is name's Quinn."

Fraser stared, then stood up and grinned wolfishly. "We've got our bait, by God."

Two minutes later the lift doors slid open. Quinn walked out carefully into the foyer and looked down the great sitting room to where three figures stood. He wore rumpled corduroy trousers and a bulky sheepskin jacket. One hand held a battered travelling case. His face was pallid and shiny, eyes bright but wandering, as if he had difficulty in making them focus. He put down the case, stumbled slightly as he straightened up, then moved forward to the low iron balustrade.

Modesty said, "Help him down the steps, Willie. Hallo, Quinn."

Quinn took the steps warily, then shook off Willie's hand. "I can manage, my good fellow." He put his hands in his pockets and looked about him, then made a breathy attempt to whistle. "Oh, my word. A nice little pad. And you run a hat-shop in Kensington, eh?"

She smiled and moved towards him. "Come and sit down, Quinn."

He allowed her to lead him to the chesterfield, and slumped down heavily. "Who are all these men?"

"All friends of mine. Would you like some coffee?"

"Aha! You're a coffee-maker to boot, eh?" He grinned and pointed a faltering finger at her. "First I thought you were a dancer. The legs, see? Jesus, they're good. Then I thought you were a doctor. Then the hat-shop bit, and then . . . what was it? Oh, I know. A secret agent." He giggled. "Wham, bam, thank you ma'am, and another Redskin bit the dust."

Modesty said, "How's your head now?"

"The head? Marvellous. A bit muzzy just at this moment, but that's from drinking black velvet. And the arm. Look." He held up his left hand and waved it about. "Good as new. Intensive treatment from the good Dr. Durand. What a pad he's got there. And all free. I asked him about that. 'I'm a philanthropist,' he says. 'Bollocks,' I told him, not knowing the French, 'it's little old Modesty the Mystery who's picking up the tab, and just why would she do that?' So he said, 'She must have fallen under the spell of that tremendous charm you have, Mr. Quinn.'"

Quinn glowered about him. "Sarcastic French sod."

Modesty sat down beside him and said, "Where are you staying?"

"Staying?" He gazed at her blearily. "I don't know. Find a hotel somewhere. I only got in this morning." He screwed up half his face in a laboured wink. "But old

Quinn's been pretty cunning. Got a mate in Fleet Street, see? Crime bloke. In the know. Drinks black velvet. So I routed him out and poured the stuff down him while I chatted him up. Down me, too." He wiped sweat from his clammy face. "I asked him, 'You know anything about a girl called Modesty Blaise? Got a hell of a straight-left, with her foot,' I told him. 'Christ,' he says, 'I can give you a million rumours, boy, but all I can tell you for sure is she's loaded, and she's been mixed up in at least three cloak-and-dagger stories we've never been allowed to print.' So I kept pumping him, see? And he told me . . ."

Quinn stopped short, catching his breath. A greenish tinge came into his face. He tried to rise, fell against Modesty, muttered, "Oh God, I'm going to be sick." And was.

Fifteen minutes later, Willie Garvin pulled him from under a warm shower where Quinn had been cursing and struggling feebly in his grasp, picked him up, laid him on a massage table, and rubbed him dry vigorously with a rough towel.

Thirty minutes later Willie came out of the penthouse guest-room and joined Modesty. She had changed into an emerald green silk wrap-over robe, let her hair down ready for bed, and was standing by the window, looking out over the darkness of the park. Fraser had gone, after one long and searing comment on Quinn.

Willie said, "He's asleep, Princess. Right out. Weng's taken 'is clothes down to the all-night cleaners. Yours too."

She turned. "Thanks, Willie love."

"Looks like we got two jobs on the go. D'you want to see Janet tomorrow anyway?"

"Yes. Even if it's only to explain that we may have to hold fire on her thing until we've got something else cleared up. I'll talk to Quinn in the morning, then we can decide

112

the next move." She thought for a moment. "You might plug in the intercom in his room. I'll switch mine on so I can hear him——just in case he wakes up and starts blundering around, wondering where he is."

"I'll do that. What do you reckon about old Tarrant?"

"We still can't be sure he's alive, Willie . . . but I hope so."

"Me too. I don't think they'll do a crash job on 'im. They'll take it slow. Get more information that way."

"All the same, we'd better find him fast."

He saw her eyes swim, and was startled for a moment. Sometimes he had known her weep briefly after a caper, in his presence only, from strain and pain and reaction. But never otherwise. For the past half hour he had been too occupied with Quinn to register the anxiety that was gnawing within him or to realise how strongly it would be reflected in her. He liked Tarrant very much, but knew that Modesty's affection for him was deeper, perhaps in a way only possible for a woman. Not that it was sexual. Simply filial.

She blinked and managed a smile. "Sorry. It's just that . . . he's not young, Willie. You know the sort of things they'll do to him. And he isn't used to——I don't know ——not so much the pain, the indignity if you like. There's little new anyone could do to us, but it's different for him."

Willie looked at the great S-shaped scar on the back of his right hand, made by a hot iron, the initial of a man now dead. He looked at Modesty, knowing the splendid body beneath the silk robe, knowing it had suffered rape and wounds, knowing it because he had three times nursed it back to health. She was right. They were neither of them new to the shattering impact brutality has upon the inner self. They had learned how to absorb it, and later forget it. But it would be different for Tarrant.

He said, "Just so long as we find 'im. He's the kind that's got a lot of gristle."

"Yes. I'm sure he has. Goodnight, Willie."

She touched his arm and moved away to her bedroom.

*   *   *

The lever flew off the Mills grenade as the barrel-shaped handful of destruction hit the deck of the aircraft. Quinn sprawled across the half-conscious Arab, head twisted to look back over his shoulder, a silent scream of horror erupting in his mind as the ugly black pomegranate rolled lurchingly down the aisle.

Futile fragments of hope flared and died in him during the eternal seconds of watching. It was the good old-fashioned Mills. Could have been made years ago. Perhaps the spring would be weak, the striker fail, or the percussion cap fail to ignite the five second safety-fuse, or . . . something fail.

The white-faced man in the aisle-seat on the port side dived forward. The rolling grenade swerved neatly to evade him, as if governed by some malevolent intelligence. It vanished under the seat where the man's wife and child huddled, and then came the frightful roar.

Nothing had failed. Except Quinn.

Over the intercom, Modesty heard Quinn's gasping moans and mumblings. She slid quickly out of bed and was halfway to the guest-room before she had the robe belted about her naked body. Willie met her in the passage. The tortured groaning faded a little, then broke out anew.

"Some nightmare, Princess. Didn't need an intercom to 'ear it."

"Yes. I'll see to him, Willie. You go back to sleep."

"Sure?"

She nodded, and turned to the half open door of Quinn's room. Putting on the light, she closed the door and moved to sit on the edge of the bed, reaching out to put her hands on his shoulders as he writhed and uttered strangled incoherencies.

"Wake up, Quinn," she said quietly, "you're having a bad dream. Come on now."

His eyes opened wide, and he jerked to a sitting position.

"Oh God . . . !" He clung to her, panting, and she patted his back gently, saying, "Poor old Quinn. That was a bad one. I don't think black velvet's your tipple."

He let her go suddenly and drew back, blinking at her, then looking about the room. She saw bewilderment slowly fade as he tacked a few fragments of drunken memory together. At last he drew a long breath, looked at her with self-disgust dawning in his eyes, and said, "Did I make an absolutely titanic fool of myself?"

"Anyone can have a nightmare."

"I meant before that."

"Well, if you could run an action replay for yourself, I don't think you'd be too happy about it. You were stoned."

"I'm sorry." He rubbed his eyes and shivered. "Some bloody giant stripped me and held me under a shower—— or did I imagine that?"

"No, that was Willie Garvin."

He thought for a moment. "Ah, yes. Duggan said about him."

"Duggan being your Fleet Street friend?"

"Yes."

"Lie down and cover up. You've got the shivers. Would you like a cigarette?"

"Please."

She took two from the box on the bedside table, lit them

both, put one in his hand, then set an ash-tray on the bed between them.

Quinn said wearily, "I don't know why I always do things wrong. I wanted to find you so I could come and thank you. Bring you some flowers or something. Then I got smashed and behaved like . . . what did I behave like?"

"Sort of cocky and hostile. More in the manner than the words."

"Cocky and hostile. Yes, that would be about right. You tell it straight, don't you?"

"You asked me." She smiled. "At least you didn't call me ducky."

"I'm glad about that." He smiled back at her, and it was a good smile without the usual hint of acid mockery. "Look, will you take it that I'm very grateful for all you did for me?"

"You're welcome. Can I get you anything? Not from the bar, but a sandwich or something if you're hungry?"

"Nothing, thanks." He hesitated. "If you'll let me loose in the kitchen I could make myself some coffee."

"Coffee at two a.m.? It'll keep you awake."

"That's the main idea." He tried to speak lightly, but his voice was uneven and she saw that his hand holding the cigarette was trembling.

She said, "Does it happen often, this nightmare?"

"Often enough." His mouth worked, and he had difficulty in drawing on the cigarette.

"Would telling about it help?"

"I thought you might have guessed. Thought the name might have rung a bell. Henry Quinn, Second Officer on the good aircraft Delta Bravo, hi-jacked on the Rome flight last September."

"There've been a lot of hi-jackings. And I was out of

touch with newspapers and radio for a couple of weeks in September."

He stared up into nothingness. "Two Arabs. They took over as we were coming into Rome. A Trident of Corsair Airlines. When we landed they demanded the release of those three terrorists the Italians held after the shoot-up at Milan last year. Or they'd blow up the plane and everyone in it, including themselves. It went on for about eighteen hours, negotiations with Italian officials, the Red Cross, all that stuff."

He tried to stub out his cigarette, but his hand was shaking so violently that she took the stub from him and crushed it in the ash-tray.

"I killed three people," he said, and closed his eyes. "One was a child."

"What do you mean?"

He had found her hand and was holding it tightly, though she was sure he was unaware of it. He said, "It was all going on, you see. Twelve hours, fourteen, sixteen. On and on. Oh Christ, I hated those bastards so much. I kept trying to feel afraid, but I couldn't. I was too mad. The passengers were bloody marvellous. This seems feeble, but I kept thinking, *How dare you! How dare you threaten all these men and women and kids, you mindless maniacs!*"

He rubbed a hand across his mouth. "You can't get nearer to it in words, but the feeling was . . . huge. Towering." He was silent for long moments, then went on, "We played it according to the rules. The crew, I mean. Safety of passengers the prime consideration. So what does that mean? Does it mean you sit tight and hope they won't blow us all up? But suppose you're wrong, and they do? I still don't know. But there came a time when one of them was outside, arguing with the Minister or whoever. And the other one was standing at the end of the aisle, holding a grenade. A Mills bomb. He hadn't pulled the pin." His eyes flickered to Modesty. "They're safe until the pin's drawn, you see."

"Yes."

"Well . . . I'd been giving one of the hostesses a spell, serving food, and I saw a chance. This Arab's s.m.g. was slung on his shoulder. He just held the grenade. I was carrying a tray, and I'd managed to wriggle a bit of steel bar out of a rack in the galley. I'd been sweating cobs for hours, trying to make up my mind whether to have a go. Mike Charnely, the Captain, he was playing it cool and I think he was worried about me, because he kept muttering, 'Don't do anything bloody stupid, Quinn.' But then I saw this chance. I'd got the bar hidden under the tray, and when I was just a couple of steps from the Arab I dropped the tray and took a bloody great swipe at his wrist."

Quinn's eyes were blank, and though his voice was low his speech became faster and more feverish. "It should have been all right. If I made him drop the grenade he was sunk. But I missed. I mean, I hit him but didn't get it quite right. He hung on to the grenade, and he jumped back, pulling at the pin, and it came free just as I smashed him on the head with the bar. I went down on top of him when he fell, and I heard the thing hit the deck, and looked round, and it was rolling, rolling, wobbling about, and this poor devil with his wife and kid dived at it. He couldn't have stopped it or got rid of it, but he was going to smother it with his body. Christ, he was brave. But it swung away under the seats and rolled on, and then came that awful bloody bellow and blast, and then the screaming——"

His teeth were chattering too violently for speech. He turned his head from side to side, struggling for control. Modesty held his hand and waited. After a few moments he stopped moving and looked up at her very intently for a full two minutes with a wondering air. His defences had fallen completely now, and though grief aged his eyes he seemed to Modesty very young and helpless.

At last he spoke again, quietly and with little expression. "It was one of those freakish things. Most of the blast went through the side of the aircraft. The man who dived wasn't hurt, neither was his wife. But the little girl and the two people in the seat behind were killed. Somebody outside was quick enough to nail the Arab there before he could do anything. Afterwards there was an inquiry. They said I was to blame for taking reckless action, and of course they were right."

He lay breathing deeply as if he had run a race, and slowly something of the old hostility crept into his face. He said, "Come on, you're supposed to say I wasn't to blame, it was just bad luck. All my friends tell me that. At least, to my face."

She said quietly, "What they think or what I think doesn't matter. It's your load, Quinn, so pick it up and carry it. Nobody else can do it for you."

He was startled. "Jesus. There speaks a hard lady. Just for the record, what *do* you think?"

"I'll tell you what I know, not think. If you'd made it, you'd have been a hero. Daring rescue by gallant pilot. Not many people stop to remember that 'daring' means there was a risk, and that it could come out either way."

"It came out the wrong way."

"Too bad. I'm a hard-liner on this, Quinn. You let people see that the hostage game works and it spreads like a plague. It's done so."

"I killed two men and a child."

"They're dying every day, under cars or bombs or in Calcutta gutters with empty bellies."

"And one or two more make no difference? That's great."

"One or two more can save one or two hundred more if it stops the plague."

"Peachy. If you don't happen to be one of the unfortunate."

She nodded. "That comes out the way it's written."

"Kismet? A fatalist?"

She smiled. "Of a sort. But not the passive sort."

His good smile came back. "I can bear witness to that. Wham, bam, etcetera." He exhaled a long breath. "Thanks for letting me slobber it all out. And for telling me to pick up my own load. That's better than soft words. I manage all right most of the time, it's just the nightmares that get me. Once you're asleep, you've got no armour. Look, would you like to know why I've been such a particularly unpleasant bastard to you?"

"Tell me."

"Well . . . the truth is, you rather over-awe me. You did right from the start. And I suppose I resent it."

"Over-awe you? Oh come on, Quinn."

"It's true. You're a bit bloody marvellous, you know. I don't just mean looks and legs and all that, but . . . oh, I don't know. The way you keep *coping* all the time. Not failing. When a chap's not all that sure of himself, it's a bit much."

She said apologetically, "Sorry. But please try not to resent me. Are you going to be good and go to sleep now?"

He shook his head, forcing a smile. "Not without my teddy bear. Too scared. Once it starts, I sometimes get a sequence of them. You go back to bed. Never mind about the coffee, I'm not sleepy now, but can I help myself to the fags?"

"Of course." She stood up, turned, hesitated, then looked back at him. "Would it help if I stayed?"

He stared uncertainly. "You mean . . . with me? Here?" He looked round. There was no couch in the room. "In bed?"

"If it would help keep the nightmares away."

She saw swift yearning touch his face, and knew he was making an effort to speak lightly as he said, "Is lucky old Quinn about to be seduced?"

"Lucky old Quinn can take his choice. He doesn't have to rise to an occasion. If he just wants a bit of warm friendly female flesh to keep him company, that's all right. It can be a great comfort." She untied the robe and let it fall. "Move over a bit."

She slid in beside him, slipped an arm under his neck, drew his head down to rest on the warm slope between breast and shoulder, and reached up to the cord-switch hanging above. "Light out?"

"Not yet." He had gasped at the first contact of their bodies, and now held her close, a hand moving wonderingly over her smooth flesh. After a little while, when she felt him awakening, she tilted his head to kiss him, and whispered, "You don't have to prove anything, Quinn. Just be happy."

Later she was surprised by his gentleness as he used her, and by his concern for her own response, a concern that she sensed sprang not from male pride but from the wish to give as well as receive. She let slip her role as a comforter, joining with him gladly in the play and counterplay of making love.

Much later, just before they slept, Quinn with his arm thrown across her, he gave a warm, dreamy little chuckle, pressed her breast gently and murmured, "Better than teddy bears. Thank you, ma'am . . ."

CHAPTER SEVEN

Réné Vaubois, head of Direction de la Surveillance du Territoire, looked at his watch and said, "This has gone more quickly than I expected."

Modesty spread the three photographs on the table. "We've been lucky. If Bourget and Garat had been carrying false identification I could have spent all day here."

"And this fellow Servalle." Vaubois tapped one of the photographs. "He was the third man?"

"Yes." She turned from Vaubois to the Sûreté man. "Can you say if there is a connection, m'sieu?"

"No question of it, mam'selle." The Inspector passed a record card to Vaubois. "They work together, these three. Marseilles based."

"Union Corse?" Vaubois asked.

"No. Independent."

"Good. Please put out an immediate call to have them picked up, Inspector. Priority red."

"For interrogation by your department?"

"Yes."

"Very well, m'sieu. One hopes for quick results, but if they have gone into hiding . . ." He gestured.

Vaubois nodded sombrely. It was now noon. Modesty Blaise had telephoned him at eight o'clock, Paris time, and he had picked her up from Orly Airport at ten. He said, "Let us hope for good fortune."

Five minutes later, sitting beside Modesty in the back of

his car as it swept along Boulevard Haussmann, Vaubois said, "You truly believe my colleague Sir Gerald may be alive?"

"I'm not satisfied that he's dead, Réné."

"Assuming your hope is correct, it will be very . . . difficult to recover him. Perhaps impossible."

"I'll think about that when I know where he is."

"You know that the D.S.T. will give all possible help." Vaubois made a regretful grimace. "The aims of my department have occasionally conflicted with those of Sir Gerald's department, but he and I always had a pleasant understanding."

"I know, Réné. If you can pick up those men and find out who sent them to deal with Quinn, will you call me at once?"

"Of course. Now, can I offer you an early lunch before taking you to Orly?"

"Thank you, Réné, but I must get back to London, and there's a flight at twelve forty-five. I've another possible lead to follow up."

"This man Quinn?"

"Yes. He's at my place now. I think he must have seen something significant, otherwise they wouldn't have bothered about him."

"Modesty, listen please. If we find cause to believe that Sir Gerald is no longer in the west, but held . . . say, in Moscow, then you must count him as lost. There is nothing to be done."

"Just let them take him to pieces?"

"I'm sorry. Yes."

"All right, Réné."

Vaubois looked at her, then swore softly. "I waste my breath."

An hour earlier, while Modesty had been looking at

photographs and dossiers in the *Renseignments Généraux* section of the Sûreté Nationale, Quinn was woken from sleep by a big man with untidy fair hair who told him that there was a bathroom en suite he could use; that his clothes, cleaned and pressed, were hanging on the clothes-valet; and that somebody called Weng would be putting up a late breakfast for him in the dining-room in half an hour.

Quinn, still half asleep, said, "Where's Modesty?"

"Paris. She'll be back later today."

The big man had gone before Quinn could collect his wits to frame another question. He got slowly out of bed. She had been there, with him, only a few hours ago. The memory of her was clear and marvellous. Paris? She was in Paris now? What the hell was going on? He'd have to ask that big bastard——what was his name? Willie Garvin. That's what Duggan had said in the boozer. Quinn decided, without quite knowing why, that he did not like Willie Garvin much.

Half an hour later, when he entered the dining-room, he found Willie Garvin sitting at the end of the table reading a newspaper, while a young Indo-Chinese set a place at one side. There was coffee, cream and milk, a rack of toast, and a chafing dish with eggs, bacon and kidneys.

Willie put down the paper and said, "Bring another cup please, Weng. I'll 'ave some coffee too. This is Mr. Quinn."

Weng bowed slightly and smiled. "Good morning, Mr. Quinn."

"Hallo." Quinn sat down. He felt suddenly ravenous.

When Weng had left, Willie Garvin said, "That black velvet's 'eavy stuff. Feeling a bit better now?"

"Very fair." Quinn served himself and began to eat. "When did Modesty go to Paris?"

"Caught the eight o'clock flight. She said to let you 'ave a good sleep."

"I did. Where did *you* sleep last night?"

"I got me own room 'ere."

"I see. No, I don't see. But never mind. Why did she suddenly shoot off to Paris?"

"To see a friend. She wants to get a line on those three blokes who came after you on the causse."

"After *me*?"

"It begins to look that way."

"Why?"

"She'll explain when she gets back. She wants to ask you a few things."

Quinn felt a flare of anger. God knew what she thought he could tell her, but was this the reason for last night? Be nice to Quinn and give him a tumble because he can tell you something you want to know?

He said, "Well, it's all been great fun. I'll just finish this and then be on my way."

Willie Garvin said, "No, you'll 'ave to 'ang on. I told you, the Princess wants to talk to you."

"*Who* does?"

"Modesty."

"Ah, your pet name for her. Very touching. But who's going to make me hang on, Garvin?"

"It's partly for your own good. We think somebody could still be looking for you, to finish what they tried to start that day when she clobbered 'em."

"Looking for me? Balls. Who's going to make me hang on?"

Willie Garvin sighed. "Let's not get to a confrontation. They upset me."

Quinn began to butter another piece of toast, feeling savage. He curved his lips in a false smile and said, "Modesty came to bed with me last night."

125

Willie nodded. "M'mm. After that nightmare. She said she'd stayed."

"A very good screw." Even as he said the words Quinn hated himself. They spoiled something good. But he kept smiling.

Willie picked up his paper. He might not have heard. Quinn said confidingly, "The thing is old man, how much should I leave on the mantelpiece. I mean, what's the usual? Would a quid be all right?"

Willie Garvin thought for a moment, then got up and patted Quinn on the shoulder. "You 'aven't quite got the idea," he said. The big hand gripped suddenly. The other hand swung, open and slightly cupped. It smacked across Quinn's cheek with a sound like a paper-bag bursting, rattling his teeth and splintering his mind with shock. But for the hand holding his shoulder, he would have fallen out of the chair. After a few seconds his reeling head steadied. He tried to stand up, but could not move. The hand was like a clamp.

Willie Garvin said patiently, "It's just a question of manners, Quinn. Look, I don't give a monkey's what you think about Modesty Blaise. I don't even care what you say about 'er. But when you've walked into 'er 'ome drunk, and been sick down 'er, when you've slept in 'er bed and she's stayed with you to help drive the nightmares away, when you're under 'er roof, sitting at 'er table . . . then don't say anything out of line about 'er to *me*. Because I'm a bit old-fashioned about manners, see?"

He let Quinn go, gave him a friendly nod, then sat down again and poured himself another cup of coffee. Quinn sat shaking. After a while he put his hands to his face and drew them slowly down his cheeks.

"Was I . . . really sick down her?" he asked in a low, uneven voice.

Willie waved a hand. "Compre'ensively. But don't worry. She's not what you'd call squeamish."

"Oh, Christ. Look, what I said just now . . . I didn't mean it. I wanted to needle you. But I didn't mean it by a million miles. I think she's . . . great. Marvellous. But I got knotted up with thinking she'd only done it because she can use me. And that hurt the stinking old Quinn ego, and started the stinking old Quinn viper-tongue going. Sorry. I really am bloody sorry."

Willie said, "She thinks you can 'elp us. But whatever she's done for you, all along the line, she'd 've done anyway."

Quinn managed a smile. "A sucker for lame dogs?"

"Sometimes. Some lame dogs. I could tell you about me, but I won't." He pushed back his chair. "We've got a few hours to kill, and the Princess said not to go out in case anyone's getting close to you. But there's a pool downstairs, and squash-courts, if you fancy working off your 'angover."

"I haven't got one." He looked at Willie tentatively. "If I say she did my hangover a lot more good than an Alka-Seltzer, you won't take that amiss?"

Willie smiled and shook his head. "If you don't fancy excercise, there's the best collection of jazz records in London, and a pretty good selection of classics."

"I haven't played squash for three years, but let's give it a whirl. And a swim after."

"Right. I'll get some gear out."

*   *   *

When Modesty arrived at two o'clock they had just finished changing after a leisurely half-hour in the residents' pool. She sniffed the atmosphere, found it friendly, and was glad.

Quinn said, "You've missed a hilarious sight. Me wearing Willie's shorts for squash. I looked like Amelia Bloomer."

She patted his arm and said, "Have you been behaving yourself, Quinn."

"After a slightly false start, yes. Willie?"

"Good as gold. You eaten, Princess?"

"I had something on the plane." She sat down on the chesterfield.

"Any luck with Réné Vaubois?"

"He's put out a red priority call to pick up those three men, but God knows how long it will take. Are you sitting comfortably, Quinn? I want to talk to you."

"So Willie said. I've been floating in the pool, trying to recap on everything that happened while I was lying on the ledge. I kept coming and going, you know, and there wasn't much anyway, but at least I've been dredging for what there was."

"Good. Now you were lying there, and for some of the time you watched that bit of road across the gorge, hoping you might signal somebody?"

"I wasn't hoping much. It only took a few seconds for a vehicle to cover that stretch, and it was on a bend, so anyone driving would have their eyes on the road. Well, anyone sane. I couldn't speak for French truck drivers."

"When I asked about a grey Peugeot, you said you didn't see it go over. But did you see it at all?"

"I don't know whether it was a Peugeot, but I saw a grey car parked there for a bit."

"Parked? You're sure?"

"Of course I'm bloody sure, darling." He smiled his nice

smile. "I'm only making bold to call you that because it bolsters my ego and stops me being over-awed, and hence resenting you. See?"

"Keep it up, then. How long was the car there?"

He shook his head. "Don't know. Too whoozy. But first the Dormobile thing arrived, then the car came later. They were there together for a bit."

"A Dormobile?"

"Well, something of the sort. I'm not a student of vans. Two nuns got out of it."

Modesty and Willie said together: "*Nuns?*"

"That's right. Why not? Nuns drive that sort of thing all over the place these days. I can't think why. But haven't you noticed?"

Modesty said slowly to Willie: "You did say the squeeze was put on Janet's sister by a nun?"

He nodded. Quinn was about to speak, but saw that they were both distant with thought. He had an odd feeling that some almost telepathic exchange was taking place between them. At last Willie said, "Maybe it's the flux again. Or maybe we 'aven't got two jobs going after all."

She said, "But——" then broke off. "No, let's get the whole story first." She turned to Quinn, and now it seemed to him that her midnight-blue eyes were almost black. "Could you start from the van arriving and take it from there?"

"All right. Well, it parked on the bend and two nuns got out. I was a bit loose in the head and thought they were penguins at first. They didn't do anything, just walked about a bit and waited. I tried to signal them, but they didn't see me. Or I suppose they didn't. Then I drifted off again. Do you mind if I have a cigarette?"

"In the box there."

He lit one, and said thoughtfully, "I've just no idea how

much time passed before I came round. The van and the nuns were still there, but now there was this grey car parked a little way behind. And there was a man beside it. He bent down and . . . well, sort of lifted the door off its hinges and put it on top of the car."

Modesty said gently, "Hold on a minute. Car doors don't just lift off."

"I know. I've been thinking about it in the pool. But that's what he *seemed* to do. He bent down and took hold of the door, and after a bit he just seemed to stand up with it in his hands and put it on top of the car."

Modesty glanced at Willie, who shook his head. She returned to Quinn. "All right, then what?"

"Nothing. I mean, there's a bit of a blank. I just have this little snap-shot in my head of the chap with the door. I believe I started looking round for my coat, so I could wave it about, and flaked out again—ah, *that's* right! But I must have come round a few minutes later, because I remember waving then. The nuns were still there, by the van, but the chap had disappeared. No he hadn't. My God, just talking seems to bring it back. There was a kind of bluff bordering the road there, and he was up on top of it. I remember now, he looked like a cross."

Modesty said, "You mean he had his arms stretched out? Like this?"

"Don't push that lovely bosom at me, I'm trying to concentrate. No, it must have been like this." He raised his arms horizontally, then bent them at the elbows to bring his hands close to his face.

Willie said, "Jesus, he was looking tnrough glasses."

Quinn blinked, then lifted his hands a little. "Hey, you're right! So the bastard did see me, but didn't do a thing about it."

Modesty said, "He did something about it all right, he

sent the muscle in next morning, to make sure of you."

Quinn looked at her, then at Willie, and finally at his cigarette. "My God," he said soberly. "I'd better start believing it."

Willie said, "You were signalling? Waving the coat?"

"Like mad."

"You said the nuns were still there by the van. And the bloke was on top of the bluff. What about the grey car?"

Quinn closed his eyes and sat very still for a long time. At last he opened them and shook his head apologetically. "I don't know. I can't *see* it there now, but I'm not sure."

Modesty said, "If you saw them drive off, you'd have noticed if the grey car was left."

"I didn't see any of that. After waving the coat for about two minutes I ran right out of juice and just flopped. I don't mean I passed out. I just lay there." He grimaced "I rather fancy I snivelled a bit. I'm pretty hot on self-pity. By the time I'd dragged myself up to have another go, the road was empty. I didn't hear the engine or anything. They'd just gone."

It was silent in the big room for a long time. Quinn watched the two faces curiously. They were blank-eyed, and he could almost hear the intensity of thinking behind those eyes.

Willie said, "Take the door off to account for the body missing."

Modesty's dark head moved in assent. "That makes it a snatch."

"Using nuns, too."

"There doesn't *have* to be a connection with the squeeze nun."

"But."

"Yes. Phoney nun and phoney nuns. A bit strong, even for your flux, Willie."

Quinn said, "I wouldn't at all mind knowing what you're talking about."

She looked through him, caught her breath, and pounded a clenched fist gently on her knee in rhythm with her words as she said softly, "Willie, Willie, Willie . . . of *course*."

Willie sat up a little, eyes bright. "You got a connection?"

"We've been assuming Tarrant was taken by an opposition group to be scoured of security information."

"Not?"

"Listen, when we were theorising about Janet's trouble we said a psychiatrist's records would be a good source for large-scale blackmail. *So what about all the stuff a man like Tarrant's got in his head?*"

Willie said in a quiet, awed voice, "Jesus wept." He got to his feet, picked up Modesty's hand and touched the back of it to his cheek. Smiling, he straightened up and looked at his watch. "J. Straik, Chateau Lancieux."

Quinn said, "What?"

Modesty expelled a long breath of relief, then focused on him. She said, "Oh, I'm sorry. We were thinking."

"I guessed that. I'm pretty sharp."

She stood up, moved behind his chair and rested her hands on his shoulders, kneading the muscles gently. "Look, Willie and I have to go away for a few days. Did you have any plans?"

"I'm a gentleman of leisure, living on capital at the moment. Not much capital, mind. I've no family left, so I'm just sort of bumming around. The only plan I've got at the moment is to have you tell me what the hell's going on."

"Would you like to stay here for a bit? Or I've a nice cottage in Wiltshire you could use. We'll arrange cover for you until this is over."

"Cover? Oh yes, I'm the man who knows too much, aren't I? Are you going to tell me what it is I've spilled that seems so important to you?"

"I can't, Quinn. It's very hush."

He stood up and turned to face her. "Don't talk a lot of cock, darling," he said pleasantly. "I've already guessed half of it. My Fleet Street mate mentioned Tarrant when he was talking about cloak-and-dagger stuff. Tarrant was in the grey car that went over, wasn't he? Well, no he wasn't, because you now think he was snatched. Something to do with blackmail information. And you're going to go galloping off to the rescue. That may not be a hundred percent right, but do I get a bronze medal for trying? Next time don't forget I'm around when you're thinking aloud."

Modesty studied him a little worriedly. Willie said, "Better tell 'im, Princess. If 'e knows it all there's less chance of 'im chatting up the Fleet Street bloke again. That could put Tarrant down before we get to 'im."

Quinn said to her quietly, "I've got three lives on my conscience, and I don't want another one. You really can rely on me."

"I know. Come and sit down with me."

Three minutes later Quinn said, "So you're going to this Chateau Lancieux, in the Pyrenees, to get him out?"

"Yes."

"Why can't the French do it? I gather you have influence there."

She looked at Willie, who lifted his shoulders and made a face, then back at Quinn. "We think we can do it better. I mean, in actually getting Tarrant out. The French would have to operate within legal limits, and that would mean an official raid on the chateau. It's not quick enough against people ready for trouble. Tarrant would end up dead."

"So what do you aim to do? Get into the chateau, shoot-up all the opposition, and pull Tarrant out?"

"No. If we can get in, and get Tarrant out without any rumpus, that's fine. The French can see to the rest of it, once he's safe."

"All right. Now, you said I could stay here or at your cottage." He looked at her blandly. "But maybe somebody's still trying to kill me. I'd be much safer under your protection, so hadn't you better take me along?"

She shook her head and stood up. "No. I'm sorry, but that's out."

"I might be useful. I could dress up as a nun and go to the chateau begging for alms. You know, casing the joint."

She gave him a puzzled look. He waved a hand and said, "Never mind. How do you aim to make this stealthy break-in?"

She shrugged. "I don't know yet. We'll have to get out there and take a good look at the situation first. Then we'll work something out."

"Meanwhile Tarrant's being questioned with a lighted match under his toes, or something of that sort?"

Willie said, "Leave it, Quinn. We'll move as fast as we can." He turned to Modesty. "Shall I slip along to White'all and put Jack Fraser in the picture?"

"Yes. Do that, Willie."

He looked at his watch. "Janet's coming at three, but I ought to be back by then. What do we tell 'er, Princess?"

Modesty made a small helpless gesture. "The same as

we've just told Quinn, I suppose. We'll be holding a Press Conference next. But she's met Tarrant, and you said she knows who he is."

"Knows 'ow to keep 'er mouth buttoned, too."

"I don't doubt that. All right. You go and see Fraser. I'll get the large-scale maps out, and the Michelin Guide."

*   *   *

Lucy Straik said, "You should just take a look at that crack in the ceiling, Poppa. Some old chatto this is. I bet it must be hundred *years* old."

Colonel Jim, sprawled above the soft moist body, lifted his head to look down at her. "Goddamit, Momma. Can't you pay a little attention?"

She giggled rather breathlessly under his weight. "I *was* payin' attention, Poppa, but honest to God, you go on so long. Must be half an *hour* ago I hit tops. You're just too greedy all the time. Maybe you should save it up a bit at your age."

"Poppa don't like that kinda talk, Momma. You start fancying something younger on the hoof, and————"

"Gee, I never meant *that*. You're great." She wrapped her arms around him. "C'mon now, let's go. Give Momma the old one-two."

"If Momma's gonna watch cracks in the ceiling she better close her eyes or turn around someway."

"*Okay*. So let me up a little. There. You're real mean today, Poppa."

"I can be, honey. If I figure you're finding Poppa a kinda chore. I'll have to liven you up some."

"You *wouldn't* let that Mr. Sexton do anything!"

"Don't count on it. Hey, just the idea's put a squib under you, huh? Right, now . . ."

There was a tap on the door. Colonel Jim swore, then lifted his voice. "Yeah? What the hell is it?"

"Sorry if you were resting," Mr. Sexton called cheerfully. "An interesting communication from London."

"I'll be in the study in five minutes, Mr. Sexton. No, make it ten."

Mr. Sexton said, "Right."

Lucy giggled. "Five, I betcha. You know Momma when she puts her mind to it."

Mr. Sexton was standing by the window when Colonel Jim came into the study, wearing a dressing gown over pyjamas, and sat down at the desk.

"You said interesting, Mr. Sexton."

"Yes. For insurance purposes I told your man in London to keep an eye on Modesty Blaise."

"Good thinking. So?"

"A stroke of luck. He made one or two calls to the apartment block where she lives, on various pretexts, and he happened to be in reception last night when a young man arrived drunk and told the porter he wanted to see Modesty Blaise. He gave his name as Quinn, and then Stenmore heard him say, 'If that doesn't ring a bell, tell her I'm the bastard she hauled out of the gorge.' "

Colonel Jim rested a big hand on the desk, fingers tapping slowly. "Reckon there's anything he could tell her?"

Mr. Sexton shrugged. "Who knows? But we were going to put him away before, to make sure."

"Yeah. Even if this Quinn guy saw something and told her, I don't see any way she could locate us. But contingency-wise we better cover ourselves. Have Stenmore watch her place real close. I want tabs on her. If she makes a move, I want to know where she's headed."

"I've told him exactly that, Colonel Jim. I also called Ferrand, in Toulouse, and told him to have some eyes standing by so that we can locate her if she heads this way. She'll have Garvin with her, of course." Mr. Sexton chuckled. "Ferrand said not call on him for any soldiers, because he wouldn't tangle with Modesty Blaise or Willie Garvin under any circumstances. But he'll finger them for us if they come into the area."

"I don't figure we need any strong-arm help, Mr. Sexton."

"Neither do I." Mr. Sexton smiled happily. "As a matter of fact, I'm very much hoping they'll come. I believe they're really very good, and it's time I had something to stretch me a little."

CHAPTER EIGHT

It was two hours since Quinn had told his tale.

Willie Garvin knelt over a map spread on the floor, measuring with a pair of dividers. Modesty was speaking in French on the telephone.

Quinn sat smoking, unobtrusively studying the woman who was watching Willie. She had arrived an hour ago, a woman as tall as Modesty and perhaps a year or so older, fresh and cool with short chestnut hair, a superb complexion, and light hazel eyes set in strong features. She wore a camel trouser-suit and walked with a slight limp. Her voice and turn of phrase held a flavour of Scotland, but no more than that.

Lady Janet Gillam. Quinn had been a little taken aback by the title; quite impressed, to his annoyance, when he gathered that she was in fact the daughter of the Earl of Strathlan and Inverdall; and delightedly incredulous when he realized that she was Willie Garvin's girl-friend. In many ways Quinn was enjoying himself as he had not enjoyed himself for a long time now. To enter the world of Modesty Blaise and Willie Garvin was, he found, an experience of unceasing interest and one which roused new curiosity in him from hour to hour. It was only marred by the thought of a man who was no more than a name to him. Tarrant.

Quinn had a lively and sensitive imagination. The concept of torture, repugnant enough to any normal mind, produced in him a reaction of physical nausea. He remembered, as a child, running from the Chamber of Horrors at Madame Tussauds because the sight of rack and thumbscrew filled his mind with sickening images and his heart with a sense of wild, unbelieving hatred.

He was keeping all thought of the man Tarrant shut carefully away. This was not too difficult, for the centre of his attention was occupied by something else; an urgent, almost desperate longing. And he was waiting for the right moment to speak.

At the moment Modesty was talking on the phone to a man who, Quinn gathered, had carried out certain illegal activities for her in the Pyrenean border area during years when she ran an organisation called *The Network*, of which Duggan had spoken that night in Fleet Street.

She put down the phone and said, "According to Viret, the Chateau Lancieux lies three kilometres from the nearest village, which is just a cluster of half-a-dozen cottages. Then you've got Niaux at eight kilometres and Lousset at fifteen. Look up the Michelin for Lousset, Willie, and I'll get Janet booked in there."

Lady Janet said, "You'll not be there yourselves, Modesty?"

"No. We'll drop you there, then take to the hills. But you'll be our emergency line of communication. We'll give you two phone numbers, one in France and one here in London."

Lady Janet's smile was a little rueful, and Modesty said, "It's not a mock-up job, honestly."

"You'll hardly be able to get in touch with me from the hills. What sort of emergency were you thinking of?"

"If we're not back before a deadline we'll give you, then you'll know something's gone wrong."

"Oh." Lady Janet looked down thoughtfully at her hands.

"Or it's just possible we might ring you from the chateau, depending on how things work out there."

Willie looked up. "There's a phone-line?"

"So Viret said. The Germans used the chateau as their headquarters for patrolling the escape routes to Spain during the war. Apparently it's changed hands several times since then, and dirt cheap because it's a white elephant. He doesn't know who's there now."

Quinn said, "Lady Janet, how did you persuade these two to take you along on this?"

"Janet, please."

"Thank you. How did you persuade them?"

She looked at Modesty. "I'm not at all sure."

Willie, a finger on the Michelin Guide, said, "There's *Le Lion Rouge*. Twelve rooms, central-'eating, bidet, bath and parking. Plain but adequate. Fairly comfortable restaurant. That do you, Jan?"

"Anywhere I don't have to get up at five and milk cows is five-star for me."

Quinn said, "Make it two rooms, Modesty."

She looked at him with suppressed impatience and said, "We've been into all that."

"Ah, but we haven't, my little wham-bam sweetheart. There are matters you wot not of. For example, have you ever done any caving? Pot-holing?" He lifted a hand. "No, don't shoot me down. I'm serious."

She looked at him suspiciously. "All right. We've done very little. Carlswark Cave in the Peak District and East-water Swallet in the Mendips. Just to see what it was like. It didn't have much appeal for either of us, so that was all."

"It's just what happens to grab you. I liked it. Haven't

140

done much this year, but it was my only hobby for about four years."

Janet said, "What does it have to do with the situation, Mr. Quinn?"

"Just Quinn, please. I'm glad you asked me that." He looked at Modesty. "What it has to do with the situation is that you want to find a sneaky way of getting into the Chateau Lancieux. And good old pot-holer Quinn can show you the way."

Willie got up from the floor. Modesty took a cigarette and sat down on the arm of the chesterfield, watching Quinn. "I knew you had something brewing up," she said. "A cave?"

"Verily a cave. If you don't know it already, that area's stiff with caves. It's a calcareous region. You've got the tourist caves at Mas d'Azil, at Labouiche, and at Niaux. But there are dozens of caves and grottos all around the Ariège. I spent three weeks there with a club one summer, and we had a French instructor who took us into half a dozen different holes that few people in the area even knew existed. There was one he called the Lancieux Cave."

Modesty said, "You mean it actually leads into the chateau?"

"No, it's a bit trickier than that. As a cave, it would be classified as moderate. That means a few tough patches here and there. We covered about a mile. I don't remember the details, except that there's one place where an underground river widens out into a small lake, and you need a rubber dinghy. But the main point is this. There were all sorts of passages leading off the main run, and about half a mile in there was a kind of water-slide on one side. Fairly broad, like a chute leading up, and with a few inches of water running down the middle of it. The instructor said he'd climbed it once, and it led to the chateau. I'm not sure

141

which part, but I suppose it would be the kitchens or the dungeons if they still exist."

Willie said, "A sort of garbage chute from the kitchens?"

Quinn rubbed his chin. "I've just remembered what made me mention dungeons. He said some old skeleton had been found at the bottom of the chute. I mean, very old. They reckoned it could only have come down from above, and was probably the remains of somebody who'd been quietly got rid of, back in whatever century. But if the corpse did come down the chute, it implies a hole at the top big enough to bung a body through."

Willie said, "There could be a grille at the top now." He looked at Modesty. "All the same, it's a bloody marvellous chance, Princess. With tools, we could lever a grille out."

Modesty nodded, and said to Quinn, "Where's the entrance to the cave?"

He laughed, and spread a hand. "Have a heart, darling. How the hell does anyone describe how to find a crack in the side of a valley in the Pyrenees? I know I didn't even *see* the chateau while we were above ground, so it must be on the other side of a ridge. But I don't know which ridge, or which crack. I can take you there. I remember the road and the track, and the lie of the land when we left the track. But I can't tell it."

Modesty stood up and inhaled on her cigarette. "Could you find it after dark?"

He shook his head positively. "No. Much too confusing. I'd want to reach the valley with half an hour of light to spare. And I'll have to come into the cave with you, to show you where the chute lies, or you could miss it."

Modesty looked at Willie. "It's tempting," she said quietly. "But it's too close, Willie. We've no right to put him in the firing line."

142

Quinn hit the arm of his chair with a fist. "Don't be bloody stupid!" he said furiously. "Look, I'm not an idiot. I'm not going to come charging in with you and start leaping about, kicking people in the jaw. I know very well that's not my line, for God's sake." He leaned forward, and she saw the gleam of damp on his brow. "There's a man being . . . being tortured, perhaps as we're sitting here. Is that so? If somebody doesn't get to him, he's finished. Now look, I've killed three innocent souls. That's good old Quinn's record. And this is probably the only chance I'll ever have to help *save* anyone. So don't stand there like a bloody pudding and tell me I mustn't!"

There was a startled silence. Lady Janet looked curiously at Modesty. She stood with eyebrows raised high and startled amusement in her face as she spoke. "Well, I'll say one thing for you, Quinn. You're original. I've never been called a pudding before."

The humour faded. She was silent for a little while, then went on slowly, "I think they'll be taking their time about breaking Tarrant. But even so, you're right, he could be getting badly hurt at this moment." She moved to the phone. "You know, there are times when I like you quite a bit, Quinn. All right, two rooms."

With a hand on the phone, she paused and looked at Willie. "Have you got all the gear we might need, down at *The Treadmill*? I mean for the caving bit."

He thought for a few moments, then nodded. "I reckon so. I'll go over it with Quinn, then run down and pick it up."

"Take Janet, so she can pack a case and get her passport. When I've booked the rooms I'll call Dave Craythorpe and see if he can fly us over to Toulouse tonight. There's an airfield there at Blagnat. If we leave by eleven, we could check the cave at first light, do a recce of the area round the castle by day, and be all set to go in tomorrow night."

Quinn said diffidently, "Couldn't you go straight in?"

"By day? No, it's too risky for Tarrant. If there's trouble, he could get hurt, so we don't want trouble. Just quietly in and quietly out. We also don't want to bring him out by the cave. He's not young and he won't be in good shape. So we have to know our getaway route by dark, and that means a long and careful day's work."

Ten minutes later, at the wheel of his Jensen heading for the M4, Willie said, "What's up, Jan?"

She gave a strained little laugh. "It's all going so fast!"

"It's got to, love. If you feel you'd rather pull out——"

"No," she said sharply. Then, very quietly, "I felt like a bloody little mouse sitting there. I've never seen that aspect of Her Highness before, and it's a bit frightening."

Willie grinned. "She's on our side, remember."

"I didn't mean that. She was so damn good it was over-powering. When you feel your personality being swamped, you don't like it, and I was beginning not to like her one bit."

"You swamped? With six 'undred years of noble Scottish blood behind you? Come off it, Jan. Head-waiters cringe when you walk in, even before they know who you are."

"They bow and scrape for you too, Willie, even with that Bow Bells accent. You know why? Confidence. You're a reflection of her." He glanced at her, but she did not look annoyed, only puzzled and perhaps wryly amused as she said, "I was just starting to hate her when Quinn called her a pudding. I thought she'd flay him, but no. She was damn near giggling inside. I could tell. She really liked him for it. And I liked her for that."

"Well, she's got a sense of 'umour, Jan. Like a kid she is sometimes."

"Aye. I should think she's like all kinds of different things sometimes, Willie."

*   *   *

At eight the next morning, Lady Janet Gillam woke in a small room with flower-pattern paper on the walls and home-woven rugs scattered on a well-polished if creaking floor, six hundred miles from London.

She had not expected to sleep, but had done so as soon as her head touched the pillow, three hours ago. She lay trying to dispel the sense of strangeness, the feeling that she was in a world not quite real.

The Cessna had taken off only a few minutes after ten. She remembered feeling taut with a blend of excitement and apprehension. Before they gained cruising height, Modesty and Willie were asleep, slumped in their back-tilted seats. Quinn caught her eye, jerked his head at them and said, "Makes you sick, doesn't it? I'm tired as hell, but I'd need a couple of sleeping pills to do that right now."

Her rueful smile showed fellow-feeling. "It's an enviable gift. I have some pills, if you want one."

"Thanks, but I'll probably be blundering about the Pyrenees by dawn, and I don't want to be in a stupor." He indicated Willie. "I've only spent a few hours with him, but I'd say you've got quite a character there."

"Yes. So have you."

"Modesty? I don't think I've exactly got her. But while it lasts I'm finding her a unique experience. Half the time she treats me as if she was my mum."

"But the other half?"

"That's quite a bit different. Mind you, there hasn't

145

really been a great deal of time overall, but she does pack it in. Do you have the feeling that you're not really here, and that you'll wake up at home any minute?"

"You too? Thank God for that, Quinn."

"Join the club." He reached out politely and shook her hand. "I've got a pocket chess set. Do you play?"

"Badly. Willie murders me." She looked at the sleeping figures. "You know what those two do? Play chess in their heads."

"Pair of bastards. You sound as if you're in my league though. How about it?"

"All right."

She played two games with Quinn, then spent an hour sitting with the pilot, Dave Craythorpe, a lanky man of about forty with thinning hair. Uncommunicative at first, his manner changed when he learned that she held a Private Pilot's Licence with an Instrument Rating, and after talking technicalities for a while he allowed her to take the controls for half an hour.

Soon after two a.m. they landed at Blagnat. Two cars were waiting for them there, delivered by a car-hire firm in Toulouse. They completed formalities, picked up the car-keys at the airfield office and drove off south. At four they stopped a mile short of Lousset, a small village by a tributary of the Ariège. Quinn took over the wheel of Willie's car, and drove on with Janet to *Le Lion Rouge*.

The patron was expecting them, but Janet felt that he would have been undisturbed by their arrival at this early hour anyway. Her French was limited but sufficient, and her ear did not have to cope with a local patois since the patron had come from Rouen twenty years earlier. She learned that since it was so late in the year only two other rooms in the inn were occupied, each by an elderly French

146

gentleman. Both were residents, and it was their habit to quarrel continually. The patron hoped that madame and m'sieu would not find this annoying, and would understand that it was not serious.

Janet explained that her brother, Mr. Quinn, had unfortunately left his brief-case at the garage in Toulouse where they had hired the car. It contained important notes for the book he was writing, and he intended to drive back there at once.

The patron clucked his sympathy, showed them their rooms, hoped that madame would sleep well after her tiring journey, and saw m'sieu off, promising he would try to ensure that the French gentlemen quarrelled quietly in the morning so that m'sieu could sleep soundly on his return.

Lying in the warm bed, and looking out through the latticed window on the new day, Janet wondered what the others were doing at this moment. A frisson of unease touched her. Apart from one occasion she had never known when Willie Garvin was engaged in something of this kind. He did not tell her, though sometimes she guessed on his return. She knew little but fragmentary details of anything he had done with Modesty. But this was happening now, and very close. Close enough for her to feel a part of it.

Her mouth twitched in a dry smile. Well, this was what she had wanted.

There was a soft tap on the door. She sat up and called, "Entrez."

The door opened and Quinn put his head round it. He was unshaven and looked tired but content. "Good morning, Sister Janet. Did I wake you?"

"No, I came round five minutes ago. Lord, it's good to see you, Quinn."

"All right if I come in?"

147

"Vanity says no, but curiosity says yes. I must look a gummy-eyed mess, but you've seen me now anyway."

Quinn pushed the door to, moved to an upright chair by the window and sat down. "To be honest," he said, "I was just thinking how bloody marvellous you look. It's grossly unfair. You're one of those people who always seem to have just stepped out of a bath even when they haven't. It must be the complexion."

She was pleased, and let her smile show it. "Country wench."

"No, you don't give that impression at all. It's a child's complexion."

"I can give you five years, Quinn."

"Really? I seem to be having a phase for older women." His grin was engaging. "You've no idea what a kick I'm getting out of chatting with the daughter of a belted earl in her boudoir. I must have a servile streak in me somewhere."

She looked at him curiously. "Willie said you could be a bit savage, but I haven't noticed it yet."

"Oh, I can, Janet, I can. I'm all bitter and twisted inside. But . . ."

"But what?"

"Well, I don't really know. Modesty was uncommonly kind to me after I'd behaved like a pig, and then Willie gave me a thundering great clout over the ear-'ole, and I've felt better ever since. Do you want breakfast now?"

"I want to know what happened this morning."

"Well . . . nothing special, but it was exciting in a weird kind of way. We hid the cars about three miles from the cave entrance, and went across country on foot. Willie and Modesty were humping a great load of gear apiece, but they wouldn't let me help and it didn't seem to bother them. Do you mind if I smoke?"

"I'll have one too."

When he had lit the cigarettes he said, "They were working from a blow-up of some map. I said I only knew the way by the track, but they said we'd strike that later, and they were right, even though it was still half-dark for the first two miles. Anyway, we sighted the track, I got my bearings, and we were in this valley at first light."

"And you found the cave?"

"It only took me twenty minutes. I remembered better than I thought. And inside it was much the way I'd been trying to recollect during the flight out. There's a twisty bit at first, and a long steep descent, then a fifteen-foot pot and a traverse along a stream until you come to the stalactite chamber. That's quite a sight. It's crossed by another stream, or maybe the same one, except it's not a stream any more but a lake. We used the little inflatable boat for that, one at a time."

"It's deep?"

"God, yes. A freak thing. When I first did the cave, our instructor lowered a weight on forty-feet of cord, and didn't find bottom. It's like a water-filled pot-hole. But we'd have used the boat anyway, rather than wade. You always stay dry as long as you can when you're caving. Too much loss of body-heat once you're wet." He half closed his eyes, remembering. "Well, then there's a squeeze through a bedding plane. That was a bit tight for Willie, but he made it. After that you have to get up a ten foot pitch, and the rest is straightforward. I showed them the water-chute, the slide leading up to the chateau, and then we came out."

Lady Janet stared out through the window at the bright sunshine, trying to feel the dank iciness, to see the ancient blackness yielding to the gleam of lamplight. The cave was like some huge sprawling animal, she thought, which had lain underground for a million years. She said, "They didn't go up the slide to see if there was a grille at the top?"

"No. They'll do that tonight. They've left all the gear there and they seem pretty sure they'll cope with a grille if there is one."

"Where are they now?"

"Heading back to the castle to have a good look at it."

"Back?"

"Oh, yes. When we came out of the cave, they saw me safely to where we'd left the cars. That's when it got weird. We were crossing a series of valleys. We'd lie flat, just looking for about five minutes. Then Willie would move down and up to the next ridge. He didn't seem to hurry, but God he was covering ground fast. He'd disappear, sort of fade into the ground, and we'd watch for another couple of minutes before Modesty and I moved. They'd each got an automatic rifle, an M16 she called it. So they were covering each other at every move."

"Why was it weird?"

"Well . . . you don't exactly think of them as a cautious pair, but they were concentrating like hell and taking no chances at all."

"I find that comforting."

"So do I. And it's weird seeing them work together. They hardly talk at all, but they operate like one pair of hands."

"Yes." Lady Janet stubbed out her cigarette. "Well, I suppose that's comforting too." Quinn looked at her quickly but said nothing. After a moment she smiled and said, "I'll get up and have a bath now. You'd better catch up on some sleep, Quinn."

"Yes." He suppressed a yawn. "Will you wake me at noon?"

"All right. When are Modesty and Willie going to get any sleep?"

"Between dusk and when they aim to enter the chateau, about three a.m. They'll sleep just inside the cave. We left sleeping bags, food and some gear there."

She closed her eyes for a moment, then opened them again. "I'm glad you brought your pocket chess, Quinn. I don't fancy you or I will be sleeping much tonight."

* * *

Lying prone on a table pushed against the window, Mr. Sexton lowered the field-glasses and murmured, "They're as good as their reputation, which is very good indeed."

Colonel Jim said, "You still can't spot 'em?"

"Not a sign." Mr. Sexton slid back off the table and moved away from the window. "And I've been scanning from different positions for a couple of hours now."

Mellish looked up from the notes he was studying. "They may not be out there."

"They're out there all right." Mr. Sexton smiled. "They're making a very careful reconnaissance to find the best way in and the best way out. The only thing that puzzles me is why they've brought in that pair at *Le Lion Rouge*. Blaise and Garvin always work alone."

Colonel Jim rubbed a big hand against a heavy jowl. "When d'you figure they'll try it?"

"Oh, tonight. They know Tarrant's on the griddle, so they're up against time."

"That's my thinking, too. Question is, how they'll try it."

Mr. Sexton shrugged. "There are various possibilities, none very good, and we'll be ready for them all." He looked at his watch. "Clare and Angel should be back soon, and we might learn something useful then."

"Yeah." Colonel Jim mixed himself a drink, frowning. "What's bugging me is how they homed-in on us here. Maybe this Quinn saw something when you picked up Tarrant, but that wouldn't give 'em the chateau. So where's the leak?"

"It's certainly a question that needs answering," agreed Mr. Sexton cheerfully. "But once we've got Blaise and Garvin we'll soon find out."

*   *   *

Lady Janet and Quinn sat in the small lounge of *Le Lion Rouge*. They had finished lunch an hour ago, a lunch made entertaining by the energetic quarrelling of the two elderly Frenchmen the patron had spoken of. These two had now retired to an enclosed sun terrace at the back of the inn and were playing an acrimonious game of cards.

Lady Janet said, "Will you take another flying job?"

"I don't know." Quinn looked at the dregs in his coffee cup. "I haven't thought much about it. Airlines don't like pilots who get their passengers killed off. Would *you* like to fly with a chap who'd done that?"

"It wouldn't worry me. I think you had awful bad luck. But if the airlines feel that way, there are other flying jobs. I've a brother-in-law in the States who might help. He owns an air-freight company, among other things."

"You're very kind." He looked at her in silence for a while, his young face curious. "It must be a bit rotten for you. About Modesty and Willie. I don't mean now, I mean generally."

For a moment she stared him down, the cold pride of

generations of Covenanters in her eyes. "I've no wish for sympathy, Quinn."

"I'm sorry——"

She raised a hand to stop him, her expression changing. "No, I didn't mean to snap at you. I'm a wee bit over-touchy on that point, maybe. All right, it's something I've learned to live with. When I first met her and saw what she was to Willie, I had a bad attack of the hates. I think any woman would have. But that's long over now."

"You like her?"

Lady Janet lifted an eyebrow at him, then gave a small shrug. "I respect her. She never competes, never patronises, never uses her influence over Willie or so much as lets it show. I value her goodwill. It comes to me through Willie, but it's no less real for that, and it's a very positive thing. But we'll never be cosy intimates, having long sessions of girl-talk together."

She paused, thinking, then went on slowly. "There's another thing, I like Willie better than any man I've known. He's very intelligent and kind, and he has a great gift for understanding a woman." She half-smiled. "Above all, he cheers you up, and there aren't too many you can say that about these days. But he wasn't always the way he is now, Quinn. He says he used to be a very nasty character indeed, until Modesty came along and bought him out of gaol somewhere out East, years ago."

"That's when he started working for her?"

"Yes. As far as I can make out, it was something like being reborn for Willie. So whatever he is now, she made him that way, and I've her to thank for it."

Quinn eyed her with respect and said thoughtfully, "Not many women would, though." He looked about him and lowered his voice. "This waiting's a hell of a business, isn't it?"

153

"Awful." She looked at her watch. Tomorrow at noon, if there had been no word from Modesty and Willie, she was to make two phone-calls. Both were restricted numbers, one for a man called Vaubois in Paris, another for a man called Fraser in London. She was simply to say that Modesty and Willie had gone into the Chateau Lancieux to find their friend, and had not returned.

Lady Janet felt slightly sick, imagining how it would be next day, as the morning wore on, if no word came.

Quinn said, "Have you hurt your foot? I noticed you limping a bit."

"I've half a leg missing. This one. I lost it in a car smash a few years back."

"Oh, Lord." He rubbed his eyes with finger and thumb. "Sorry, love. Old Quinn isn't exactly a master of tact."

"It was a natural question. Old Quinn worries too much, probably because he's still pretty young."

"I'm going to put on about ten years in the next twenty hours."

"And I'll be a hag by midnight. Do you know exactly what they aim to do, once they get in?"

"Not exactly. But I gather the general aim is to locate the baddies and immobilise them, then find Tarrant at leisure, phone us here to stop worrying, and bring him away."

"How does the immobilising bit work?"

"Quietly, they hope. They have an interesting range of equipment, including ether sprays and suchlike, but if they run into anyone on the hoof I suppose they'll be rather brusque with them." He reflected for a moment or two. "I've actually seen Modesty flatten three men in about five seconds. If Willie's as good, which I don't doubt, then we've every reason to feel encouraged, haven't we."

She patted his hand. "Keep telling me that every hour on the hour."

The patron entered the lounge. "Excuse me, madame. An English lady has come. She speaks no French and I do not understand what she desires. Would you have the kindness to speak to her?"

At the first mention of an English lady, Quinn and Janet had stood up, excitement leaping between them. Now they exchanged a wry look, and Quinn said, "It couldn't have been Modesty anyway. Much too soon."

"We'd better go and see what she wants."

A woman was waiting in the small courtyard. She wore a light motoring coat and a head-scarf. The hair peeping from beneath the scarf was sandy-gold. The features were strong, but the thin high-bridged nose gave a slightly predatory impression.

Lady Janet said, "Can we help you? I speak a little French."

The wide-set eyes lit up with relief. "Lord above, you're Scottish, surely?"

Lady Janet smiled politely. "We seem to get everywhere, don't we? What's the trouble?"

"I'm travelling with my niece, and we've broken down a few hundred yards along the road. It's my own silly fault, I'm afraid. They told me at the garage where we hired the car that the needle on the fuel-gauge was reading proud, but I forgot."

Quinn said, "It's just petrol?"

"Aye, I'm sure it is. I had a spare can, and put that in, but the battery ran flat before enough petrol came through to the carburretor—at least that's what Angelica said. I'm a fool with such things."

"There's a little garage here," said Lady Janet. "They'll give you a tow-start."

"My dear, I've been there. The wee man's out and his wife says he'll not be back for two hours."

Quinn said, "Never mind. We'll drive you back and give you a tow."

"Och, that's awfully kind of you."

Five minutes later, where the road dipped in a long hollow, Quinn pulled in front of a blue estate car, a Citroen Safari, and backed up to it. A pretty girl in a short white dress stood on the verge beside the car. Quinn opened his door to get out, then heard a little gasp. He turned his head and froze. In the passenger seat beside him, Janet sat with her head tilted awkwardly back, her face draining of colour. The Scotswoman sitting behind her said, "Stay where you are please, Mr. Quinn." She was holding Janet by the hair with one hand, pulling her head back. In the other hand was a slim knife, its point pricking the side of Janet's neck. The woman said, "I've only to push it in just a wee half-inch and she's dead, Mr. Quinn."

The girl in the white dress stood by Quinn's door now. She giggled and said, "She'll bleeding well do it, too, you can bet your balls on that, whacker."

"We'll have no smut, thank you, Angel," the Scotswoman said severely. "Get back in the car and don't drive too fast. Mr. Quinn, you'll follow her. I wouldn't advise any foolishness, like braking suddenly. It just needs a quick jab in this big artery here, you understand? We'll be stopping in a mile or two, to leave your car and change to ours, and you'll be given no chance for heroics, Mr. Quinn. Angel has a silenced gun in that handbag. Now, have I made everything quite clear?"

White-faced, hands shaking on the wheel, Quinn nodded slowly. Angel slammed the door, and from the corner of his eye he saw Janet wince as the knife pricked her neck with the shudder of the car. He watched the Citroen pull out past him, then switched on and moved off carefully. His limbs felt leaden, and his mind was in chaos.

*   *   *

Fifty minutes later, lying face to face with Janet on a thick car rug spread on the Safari floor, their arms passed about each other's body and their wrists manacled, Quinn glimpsed the chateau through the off-side window. It stood halfway up the long slope they were now mounting by a dusty track which zig-zagged up from the valley. The Scotswoman was driving, unbelievably delivering a monologue about a crochet pattern to the girl beside her, Angel, who seemed from her lack of response to be not even mildly interested.

It came to Quinn that from somewhere in the valley Modesty Blaise and Willie Garvin would be watching at this moment. They would have seen the Citroen leave the chateau, and were now marking its return. If they were using glasses, if they spotted him in the car . . .

Hampered by Janet's weight on his arm, he tried to lift his head and shoulders. Without turning round Angel said, "You want to know what I'll do if you don't keep your bleedin' 'ead down, Quinnie?" He twisted his head and saw her eyes in the mirror. She had adjusted it so that she could watch them in the back. To Quinn those eyes were an outrage in the pretty young face. They held glints of childish pleasure in things unspeakable, the amusement of a small devil in hell.

She said, "What I'll do is 'op over there and twist me piano wire round that toffee-nosed bird's neck. Then you can watch 'er tongue turn black, Quinnie. You ever seen that? It's a real giggle." She sniggered and nudged the woman beside her. "Go on, let's 'ave a bit of fun anyway,

Clare. We can always say she started yelling or something."

"You'll do no such thing, Angel dear," Clare said firmly. "I'll not tell lies to Colonel Jim for you. He said to fetch them back in prime condition, and in prime condition we'll fetch them back, young lady."

"Ah, bollocks," Angel said sulkily.

Quinn rested his head, dazed with horror. Janet's face was only a few inches from his. She was still pale, but there was a dour set to her mouth, and though her eyes held no hope they were calm. She moved to touch his cheek with her lips briefly, then drew back her head again and whispered, "Hang on, Quinn."

It was the voice of the aristocrat in the tumbril. There was nothing left to cling to, except pride.

CHAPTER NINE

Modesty Blaise woke up and lay quietly in her sleeping-bag for a few seconds in the total darkness. Beside her Willie stirred and said, "Two o'clock, Princess?"

"It should be. Just a moment." She flashed the beam of a pencil-torch on her watch. "Five minutes to. Light the lamp, Willie."

He sat up, and she held the beam on the pressure lamp for him while he lit it. They were fifty yards from the cave entrance, on a broad stretch of dry rock and with a sharp dog-leg of tunnel between them and the opening in the valley-side. Under their denim shirts and slacks they both wore woollen tights and string vests. Even so it was cold when they emerged from the warmth of the sleeping-bags.

They put on light quilted jackets, combat boots, and nylon overalls, then rolled up the sleeping-bags and set them in a vertical crevice. Willie rested a hand on a long canvas bag with shoulder-straps attached, and said, "We taking the rifles?"

She thought for a moment, then shook her head. "They're a damn nuisance to carry on a sneak-job, and if it does come to a shoot-out we'll be in the close-quarter business." A Colt .32 was holstered on her thigh, beneath the jacket and overalls which she would be taking off once they were inside the chateau.

Willie carried two throwing-knives. Usually he wore them in twin sheaths strapped in echelon on his left breast.

Tonight, because there was an awkward squeeze to face, he carried one knife at each hip under the overalls. They were from a range of knives he made with his own hands. These two had a modified Bowie-style tip with a straight back-edge. The blade was diamond-shaped in cross-section for strength, carried a quarter-inch brass strip on the back, and was blued to cut reflection at night. The full tang was set in a haft of Gerber Armorhide, a metal alloy with a finish like sharkskin, moulded with a concave sweep between the butt and the brass face where the tang entered the haft. Both knives had been carefully balanced to make a full revolution in twelve feet with a normal throw, but this could be varied by wrist-action at the moment of release. His accuracy with them was incomparable.

Modesty put a bulging haversack in the crevice with the rifles and sleeping-bags, looked at her watch and said, "Two-fifteen, Willie."

"Right." He swung a rucksack on to his back, and together they began the journey into the Lancieux Cave. Electric lamps were clipped to the front of their plastic helmets. Willie had put out the pressure lamp and was carrying it as a reserve. The cold grew more penetrating as they moved on, but they registered it only on their exposed hands and faces.

Modesty led the way. There was no obvious main route, but the way Quinn had taken was fixed in her mind. Sometimes they moved through narrow passages, sometimes the walls fell back. Underfoot the rock was wrinkled and pitted, demanding wariness. The convoluted maze was no man-made thing with level floors and vertical walls to serve the two small creatures now violating its ancient privacy. It had been shaped by Nature's freakish hand over infinite millennia and many an Ice-Age.

Yet when they had descended the fifteen-foot pot and

traversed the sloping wall that leaned outwards from a shallow stream, they reached a huge stalactite chamber which seemed to echo man's architecture, though it had been shaped eons before man's forebears used the first primitive tool. The roof rose in a vast dome seventy feet high. The stalactites that hung from it were small, few more than an arm's length, but they were tightly clustered and glinted like great silver needles in the lamplight. There were no stalagmites rising from the floor. The walls were wrinkled like curtains. Around the perimeter shimmered white patches of the calcite deposit called moonmilk.

The floor of the chamber was split by what might have been a wide stream but was in fact a pool of unknown depth. Twenty-three feet wide, it extended from wall to wall. The banks of rock did not slope gently into the pool, but dropped abruptly from eighteen inches above the surface. Whatever the source of the waters that fed it, and whatever the outlet, both were hidden. On the surface, no current was perceptible.

The miniature rubber dinghy had been left inflated and tucked out of sight in a hollow close to the wall of the chamber. Willie set it on the water. Modesty got in very carefully, facing the way they had come, then paddled with her hands to send the little craft drifting across to the far side. Willie held the end of a thin nylon rope attached to the stern. When Modesty had climbed out he drew the rope in, made the crossing himself, and set the dinghy behind a low outcrop of rock. Beyond the pool lay a stretch of flat ground giving way to a slope of irregular dripstone steps which rose to the far wall of the chamber.

Three rifts pierced this wall. Modesty led the way into the smallest, which lay on the right and offered a narrow triangular passage through which they crawled for eighty yards on hands and knees. It ended in a grotto with a slot-like, almost horizontal opening between two layers of rock. This bedding-plane squeeze extended for fifteen yards, and five minutes passed while Willie edged his bulk through inch by inch. Beyond the squeeze the going was easy, apart from the ascent of a ten-foot pitch. Here a short electron ladder had been set up during their trip with Quinn, using a maypole of heavy-duty aluminium alloy.

A hundred yards beyond the pitch lay the point where the slide from the chateau pierced the passage at an angle. The floor of the side was five feet broad. Down its centre ran a trough or depression carrying a rapid flow of water a foot deep. The water debouched into the passage where Modesty and Willie stood, spreading to fill a shallow stream-bed at their feet as it crossed the passage diagonally, to vanish into a swallet some distance from them on the far side.

They had left ropes, pitons and a copper-headed hammer beneath an undercut in the rock when Quinn had brought them to this point twenty hours earlier. He had not been able to tell them the length of the slide, but after studying it they had assumed that it ran fairly straight and at a rising angle of no more than forty degrees overall.

Willie put the pressure lamp in a crevice to one side of the chute, set down his rucksack and looked at Modesty. She nodded, and bent to pick up a coil of rope and the canvas bag containing the pitons and hammer. Willie eased himself carefully into a face-down position to the left of the tumbling water, where there was a slightly greater width than was offered on the other side of the trough, and began seeking niches in the slimy rock for fingertips and boot-tips.

After a few moments he began to edge up the slope like some monstrous crawling insect. When he had gained a few yards, Modesty started after him. One end of a long rope was looped round her elbow. The other end was tied to the rucksack and to the bag with the pitons and hammer. The hope was that the pitons would not be needed. If they were, the soft copperhead of the hammer would cut noise to a minimum.

After thirty feet Willie paused for a while, then turned on his back. In the light of her helmet-lamp Modesty saw that for a few feet the floor of the slide rose steeply; but the roof was low here, and stippled with nodules, making it possible to use hands and feet for edging up the slope with a chimneying technique.

Beyond the steep incline the slide resumed its forty degree gradient, and after another twenty feet Willie stopped again. The floor was wider here. He edged over and beckoned. Modesty came up beside him. Four feet ahead of them was a vertical wall of rock, the height of a man. The lower part of it was natural, the stream emerging from a submerged opening at the base of the wall. At a height of three feet the wall became man-made, of rough-hewn stone blocks bonded by mortar. Centred above the stream at this point was a slot like a giant letterbox, four feet wide and half as deep. There was no grille, but set in the thickness of the wall were three stubs of rusting iron, the bases of heavy bars which had once guarded the aperture.

Modesty wriggled forward, hooked a hand over the edge of the slot, and stood up, straddling the gushing water. Slipping the loop of rope from her arm, she hooked it over one of the iron stubs, unclipped the lamp from her helmet, and bent forward across the two-foot thickness of the wall. The beam of the lamp showed a cobwebbed cellar. Dust lay thickly on the flagstones. To one side was a short flight of stone steps leading to a heavy wooden door. The cellar was vaulted, and the light of her lamp could not penetrate the full extent of it, but this section seemed to have been used as a workshop at some time, probably during the German occupation. Along one wall stood a massive wooden bench with a vice bolted to the front of it. On the wall above it were racks for tools, empty now. Under the bench stood a cluster of rusting jerricans, bottles, cans of paint and grease, and a variety of screw-top containers. Two large and grimy high-voltage bulbs hung from flex above the bench.

She drew back, nodded to Willie, then threw one leg over the edge of the slot and wriggled through, swivelling on her belly to lower her feet to the cellar floor. She stood up, moved the beam slowly round, then bent and beckoned to Willie.

He was halfway through the slot, and swivelling to bring his legs round, when the lights in the cellar went on. Head twisted awkwardly, he saw in the limited area of vision offered by the slot that a man had moved out from behind the nearest pillar, a fair, bearded, smiling man in a black blazer. Modesty had dropped the lamp and was moving fast. She had already covered half the distance that lay between her and the smiling man. The instant surge of alarm in Willie eased a little. The man was empty-handed and alone. She would have him before he could draw breath to shout.

Swinging round, he slithered backwards through the slot, and as his feet touched the floor he heard the sound of a soft impact, a gasp, and the scuffling thud of a body crumpling to the floor.

He straightened up and turned, whispering, "Blimey, Princess, d'you reckon they——?" Shock hit him, a series of shocks compressed into high frequency. She lay huddled limply on the dusty floor, her helmet rolling away. The bearded man was in mid-air, hurtling at him in a huge leap, poised to perfection, one foot driving out like a piston to strike under the heart.

There was no time for thought. Instinct twitched his body in an awkward, unbalanced evasion. The foot scored across his ribs in a glancing blow and he stumbled sideways, fighting for control, desperately aware that the bulky clothing hampered his speed and that he faced an opponent of dazzling skill. The bearded man landed perfectly, and rose again as if from a trampoline. He touched down just out of arm's reach, swayed sideways, moved in with the speed of a darting lizard, then struck almost casually with the edge of his right hand.

Still off balance, Willie Garvin caught the wrist and kicked for the knee. In one fluid movement the bearded man broke the hold, moved his leg to evade the kick and swung the same leg incredibly high to take Willie on the side of the head with the sole of the foot. Lights exploding before his eyes, Willie reeled back. The strength shown by the breaking of the wrist-grip piled new shock upon all that had gone before. He let himself go, falling so that he would hit the floor in a backward breakfall and could then try for an upward kick as the man came in. But the head-blow had confused his sense of direction. The bench was behind him now, and he fell back obliquely on to the pointed anvil of the vice.

Pain exploded in his shoulder with paralysing effect. He lurched sideways, clawing for a hold on the bench, and lunging feebly with one foot at the blurred figure that swam into his vision. The man in the black blazer brushed the kick aside, then chopped with carefully controlled force between the hinge of the jaw and the ear.

Willie Garvin slithered to the ground and lay still.

Mr. Sexton peered into the depths of the cellar where the light failed to penetrate, and said, "All over, Colonel Jim."

Colonel Jim moved out of the shadows. Da Cruz was beside him, carrying a machine pistol, a 9mm Stechkin with a 20-round staggered-row box magazine. Mr. Sexton bent over Modesty Blaise, lifted an eyelid with his thumb, then straightened up. Colonel Jim said, "They better be alive, like I told you, Mr. Sexton."

"Prime condition," Mr. Sexton said cheerfully. He glanced across at Willie Garvin. "Well, not quite. I'm afraid Garvin's damaged a little. He fell against that vice."

Colonel Jim's shark-like mouth opened in a chuckle. "That don't bother me none."

"It's annoying for me, though." Mr. Sexton fingered his short beard. "I was looking forward to a really interesting bout later."

"Didn't look like they could give you much trouble, Mr. Sexton."

The fair man's eyes twinkled. "It's all relative, but they're extremely good, you know." He glanced at Modesty. "She had no chance, of course. The element of surprise. She was scarcely expecting anyone at my level." He smiled. "There isn't anyone else at my level. But she's very fast and moved beautifully, especially so when you consider she's bundled up in a wad of clothes."

His gaze turned to Willie Garvin. "He had a fraction of a second to realise what he was up against, and I must say he reacted extraordinarily well. I'm stronger, of course, I tested that. But he has great qualities. It's very annoying about that shoulder. Even if he hasn't broken anything he'll be as stiff as a board on that side for a week or two."

Colonel Jim took a cigar from his jacket pocket and considered. "Maybe we'll be able to give you a week or two, Mr. Sexton. Depends what insurance they took out. If it was only Quinn and that Mrs. Gillam, we got no worries."

"That's excellent," Mr. Sexton said heartily. "It's stimulating to have a good store of practice material in hand."

166

The door creaked open and Mellish appeared at the top of the steps. Relief touched his face as he took in the scene. He said, "Everything all right?"

Colonel Jim held a match to his cigar. "What else? Got your needle and dope, Mellish? Good. Now here's what you do." He pointed with the cigar. "Right now you give these two a shot to keep 'em quiet for a few hours. Then Mr. Sexton carries 'em upstairs. I want 'em searched. Every stitch. The word is, they're pretty sneaky. Get Angel in on the search, Mr. Sexton. She's sneaky too."

Mellish said, "Where shall we put them when we're finished? We've only got two cells with sound doors and locks." He knelt over Modesty and opened a flat box containing disposable syringes and ampoules.

Colonel Jim said, "I want these two kept apart. Let's see now, how long have we had Tarrant in the stink-hole?"

Mellish looked up. "Over thirty hours."

"Okay. Get him out, clean him up, and find something decent for him to wear. Then, when you've finished with these two, you put Garvin in with Quinn and the Gillam girl. Blaise in with Tarrant." He paused, considering. "Yeah, do it like that. It'll work good for us, I reckon. And we'll leave 'em sweat a while. See what time and twitchy nerves can do before we start making anyone redundant."

Mellish got up and moved to Willie Garvin. Mr. Sexton said, "It's Tarrant we want to talk. The rest are expendable."

"That's right." Colonel Jim watched the needle slide in. "I figure if we take it slow and make the others redundant one at a time, he'll crack. He's tough, but kinda sensitive."

Mr. Sexton sighed contentedly. "They'll all have to go eventually, of course. Who would you like me to discharge first, Colonel Jim? I mean, when the time comes to begin."

The big man rested his cigar hand on the slope of his

belly and pondered. Slowly his mouth stretched, and an indulgent twinkle came into the granity eyes. "We'll let Momma choose," he said. "She'll like that."

*　　*　　*

An hour later, in the big bedroom she shared with Clare, Angel sat on the edge of her bed and idly swung the two-foot length of fine wire, holding one of the two wooden toggles attached to the ends. The wire touched the carved top of the thick wooden bedpost, curving round it under the centrifugal pull of the heavier toggle at the far end, and as this swung towards her, Angel caught it deftly in her free hand.

"I fancy that Garvin," she said. "He's a big 'un."

Clare looked up from her crochet and nodded towards the wire Angel now held taut round the bedpost. "Fancy him for that, you mean?"

"No, daft. Fancy a good grind with 'im." Angel gave the thin wire a jerk, then giggled. "I like big 'uns for this too, though. There's more of a kick when they're twice your size and squirming about like a live winkle on a pin. Don't matter 'ow big they are, once you get your knee in their back, they're cooked. Remember that bloke at Point Clair, the big darkie——"

"I've no wish to be reminded, Angel." Clare's nose twitched with distaste. "We all have unpleasant duties to perform from time to time, but discussion of them is coarse and unladylike."

Angel swung the wire again. "I don't see anything un-pleasant about 'em."

"You lack breeding, dear, but we won't argue the matter. Do you know what plans Colonel Jim has for our visitors?"

Angel looked sulky. "Well, he's going to cater for Mister

168

bleeding Sexton, we can guess that. Teacher's pet, 'e is. I bet all I'll get is that gimpy red'eaded bird to see off." A malicious glint touched her muddy eyes. "Still, I can pretend it's you Clare, eh? After all, she's Scotch too."

"I wish you'd not say *Scotch*, Angel. Scottish. And I wasn't asking about disposal, I was asking how Colonel Jim proposed to make use of them."

"Going to use 'em for squeezing Tarrant of course."

"Aye, but how?"

"Let 'em sweat a bit, then 'ave Mr. Sexton knock one of 'em off in front of the rest, just to show we mean business. Let 'em sweat again, then pick another of 'em and put the screws on slow, with Tarrant there. And so on, I suppose."

Clare nodded, lips pursed judiciously. "Sir Gerald is a gentleman," she said. "I'd imagine he would react best to sight of one of the ladies under treatment by Mr. Sexton. I must confess to a wee hope that it'll not be Lady Janet. As a compatriot, I'm bound to prefer that she has a nice quick end." She smiled archly. "Sir Gerald Tarrant and Lady Janet Gillam. My word, but we've such distinguished company just now."

She held out the crochet-work at arm's length and studied it with her head a little to one side. "D'you not think this a pretty pattern, Angel dear?"

CHAPTER TEN

Willie Garvin's first awareness was of pain. The whole of his left shoulder and back throbbed. He kept his rate of breathing unchanged and lay still.

The cellar. Modesty unconscious. The brief frantic fight against the smiling man with the golden beard. A master. Unbelievable. Then falling back . . . against something. Paralysing pain.

And now. Lying on what felt like a thin straw palliasse. Hard floor beneath.

Alone? No. Faint sound of clothes rustling in movement. Breathing. A voice said dully, "What time is it?"

Quinn's voice.

As Willie opened his eyes Janet said, "I don't know, they took my watch with everything else. About noon, I think." She sat beside him on another palliasse, her back to the wall, looking away towards Quinn, who sat facing her across the corner of the long narrow cell, arms wrapped about his knees. She looked down at Willie and gave a little start. His right arm moved quickly to touch his fingers to her mouth, warning her to silence. She flinched, and he saw dried blood on her swollen lower lip.

Painfully he sat up, flapping a hand at Quinn to prevent him speaking. The nylon overall and quilted jacket were gone. So were the knives. His shirt hung loose, his combat boots were unlaced, his belt unbuckled. He knew he had been carefully and expertly searched.

Janet and Quinn, here in the Chateau Lancieux. So that was it. Keeping shock from his face, he gave a reassuring nod and got to his feet, buckling his belt. Carefully he moved his left arm, up, forward, back. Stiff. The shoulder-blade badly bruised. Plenty of pain but fair mobility. Nothing broken.

The light was bright, and came from a single large bulb hanging from six inches of flex. He began to move slowly round the cell, eyes probing every inch of wall and ceiling. When he was satisfied he examined the floor and the door. The door was very solid and had one large key-hole. The stops were on this side, so the door opened outwards. He wondered if there was a drop-bar on the other side.

At least the cell wasn't bugged, unless there was a pick-up clamped outside the door, but that wouldn't yield much providing they spoke in whispers. His examination had taken ten minutes. During that time Janet and Quinn had not moved, had simply watched.

He sat down beside Janet again, took her hand, and beckoned Quinn to join them. Quinn rose from his pal-liasse. His eyes were feverish and his pale face twitched uncontrollably.

Willie said, "No bugs, but talk soft." He looked at Janet. "About noon, you reckon?"

"Yes." Her hand was shaking as it gripped his. "They brought you in hours ago."

"Modesty?"

"In another cell. With Tarrant, I think. We heard them say something like that when they were carrying you in."

Relief eased the tightness in Willie's chest, and he let out a slow breath. "When did they get you, Jan?"

"Yesterday, at *Le Lion Rouge*, just after lunch. A woman came, a Scotswoman . . ." She told him what had happened, and though her low voice did not falter he could feel the tension quivering in the sinews of her hand. "I'm sorry, Willie. We just walked into it. We're not very . . . experienced in this sort of thing."

He said gently, "Breathe deep and slow, and try to unwind, love. You're burning up too much juice. You too, Quinn. Push the air right down deep, and it'll relax your belly."

Quinn had not uttered a word yet. While Janet spoke he had knelt upright on the palliasse, arms hanging by his sides, never taking his over-bright eyes from Willie's face. Now he said very distinctly, "I told them, Willie. They knew you were coming, but not how. I told them."

Willie turned his head to look at Janet, lifting her hand and touching it to his lips. "They give you a bad time, Jan?"

Before she could answer Quinn said, "There's a man named Sexton. Mr. Sexton, they all call him. They asked what you were planning to do, and we pretended we didn't know. Then Sexton stood behind Janet and reached in front of her. He smiled all the time. She didn't make a sound, but she was . . . writhing. She bit through her lip. And then, just as she passed out . . . there was this awful sound. I thought he'd killed her. But after a minute or two she came round, and he was going to do it again. So I told them."

Willie nodded. "I'd 'ave told 'em sooner."

"What?" Quinn blinked and shook his head as if trying to clear it.

"You got no choice, Quinn, not when they just want one simple answer. They can always rip it out of you. It's different with Tarrant, they daren't do a crash job on 'im." He felt sorry for Quinn. The boy must have been suffering agonies since yesterday, seeing himself as a betrayer. No point now in saying that he should have babbled a false

172

story, should have told them the plan was for a spot-landing by parachute on the roof an hour before dawn. That might have done. But Quinn could never have concocted a convincing lie under pressure, could never have made it stick.

Willie feigned a little start of surprise and said, "Christ, 'ave you been *blaming* yourself, Quinn?"

"What the hell do you think?" Quinn's voice was a savage whisper, but there was a small, desperate note of hope in it.

"I think you ought to kick me and the Princess right in the teeth," Willie said. And that was true enough he thought bleakly. As they stared at him he went on, "We're the only ones to blame. The clever pair. We know it all. Except we slipped up right from the start. Before the start."

Janet said, "I don't see what you mean."

"We knew they'd tried to knock Quinn off, and we knew they might still be after 'im, just in case 'e'd seen anything that day they nabbed Tarrant. And they were, Jan. Someone tailed Quinn to Modesty's place. Or maybe they were watching it anyway. Those three she clobbered on the causse must've twigged who she was. So Quinn arrives, and within twenty-four hours we all go rushing off to a private airfield, never even looking over our shoulders. It'd take a smart bloke about ten minutes to find out what flight-plan Dave Craythorpe filed. Then this smart bloke gets on the blower and says, 'They're landing at Blagnat.'" Willie exhaled disgustedly. "They've 'ad tabs on us all the way."

There was a long silence, then Quinn said slowly, "Well . . . that makes me feel a bit better."

"Don't get over the moon about it." Willie rotated his shoulder. "There's a lot of aggravation ahead, and we start from 'ere. Who's to blame makes no difference." He looked at Janet. "Is Sexton the fair bloke with a beard?"

"Yes, that's him, Willie."

"He's the only one I've seen. Fastest thing on two feet I've ever seen, too." He massaged the shoulder, clamping down on the sense of shock that came with remembering those brief moments in the cellar. "He caught us on the 'op, and took us out in five seconds flat. Is Sexton the boss-man?"

Janet shook her head. "No, that's an American. They call him Colonel Jim. We don't know his other name."

"I expect it's Straik. J. Straik. You seen anyone else?"

"There's his wife. He calls her Momma. She's a sort of B-picture southern belle. And two women, Clare and Angel. I think they may have been the nun-women, Willie. There's an Englishman, middle-aged and rather jumpy, but I didn't hear his name spoken. And a half Chinesey looking man called da Cruz. Portuguese, I suppose. There may be others. I don't know."

Quinn said, "When Sexton brought us down here he talked to Angel about someone being on guard. It sounded like Ee-tow."

"Ito? Japanese?"

Quinn shrugged. "Maybe. We haven't seen him."

Janet said in a low voice, "Willie, you were saying just now we have to start from here. Is there really any chance?"

"There's always chances, Jan. Things don't often go right all the way, and then you 'ave to improvise a bit." He brought his right foot up to lie across his left thigh and began to probe with sinewy fingers at the welt of the sole. "It's a pity I didn't let you come on the Macao thing instead of this one. That was a beauty." He glanced at the door. "It's a mortice lock, and pretty new, but I can fix it if——"

174

He broke off as the composition sole separated and peeled away. Within the half-thickness of the sole were several curiously contoured hollows, empty. Willie grimaced. "I 'ad some pick-locks in there." He matched the studs and sockets which clipped the two layers of the sole together, then stood up and put his weight on the foot to clip them together.

Janet and Quinn watched as he fingered the cuffs of his shirt, the collar, then unbuckled his belt and checked the waistband of his slacks. He shook his head and said, "They didn't even miss the sling in me waistband. The Princess was carrying a few things, but they'll 'ave done a strip job on 'er, too."

Quinn said, "Well . . . that's it, then."

Willie glowered at him. "Just keep up the deep breathing and don't get morbid. Go on, I bloody mean it, Quinn. Stand up. Breathe right out, nice and slow. Now suck it in. Slower. That's right. Shove it in till your lungs creak. Good. Out again. Now keep that up for ten minutes and don't talk. Come on, Jan, you too." He reached down to help her to her feet. She began an effortful smile, then saw that he was serious and stood with her back to the wall, watching Quinn and trying to match her breathing with his.

Willie moved to the door, knelt to peer closely at the lock, shook his head regretfully, and moved back to the corner where Quinn and Janet stood. They looked at him with wide bewildered eyes, breathing obediently, like children performing some baffling adult ritual which would make everything come right because a grown-up had said so.

"Just carry on and listen," Willie said softly. "You got to understand the set-up, then we'll all 'ave a better chance when it comes to the crunch. They aim to knock us off in the end. Can't afford to do anything else. We're only alive now because they can use us in some way, probably to lever stuff out of Tarrant. At a guess I'd say they'll get us altogether some time early on, to see 'ow we react with one another. You two stay quiet. That means you watch your tongue, Quinn. Don't be surprised if the Princess starts a cat-and-dog fight with me, blaming each other for getting nailed. It's a good principle, letting the opposition think you're cracking a bit. Another thing, maybe they won't feed us, but if they do, eat while you've got the chance."

He paused, gathering his thoughts. There was a filthy taste in his mouth, he was very dry, and his shoulder throbbed. When he had time to sit quietly and concentrate he would abate the pain, setting it at a distance so that it seemed not to be a part of him.

He smiled and said, "Somewhere along the line we'll get a chance. I got no idea what shape it'll be, or 'ow good. It might be pretty thin, but it'll come. If it's while we're together, I'll get the sign from Modesty. I'll be getting signals from 'er any time we're together, telling me what line to play. Now listen. Don't live on your nerves waiting for it. Try and relax. If ever you 'ear me say, '*I could do with a beer*,' you'll know something's going to pop any second. Don't move till we've started it. Then if there's anyone near enough, kick 'em in the slats. If not, duck for the nearest cover and leave it to me and the Princess."

He paused again, aware that there were a hundred varieties of opportunity which might occur under different circumstances, and that none of the circumstances could be even guessed at yet. But at least he had done his best to lay down a basic guide-line, and it would help Janet and Quinn to have a positive sense of hope, however slender. He said, "All right, you can ease up on the breathing."

Janet moved forward, put her arms round him and rested her head on his shoulder. Quinn leaned back against the wall. After a moment or two he said gently, "I think you're

176

talking a lot of balls, Willie, but I could be wrong. I thought the same about the deep breathing, but it seems to have worked." He forced a tired smile. "I'm not exactly happy, you understand, but at least I don't feel that my guts are turning to vinegar."

"It's a panic-killer, the breathing. Sovereign remedy. We'll 'ave ten minutes in every hour. Now let's sit down. Jan, I want you to go over the opposition again, one at a time. What they look like and act like, what impression they make on you. And Quinn can chip in with 'is own ideas as we go along."

Janet said, "We haven't seen much of them, Willie."

"Never mind. Let's 'ave all you can remember. I want to get the feel of 'em."

*   *   *

Tarrant looked at the faint outlines of the sketch he had made with a wet finger on the surface of the table.

"That's about all," he said. "There's a lot of the chateau I haven't seen, of course."

"Never mind, this is quite a bit." Modesty's hand moved over the crude sketch, touching the table lightly. "We're in this section, a corridor with cells on one side, most of them without doors. A kind of open hall here, in the middle of the run, and you think Willie and the others are locked up in the end cell, here, where the corridor dead-ends?"

"That's right. I heard movement along there soon after Sexton carried you in."

"All right, we'll assume it. At the other end, a door and steps leading up to the ground floor. Kitchen on the left, here, and you think the access to the cellar is by steps down on the far side of the kitchen."

177

"That's my impression, Modesty. I'm not quite sure why."

"Something you've seen or heard without quite registering it at the time. Now, the dining-room here, and a big sitting-room on the north side. Staircase to a sort of mezzanine, where this gallery looks down on Sexton's gym."

"He calls it his consulting room when I'm taken there for treatment."

She turned her head to look at Tarrant. He wore a garment which was like a one-piece track suit of thick navy blue blanket-material. His greying moustache straggled a little, untrimmed. His cheeks were hollow, the eyes deep-sunk, his movements slow and careful like those of a man plagued by rheumatism. He was freshly bathed, but she knew that for thirty hours he had been huddled in an oubliette, a tiny airless chamber, left to suffer hunger and thirst in his own stench.

She slipped her hand under his arm and pressed it gently, then looked at the sketch again. "You haven't been higher than the mezzanine?"

"No. I imagine they're using only some of the bedrooms."

"When did you know they'd got Lady Janet and Quinn?"

"Sometime yesterday. Soon after it happened, I suppose. Sexton came in and called to me down in the stink-hole. He said you were coming in through some cave, and he'd be waiting for you."

"Did they know about the cave before?"

"Vaguely, from what Clare said. She came and talked at me later. One of her well-bred horror sessions. The agent showed them the disposal chute in the cellar when they first rented the place. Sexton went down to have a look yesterday evening. He got as far as some sort of pool. Said he didn't fancy a cold swim unless it was necessary."

She thought for a moment. "Did that surprise you?"

"Surprise me? I'm not sure. I was too . . . dismayed to know you were walking into a trap to think of much else. Perhaps it surprises me a little now. I tend to think of Sexton as a machine. Invulnerable."

"Do you know where he comes from?"

"Not precisely. But I gather most of his life was spent in the Far East."

"I see."

Tarrant wondered why the point interested her. He was very tired, yet his mind was crystal clear as if from a stimulant drug.

It was seven hours since Sexton had carried her into the cell, Angel following with a palliasse. Her clothes were in disarray, as if she had been stripped and clumsily dressed again while unconscious. Sexton laid her on the palliasse, straightened up and looked down at her with interest. "She came well prepared," he said. "You'd be surprised what we found on her." He made Tarrant get off the bunk and examined it closely, then the table.

"No nails," he said. "Good solid jointing. I can't believe the ingenious lady will find much help here."

When they had gone, Tarrant buttoned her clothes and arranged her in what seemed a comfortable position. He knew he had not the strength to lift her to the bunk. Sadness was like a cold lump in his chest. Foolishly he found himself wishing that he had not hoped for her to come.

When she woke at last from the drugged sleep, Tarrant had been given more than enough time to bury his despair and rehearse the demeanour of a man still of good spirit and cautiously hopeful. Although he did not know it, the pattern of her awakening followed the same pattern as Wilie Garvin's. She did not open her eyes until she was fully conscious, and then quickly motioned him to silence. She sat up, taking brief stock of her surroundings and studying him for what seemed a long time. He saw pity and anger in her gaze when she knelt up and rested her hand on his shoulder for a moment, and he realised that he must look far worse than he had imagined.

She touched fingers to his lips for continued silence, then all feeling vanished from her face to be replaced by a cold, almost brutal speculation as she began to search herself, feeling in her pockets, in the various hems of her shirt, in the loosened club of hair held by thick rubber bands at the nape of her neck, and finally sitting down to remove the sole from one of her boots. The search produced nothing, but if she was disappointed she gave no sign. She stood up and began to move slowly round the cell. It was not until she had examined it minutely that she spoke at last. Sitting on the bunk beside him, her voice a low whisper, she began a series of questions.

As one who had de-briefed many agents in his time, Tarrant saw her purpose and shaped his answers to it. Over and above the cold facts of their situation, she was seeking the intangibles of impression and insight. Carefully Tarrant described Colonel Jim and each one of his company, adding as much as he had been able to gather concerning inter-relationships between them.

Then came an account of his treatment at their hands, and finally she had asked him to sketch as much of the layout of the chateau as he had been able to see. She stood gazing absently down at the barely visible wet-finger sketch now, and said, "Have you noticed any kind of alarm system?"

"I believe all outer doors and windows are wired," he said. "Da Cruz and one of the Japanese were testing recently when I was being brought back after a session with

Mellish and Colonel Jim. Da Cruz spoke of 'trying the stairs', so possibly there's an internal alarm on the main staircase at least."

She rubbed a palm across the table, then drew him to the bunk to sit down again and said, "This man Sexton. I only glimpsed him for a couple of seconds, and I under-rated him badly. He put me out with a counter very few experts could bring off. Have you had any chance to watch him in action?"

"Yes, before a painful session in the gym, two days ago. He was working-out with the three Japanese."

"We obviously didn't extend him much in the cellar, but he had one or two advantages then, and a little goes a long way in top-class competition. How good is he?"

Tarrant considered grimly. "I think few men can be as strong. But he's more than simply strong. Unarmed combat is his religion, and he's spent his life at it."

"Comparisons. You've seen me work out with Willie."

"I think he must be faster. He has beautiful fluency. I would say his technique was complete. He claims, and not boastfully, to be the best in the world. I think it may be true."

She nodded. There were few men whose judgment in such a matter she would have relied on, but Tarrant was one of them, and for a particular reason. He was a skilled fencer, who in his twenties had fenced for England. No other sport is so demanding upon the eye of the watcher. To the layman, a long engagement is little more than a blur. Only the fencer can follow and itemise the sequence of blade on blade. And this faculty would make Tarrant a reliable judge of Sexton's skill in combat.

He said, "Why do you ask?"

She gave a little shrug. "A man like that craves to prove

himself against the best opposition. I just have a feeling Willie or I might be on the list."

"God forbid," Tarrant said fervently.

"I'll go along with that." She smiled briefly. "Willie and I don't want to prove anything."

Tarrant said, "There's something I haven't yet told you. I'm afraid Willie's hurt."

She did not move, but he was watching her eyes and saw shock hit her. Then she had absorbed it, and it was gone. "Badly?"

"I don't know. It's his shoulder. Apparently there was a brief battle with Sexton, and Willie fell against a bench or something."

"That wouldn't—oh, there was a big vice on it."

"Sexton seemed mildly annoyed by the incident."

"Yes . . . that fits, if he wants competition. Still, it sounds as if Willie has only one arm out of action."

Tarrant stared. The hint of relief in her eyes seemed quite genuine. He said, "You find it comforting?"

"I'd rather have Willie around with one arm than anyone else with two," she said almost idly, as if thinking of something else. Tarrant sat watching her with growing fascination. In the past he had often wondered exactly how she would appear at the crunch of a mission which had gone wrong. It had long been a source of irritaton to him that his French colleague, Vaubois, had once seen her in action. Tarrant had never done so, except at practice with Willie. Now he was seeing her, if not in action then in the toils of a disastrous mission which would probably be fatal, and he found it difficult to describe her manner. 'Absorbed' was the only word that came to his mind, but it was inadequate. Negatives were easier. Not defiant, not optimistic, not pessimistic, not grim. Just totally absorbed by the problem. He remembered watching the pole-vault in the

Olympics, remembered the long minutes of concentration before the vaulter at last began his run. It was something like that.

She said, "They're bound to have covered the situation at *Le Lion Rouge.*"

"Yes. That was included in Clare's monologue. A couple of hours after she got back here with Lady Janet and Quinn she phoned the inn and spoke to the patron as Lady Janet. I suppose they'd have a rather similar French accent, both being Scottish. She said Mr. Quinn had been taken ill while getting the other car going, that he had a heart condition and she'd driven him straight to hospital in Toulouse. An English friend would be calling to settle the bill and pick up their bags. Mellish drove down in the Simca during the evening and did just that."

"They're thorough."

"Very." He looked at her. "Does Fraser know you were coming here to the Chateau Lancieux?"

"Yes. When he doesn't get a call from us today he'll start worrying, but he won't take any action for a while."

Tarrant nodded ruefully. Fraser was a cool man who knew well enough how easily a mission could be delayed by small factors. If you panicked and interfered with an operation too early, you could blow the whole thing. So Fraser would hold his hand until he was certain something had gone seriously wrong. And then? A call to Réné Vaubois, who would send in a team. Tarrant shrugged mentally. At the first hint of trouble Colonel Jim would kill off his captives. The labyrinth of caves would make an ideal place for Mr. Sexton to dispose of the bodies.

He said slowly, "My dear . . . I've no personal experience of this kind of situation. Will you tell me honestly what you think our chances are?"

She looked at him, a little puzzled. "I can't, Sir Gerald.

I won't know what they are until it's all over. I only know there'll be chances. But there are so many variables, depending on how the opposition handle us, it's impossible even to imagine them. At the moment there's no point in trying to plan in any specific sense. We just have to be quick enough to see the chance that's worth taking."

"I'm afraid," he said slowly, "that's something which is to your address and Willie's, rather than mine." He had hoped for something more, and was trying to conceal his disappointment.

"We might do very well," she said, "if only we could get our hands on a little piece of stiff wire."

"The lock?" He stared at her. "But there's a drop-bar on the outside."

"Then we'd need at least ten inches of wire for that." She looked about the cell. "There's nothing here, and I expect Willie's having no better luck. What do they give you when they feed you?"

"Soup and bread."

"I meant utensils."

"Oh. A plastic bowl and spoon. Taken away after five minutes."

"That doesn't offer much, then. But bear the thought in mind any time they take you out of the cell. I know they're not likely to leave convenient bits of wire about, but if you spot anything that might remotely be useful, try to get hold of it. The others will be doing the same. Willie will tell them."

She stopped speaking and sat for a minute in silence. Then the look of concentration cleared from her face and she gave him the same sort of smile she might have given across the table if they had been dining in her apartment.

"Would you like to sleep now? Or talk? Or play a little chess?"

184

For a moment Tarrant wondered if he were dreaming. He fought against the sense of unreality and said, "I don't think I could sleep just now, I feel rather over-stimulated."

"That won't do. You'll get adrenalin fatigue. We'll play a little therapeutic chess to damp you down. How far can you go in your head?"

Tarrant said apologetically, "About two moves, I imagine. It's something I haven't tried."

"Never mind. We'll start by using the flag-stones as a board, and set up an end-game with two or three pawns and . . . say a rook and bishop each." She stood up and began to move across the cell, counting the flags.

Tarrant watched her dully. She meant well, of course, but if she thought to drag his mind from the enclosed world of dread and despair in which he had lived these many days past, then she was wildly mistaken.

Yet twenty minutes later, as he sat with narrowed eyes fixed on the flags, struggling to hold his visualisation of the imaginery chess pieces and their relative positions, the most important thing in the world for him was to find some way to prevent the threat of Modesty queening one of her pawns.

CHAPTER ELEVEN

Tarrant roused from sleep at the touch of Modesty's hand on his shoulder. Something was going on in the passage outside the cell. He sat up painfully and put his feet to the floor.

Willie's voice was suddenly raised in fury, "Watch it Quinn, you stupid bastard—that shoulder's bust! You jog me again and I'll kick your nuts off!" A laugh, and a half-heard voice which Tarrant knew was Sexton's. The sound of movement faded along the passage.

"That was Willie acting up for my benefit," Modesty whispered. "Nuts was a negative. He's playing his shoulder as worse than it is. Sounds as if they're all being taken upstairs."

Tarrant rubbed his eyes, realising with a sense of oppressive shame that this was the first time he had thought about Lady Janet. He remembered meeting her, and taking an immediate liking to the tall Scottish girl. There was the man with her, too, the young man who had brought Modesty and Willie in through the cave. They were innocents who had strayed into the battle-ground, but that would not save them. He said, "Lady Janet . . . and this man Quinn. Poor devils."

"I know. And they complicate the situation."

"So do I, my dear. I'm half a cripple just now. You're carrying too many passengers."

She tilted her head, listening. "Someone's coming back."

Thirty seconds later they heard the key thrust in the lock and turned. The drop-bar was lifted and the door swung open. A Japanese holding a machine-pistol stood well back across the passage. Mr. Sexton's head appeared round the edge of the door. He gestured to the pistol and said, "I deplore this needless precaution, but Colonel Jim insisted. Just remain seated, please." He moved into the cell, then took a step to one side, leaving a clear field of fire.

Modesty studied him carefully, noting the thick deltoid muscles which lifted the shoulders of the blazer. She guessed that the whole of his body was similarly muscled, and the way he moved confirmed Tarrant's description of him.

He was studying her with equal and more open interest, and began to smile happily as he said, "Let me put you in the picture. Your friends are above now, making a much needed toilet—under supervision of course. As Tarrant will have noticed, we've removed his soil-bucket. Colonel Jim, being a product of the Bible Belt, retains one or two old-fashioned notions about ladies and gentlemen confined together. Some things strike him as not being fittin' or decent, to use his own words. Apart from scatological matters, however, he's contrived to shed all other inhibitions of his upbringing. So if you, Miss Blaise, make a foolish move, Ito will shoot."

Mr. Sexton chuckled, and pointed to the ceiling. "On hearing this, his compatriot, Muro, will at once gun down your friends upstairs. The reverse applies should *they* make any foolish move. Tarrant will be preserved, of course. We have need of him. Now, do you feel you've grasped the situation clearly?"

Modesty said, "Yes. Did you ever train under Saragam?"

Mr. Sexton's eyes widened with pleasure. "You know him? Splendid. Yes indeed, I spent a year under him in

Bangkok, until there was no more he could teach me. But that was in my youth. What made you ask?"

She rubbed the side of her neck, where a yellowing bruise showed. "That counter you used in the cellar. It had Saragam's style."

"Perhaps so. Of course, you could scarcely name a master of any system of combat I haven't trained under. But I flatter myself I've gone some way beyond them all. Very perceptive of you to have noticed a hint of Saragam, particularly in such a brief encounter." Mr. Sexton looked at his watch. "What an interesting chat we could have. But Colonel Jim is waiting, and I don't doubt you'd be glad to enjoy the pleasures of the powder-room before we begin the evening's entertainment."

Tarrant felt his stomach clench in a tight ball, and said, "What have you in mind?"

Mr. Sexton gave him an innocent look. "Nothing very exciting, I'm afraid. We have to make our own entertainment here. But I thought Miss Blaise and her friends might be interested to watch me give a little demonstration in the gym before we all dine together."

Tarrant relaxed a little. "Am I to take part in the entertainment."

Mr. Sexton smiled and shook his head. "Not this time."

*　　*　　*

Willie Garvin followed Quinn and Janet along one side of the gallery which looked down on the brightly lit hall below. His left hand was tucked into his shirt-front, and he shuffled along slowly, as if the slightest movement sent spears of agony through his shoulder.

Colonel Jim and his wife stood at one end of the gallery. She held a tall drink in her hand. Willie knew them at once from Janet's description. He studied Colonel Jim, and felt a little chill touch his spine. The eyes were bad. Bad in a different way from Angel's, the kid who walked behind them now with the machine-pistol, keeping a safe distance. Angel's eyes were bad because she was a warped human. Colonel Jim's because he was a creature in whom the concept of humanity did not exist, whose mind held no place for it. Willie had seen one or two like him before. Just one or two, but enough to recognise the species. He glanced at Quinn and Janet. They were holding up well, Quinn dourly calm, Janet aloofly so.

There was movement on the far gallery. Modesty and Tarrant were being shepherded in by another gun-carrying woman and a thin sandy-haired man. That would be Clare and Mellish. Willie studied Tarrant for a moment. He looked gaunt and sallow, and though he tried to move steadily he could not hide his weakness. Hammering down the spurt of anxiety that started to rise within him Willie thought bleakly, "God Almighty, we're a bunch of cripples."

Modesty tilted her head a fraction to one side. Willie rubbed his slung arm slowly, then touched his right eye with three fingers, telling her that his arm was only thirty percent out of action. She rested her hands on the rail and studied the gym below. Willie did the same.

Da Cruz entered the gallery through a door behind Colonel Jim and said, "They're just about ready."

Lucy Straik said plaintively, "You mean it's only a demo? Gee, I thought you were gonna have Mr. Sexton knock one of 'em off, Poppa."

"Just take it easy, Momma." He slipped an arm round her plump waist. "You're always in too much hurry with everything."

"But you *said* so."

"I said you could take your pick, Momma, and so you can. But Jesus, you didn't hardly even get to take a look at the field yet."

Lucy Straik looked along the gallery, to one side then the other. She sipped her drink. "*I'm* not crazy about knocking folks off," she announced virtuously. "It's just *anything* makes a change in this dump, that's all. I mean, anyone gets fed up with being bored, don't they? Why can't we go and see Paris or somewhere?"

"You just stop talking dumb, Momma," Colonel Jim said amiably. "Once I got this project running we'll take a real nice vacation."

A door opened in the hall below, and Mr. Sexton walked in. Three Japanese followed. They were big men, only two or three inches shorter than the Englishman. All wore singlets, loose slacks ending well above the ankle, and plimsolls. Within a few moments the gym was full of movement. Mr. Sexton began a routine on the horizontal bar. One of the Japanese took the parallel bars, and the other two the vaulting horse. It was a dazzling display, worthy of professional acrobats. The four men interchanged, switching from one piece of apparatus to another, never still, throwing handsprings and somersaults, forward and reverse, spinning and bounding tirelessly.

After five minutes they stopped and removed their singlets and plimsolls. Mr. Sexton took the thick rope which hung from the centre-beam of the high ceiling and looped it to one side behind the vaulting horse, leaving the big mat in the centre clear. He returned to the mat and stood waiting. His body was golden and the muscles moved beneath the skin like rounded steel plates and flexible cables, perfectly machined, gliding in oil.

One of the Japanese handed him an iron bar. He held it in front of him, concentrating for a full thirty seconds.

Then the great deltoid muscles leapt up, biceps and triceps bunched smoothly. The bar yielded, and was bent steadily into a U-shape.

Quinn gazed down with tired, red-rimmed eyes, and thought drearily, "I was right . . . he just tore the door off Tarrant's car that day. Oh God, they're going to throw Modesty to him, I know they are."

Lucy Straik sipped her drink and sniffed. She had seen it all before.

Lady Janet dragged her eyes from the terrible golden man below and glanced at Willie. She could read nothing in his face, but his eyes roved the whole area of the gym constantly, and every few seconds he looked sharply across at Modesty on the far gallery. Following his gaze, Janet felt an inward lurch of new despair as she saw that Modesty's calm had begun to give way. Her hands were moving nervously, fingers fluttering a little. She tapped the rail, brushed her cheek, linked her hands and separated them again, fidgeting as if unable to control her nerves.

Mr. Sexton's performance continued. He broke a two-inch plank with the edge of his hand, and another by a bare-foot kick. He smashed bricks and a stack of tiles. One of the Japanese swept the surface of the mat with a soft broom, and Mr. Sexton took up his position again. A Japanese advanced to face him and the first combat began.

It was a demonstration match. The kicks, chops and punches were pulled at the last instant, the throws and holds performed without that final savagery which would have crippled or killed. But even to the inexperienced eye Mr. Sexton's superiority was clear. His opponent submitted after sixty seconds, and the second Japanese took his place.

The style was slightly different this time, though only Modesty and Willie among the spectators could have analysed the difference of technique. The result was the same, and so it was again with the third of Mr. Sexton's sparring partners.

Finally the three came at him together, and it was only then that Mr. Sexton really exerted himself. Watching the scene, Quinn had the odd sensation he had known that day on the causse, when Modesty had gone into action against the three men. It seemed to him that the Japanese were moving at great speed and Mr. Sexton unhurriedly; yet his flowing, seemingly leisured movements outpaced those of his opponents. It was an eerie and chilling demonstration of mastery.

Quinn was unable to judge what was deemed to be a disabling blow or throw, but after two minutes one Japanese retired, followed quickly by another, and the third submitted in Mr. Sexton's grasp. The bearded man stepped back, smiled, and looked up to where Modesty stood.

"I hope you found it interesting, Miss Blaise. A long way beyond Saragam, wouldn't you say?"

She was still again now, but did not speak. Lucy Straik said, "I'm hungry, Poppa. When the hell we gonna eat?"

Colonel Jim said, "Momma's hungry, Mr. Sexton. Have your boys hustle things along."

Mr. Sexton grinned. "Ten minutes, Colonel Jim. Just time for a shower. Dinner's ready to serve." He glanced to each side of the balcony. "Clare, Angel, take our guests along and make sure you keep them in two separate groups, one in the dining room, one in the sitting room until we're all ready for table."

Angel muttered under her breath. "Big-'ead." Then to Willie, "Go on, Gorgeous. That way." She nodded her head. "Young Pink-eyes beside you, and Lil the limp be'ind. I'll shoot 'er first if there's any funny business."

Willie eyed her with interest and said quietly, "Just so

long as you don't shoot *me*, love. Waste of a good 'ot-blooded lad, that'd be. Maybe I'll get to show you some-time."

Angel gave a snort of laughter, tinged with regret. "You should live so long."

*   *   *

Dinner was almost at an end. Colonel Jim and his company sat at one end of the long table, with Lady Janet among them. At the other end, Modesty and Tarrant sat facing Willie and Quinn. The Japanese called Ito stood three paces behind Modesty, holding a machine-pistol. It was at Lucy Straik's demand that Janet had been separated from the others. Her reasons became apparent only when she began to ply Janet in a querulous manner with questions about what she called the British Nobility, questions which Janet answered briefly and in a neutral voice. On first entering the room Willie Garvin had glared bitterly at Modesty, called her a stupid bitch and begun blasphemously to enumerate her failings. Colonel Jim had stopped the flow of vituperation, informing him coldly that a lady was present, and indicating Lucy Straik. Modesty had not spoken at all, and both Tarrant and Quinn had followed her lead. The dinner was simple but good, with steak as the main course, and they had all eaten everything offered.

Lucy Straik was saying to Janet, "You mean you just *inherit* being a lord and all that?"

"Yes. Unless a new title's created."

"What's that other thing, then? An earl. How does any-one get to be an earl?"

"He can be created an earl by the sovereign. Usually he inherits it."

"Some people! Fancy just being a nobility as easy as that, Poppa."

"Don't cut any ice with me, Momma."

"Well, I'd like if it was *me*, I guess." To Janet, "If your pop's an earl, do *you* get his title when he kicks off?"

"No. But in the absence of male issue it passes down through the female line."

Angel giggled. "It won't pass down your line, ducky."

Janet said without expression, "Then it will continue through my sister. Or failing her, a more distant relative."

"Hey!" Lucy Straik's eyes were round. "My folks came from England, like maybe a hundred years ago. So I could be some sorta long lost cousin of some old duke or earl, couldn't I, Poppa? I read about that in a book once."

Twenty generations of high-born Scots stared from Lady Janet Gillam's eyes as she said, "You?"

Willie Garvin winced, inwardly cursing the momentary rising of the proud blood. Lucy Straik scowled and said venomously, "You don't wanna talk to me like that, honey. Not the spot *you're* in."

Willie said loudly, "Look, 'aven't you got any Garibaldi biscuits in the 'ouse?"

There was a baffled silence, then Colonel Jim said, "What biscuits?"

"Garibaldi," Willie repeated peevishly. "Little oblong ones, with currants in. I know it's funny, but I always like to finish up with Garibaldi biscuits." He leaned forward, head turned to look confidingly at the blank faces. "As a matter of fact I've liked 'em ever since I was a kid. I remember when I was a little boy I used to say, 'Mummy, I 'ope they 'ave Garibaldi biscuits in Heaven.'" He sat back. "So I just wondered if you'd got any, see?"

Angel sniggered suddenly. Colonel Jim looked at Mr.

Sexton and said, "Is he some kinda nut? What the hell's he talking about?"

Mr. Sexton smiled. "It's humour of a sort, Colonel Jim. I've no doubt we can cure him."

"Yeah. You're the doctor." What passed for Colonel Jim's lips stretched in a smile, and he made the strange clucking sound which was his chuckle.

Tarrant saw Modesty's hand move slightly as it rested on the table, the index finger crossing the thumb. Willie had drawn breath to speak again, but flickered a glance at the hand and subsided. It dawned on Tarrant that she had just told Willie not to draw the fire from Janet any further, or at least not to draw it upon himself.

Tarrant ate slowly, forcing the food down. This meal presaged something bad; that was in the text of Colonel Jim's policy, part of the soft/hard technique. The captives would be used as levers to make him talk, but he knew that to talk would save nobody. He also knew with dreadful certainty, and had told Modesty, that somebody was due to die before ever the leverage began. Colonel Jim believed in demonstration, and had sufficient hostages to play with.

At the far end of the table Lucy Straik sulked. Colonel Jim brooded. Clare began to inflict her own long and inaccurate explanation of the system of Scottish nobility on an uninterested da Cruz. Mellish fidgeted. Angel's eyes darted from face to face with malicious glee. Lady Janet ate mechanically, like an unwilling automaton under orders, looking blankly ahead of her. And Mr. Sexton leaned back, smiling absently as he toyed with a glass of water.

Across the table from Tarrant, Quinn ate with trembling hands, eyes blinking every few seconds in a dead-white face. Tarrant had the impression that it was fury rather than fear which shook him. Modesty behaved as if she were sitting at table alone, and Willie was doing the same now.

Five minutes later Colonel Jim pushed aside his coffee-cup and said, "Well, Momma. Who's it going to be?"

Lucy Straik's bulging eyes glinted, and her full mouth thinned. "Her," she said, and nodded at Janet. "Give her to Angel."

"Me?" Angel grinned with pleased surprise. "Coo, that's ever so nice of you, Mrs. Straik. I'll pop and get me wire."

It was as Angel started to rise that Modesty spoke for the first time. Looking across at Willie, speaking as if nobody else were present, she said conversationally but very clearly, "I knew that fat cow would pick your Scotch bit of tail. It's a pity in one way. I was hoping for a chance to show that muscle-bound bastard how much he doesn't know."

The whole table froze, except for Willie, who said in a sour voice, "You bloody well messed it when you 'ad the chance."

She put a last morsel of cheese in her mouth and said contemptuously. "On equal terms I'd kill him. For God's sake, you saw him prancing about in his Jacques Tatti trousers. He's too limited."

Grudgingly Willie said, "I know that, but——"

Lucy Straik was on her feet, face crimson, shouting. "You heard what she *called* me, Poppa? Fat, she said! I'm changing my mind and I'll have *her*. You tell Mr. Sexton to fix her right *now*!"

Mr. Sexton put down his glass very carefully. For once he was not smiling. He shot one blazing glance down the table, then looked at Colonel Jim. Little flecks of gold glinted in the blue of his eyes as he said quietly, "I second that motion, Colonel Jim. But not tonight. She's had an exacting twenty-four hours and I don't want her to be at the slightest disadvantage . . . even against my limited skills."

Colonel Jim rubbed his big jaw and gazed down the table with empty grey eyes. "Momma wants it now."

Mr. Sexton's smile came back, but there was a tightness about it. "Mrs. Straik has all the sweet impulsiveness of a child," he said. "But I'm sure you can persuade her that there's much pleasure in anticipation."

"Yeah." Colonel Jim nodded slowly. "Yeah, that's right about anticipation, Mr. Sexton." He reached out and squeezed his wife's thigh, leering at her like an impassioned crocodile. "We'll make it tomorrow morning, Momma. Say about ten, so you don't have to hurry up outa bed."

She pouted sulkily. "That's not what you said."

"It's what I'm saying now, Momma, so hush-up and don't argue. I wanna go to bed."

He took her wrist and rose to his feet. "Ten o'clock, Mr. Sexton." He nodded to the table. " 'Night, folks."

CHAPTER TWELVE

Quinn sat clasping his knees and said absently, "I tried to pinch a fork, but that Jap was watching every second."

Janet sat beside him, legs outstretched, her back against the wall. There were dark smudges of strain under her closed eyes. She said slowly, "What did that girl mean . . . about going to get her wire?"

Willie, pacing the cell and exercising his stiff shoulder, shot a warning glance at Quinn and said, "Forget it, Jan. We got more important things to think about now."

Quinn sighed. He seemed to have passed through fear and anger, out into a calm void, like a ship in the eye of a hurricane. He said, "We're not idiots, Willie. We know why she needled Sexton. Just tell us one thing without wrapping it up. Does Modesty have any chance at all against him?"

Willie sat down cross-legged, facing them. Janet opened her eyes. He said very softly, "I'm not going to wrap anything up, so listen. Number one, you don't know the big reason why she needled Sexton, you only know why she picked that moment to do it."

Janet said, "The girl was going to strangle me, wasn't she?"

"Shut up and listen, Jan. Number two, you want to know what chance she's got, so I'll tell you the form. Sexton's a fanatic. He's a natural to start with, and 'e's spent a life-time training to make 'imself the best ever. He's

198

not muscle-bound. The Princess threw that in because she knew it'd make 'im mad. He's about ten percent faster than she is, and a mile stronger. He moves like a Swiss watch, and 'is timing's the best I've ever seen."

Quinn whispered, "Dear Christ . . ."

"That's 'alf the picture. Now I'll give you the other 'alf. First, when it comes to the real thing, I don't reckon Sexton's ever 'ad to fight against odds for 'is life, it's always been a walkover. Modesty's been up against odds since she was a kid, and she knows all about it. When she fights going away on the back-pedal it's like trying to nail a ghost. She's got . . . reserves, resources. And when it comes to making use of terrain and externals she's so bloody sneaky you'd never believe it."

Quinn said, "I don't know what you mean by externals. Are you saying she can beat him?"

Willie half closed his eyes, gazing at the blank wall. "I don't know," he said at last. "On form, and fighting on Sexton's 'ome ground in that gym, the odds are too big. But it's academic anyway. If she did break Sexton, she wouldn't last ten seconds. They'd gun 'er down."

A trickle of sweat ran down the side of Janet's face. "You mean she was just . . . buying time?"

"A bit more than that." Willie edged closer and lowered his voice to a bare whisper. "We fixed this up while we were watching the demo. She signalled me. It's a thin chance, but we've ridden out of trouble on thin chances before, so you needn't think it's a non-starter. She could only flash me the main points, but I know 'ow she works so I can fill in the rest. Now look . . ."

His finger traced imaginary lines on the palliasse. "This is the gym, and we can reckon the same situation as today. We'll be 'ere on the gallery, Angel covering us. Tarrant on the other side, Clare covering 'im. Colonel Jim and 'is good lady 'ere." His finger moved again. "Probably da Cruz and Mellish somewhere around, but that doesn't matter. The key things are the two Stechkins, the machine-pistols Angel and Clare carry. All right so far?"

He looked up. Janet and Quinn nodded. Their eyes were very wide.

"Good. Now I can't say just what's going to 'appen when the fight starts. Maybe the Princess will catch 'im on the 'op and shake 'im a bit. The main thing is that early on, maybe after a minute, she'll break and run."

"Run?" Quinn whispered. "*Where?*"

"For the vaulting 'orse." Willie pointed. "She wants a diversion just before that, so this is where you come in, Jan. She'll throw me a signal. You watch *me*, not the fight. When I shake my 'ead like this, you start screaming like you've gone into 'ysterics. Loud, Jan, a proper screech. And keep it up. You got no idea what a sudden terrific screaming noise can do when it's unexpected. It gets to the nerves and freezes 'em for 'alf a second or so."

His finger moved on the palliasse. "That's when the Princess jumps for the 'orse, takes off from that to grab the gallery rail 'ere, right by Clare and Tarrant, and comes swinging over the top. With any luck she'll be close enough to turn the rail-vault into a drop-kick, and nail Clare while she's still frozen. That's when I go for Angel, and you two keep out of the way. Drop flat."

There was a long silence, then Quinn said softly, "You're both mad. Raving bloody mad. It's Hollywood stuff."

Willie shook his head. "The mechanics are right. The 'orse is placed in just the best position, so she'll be out of Clare's sight until she comes whistling over the gallery rail. And Modesty's as good a gymnast as Sexton. It'll all be quick as a whip, Quinn, so don't 'ang about on dropping flat. There's another thing working for us, too. I doubt if Angel and Clare 'ave ever fired those Stechkins, and they're buggers for accuracy without a shoulder-stock on 'em. You got to 'old 'em down 'ard, or you find you're blasting 'oles in the ceiling. So even if one of 'em gets to squeezing the trigger we still got a good chance. And once we've got the pistols it's a new story. Modesty's a crack-shot. She'll knock Sexton off first go. And I'll 'ave mine shoved up Colonel Jim's nose before 'e knows what's 'appening."

Again there was a long silence. Quinn began to breathe deeply. After a while he said, "You make it sound feasible, Willie. But there are about a thousand 'ifs', and any one of them could bitch the whole thing."

Willie shrugged. "Not a thousand. About ten. I'm not pretending it's rosy, but it's the best chance we're going to get."

Janet felt Quinn's hand find hers and grasp it. She returned the pressure, watching Willie, who sat staring down at the palliasse as if visualising once again the set-up in the gym. With a flicker of pallid humour she remembered that she had wanted to know what it was like for him and Modesty in this strange dark area of their lives. Now she had found out. She did not think she would have much time left in which to reflect on her discovery.

Fifty yards away at the other end of the corridor, Tarrant lay on his bunk, eyes closed against the light. Modesty was asleep on the palliasse. He had wanted her to take the bunk, but she had assured him with a smile that the floor would do very well for her and she wanted him to get as much rest as possible for tomorrow.

She had explained the plan carefully, and now Tarrant felt the cold relief of a man who knows the worst at last. He did not believe that any of them would live, but it was something to feel that a term had been set to this nightmare. He opened his eyes, turning his head to look down at her. She was breathing evenly. Sleep had smoothed the hardness from her face, restoring it to the face of the young woman he knew at home. It was unlined except for little crow's-feet at the corners of the eyes. She laughed rarely, but had a habit of crinkling her eyes when she smiled, and this had left its mark. A mark Tarrant found oddly moving at this moment.

He thought of her facing Sexton's quick and dreadful hands tomorrow, and he shuddered. If she left it too late to break and run . . .

He closed his eyes again, and sweat broke out on his body.

* * *

Willie Garvin found himself awake, which he had not intended. His internal clock, which was very accurate, told him that it was no later than two-thirty. He lifted his head. Quinn lay awake. Janet was sitting up, lower lip caught between her teeth, rubbing her knee.

Willie said, "The leg playing up, love?"

She nodded. "I haven't had it off for two days, and——"

"Bloody fool!" The words broke from Willie in a shocked whisper. He came bolt upright and clasped his hands to the sides of his head. "I ought to be *shot!*"

Quinn pushed himself up on one elbow and said wearily, "You probably will be in a few hours. But why especially?"

"The leg." Willie looked at Janet, excitement flaring in his eyes. "Is it the new one, Jan? With the articulated foot?"

"Yes——"

"It's got two wire braces running down to the pivot.

Wire, Jan." He closed his eyes briefly and gave an angry shake of his head. "Wire. We've 'ad it with us all the time. Get it off, love. Quick."

She said uncertainly, "Willie, I . . . I can't walk without it, I'm helpless."

"You're going to ride out of 'ere with any luck. To-night."

She looked at him, then leaned forward and drew up the trouser-leg. Quinn was sitting up now. He looked away quickly. Irrational though it was, he knew that being so crippled must bring a sense of humiliation, perhaps especially to a woman.

When he looked again Willie held the contraption in his hands and Janet sat with the trouser-leg lying flat and empty below the knee, watching. The leg was not solid but made from several broad strips of thick sheet metal, varying in width, skilfully curved for shape and added strength. The false foot was solid, and free to pivot through a few degrees at the ankle.

Willie said, "It's steel wire and a bit thick, but it'll do for the lock, once I can work it out of these 'oles in the reinforced section 'ere. I'll 'ave to break it up though, Jan. I'll need a strip of the alloy for lifting that drop-bar. The wire won't be long enough."

Janet said in a low voice, "Is it a better chance than tomorrow, Willie?"

"About ten times better."

"Thank God for that. Go ahead."

It took him half an hour to work the rivet-head ends of the two wires through the holes in the tough metal. Another full hour passed in shaping the end of one into a carefully judged double-hook, like an elongated letter F. This was achieved partly by using as pliers a narrow crevice between two of the stone blocks forming the wall, and partly by gently hammering with the solid foot, now detached.

In the second wire Willie made a simple half-inch right-angle at one end, then turned to the main part of the leg and began to crush lengthwise the section of sheet-metal forming the shin, using his heel and the stone flags as the jaws of a vice. His fingers were bleeding now. Janet and Quinn sat watching in silence, holding hands but scarcely aware of it. After what seemed an age, Willie held a thin flat strip of metal in his hands, half an inch wide and ten inches long, one edge smooth, the other rough where he had broken it by constant bending. He wiped sweat from his brow and moved to crouch by the door, setting down the strip of metal and picking up the probes.

Quinn whispered, "What time is it, Willie?"

"About four-thirty. Sunrise at around seven. Don't talk for a bit." Holding a probe in each hand, he inserted them in the key-hole very gently. Five seconds later he was snatching up the strip of metal and darting across the cell. *"Something's 'appening along the passage. Lie down and get that chunk of leg out of sight."*

He thrust the probes and metal strip into Quinn's hands, then moved quickly back to crouch by the door, an ear pressed against it, eyes closed. After two minutes he exhaled a long breath and stood up, frowning.

Janet whispered. "What was it, Willie?"

"Not sure. They came to the other cell, and I 'eard Sexton's voice. Then they went away. I can't figure it."

"Maybe . . ." Quinn hesitated.

"Go on."

"Well, it's basically Tarrant they're working on. They've been . . . interrogating him. Maybe Sexton's taken him away for a session. You know, in the early hours, when you're at low ebb. That's a favourite time, isn't it?"

Willie nodded slowly. "I 'aven't got a better idea, so let's gamble on that and reckon they won't look in on us. I'll get the lock open and give 'em 'alf an hour before I start on the bar."

Twenty-five minutes later, crouched by the door, he heard renewed sounds of activity along the passage. Then silence again. The lock was open now, the probes in his pocket. He picked up the metal strip. The problem was to force one end of the strip round the right-angle formed by the stop of the door-frame, so that it would protrude sufficiently to catch under the drop-bar when the strip was eased upwards. Fortunately there was a good half-inch of play in the door, now that the tongue of the lock had been withdrawn, and this offered room for manœuvre.

Twice he forced the strip partly through the right-angled gap, only to have the end gouge into the wood of the frame and jam there. He withdrew the metal and spent five minutes rubbing the corners on stone, to round them a little, then tried again. The strip bent, slid through, jammed, came free, and moved again as Willie thrust hard.

Very cautiously he slid the strip upwards, felt the metal catch the drop-bar, and lifted slowly. He pushed. The door opened an inch or two. He snaked a hand round the edge, gripped the drop-bar and lowered it to the bottom of its retaining bracket without a sound. Relief swept through him.

He turned and grinned. Quinn was kneeling up, still holding Janet's hand. They were both staring solemnly, like children watching their first puppet show and trying to associate it with reality. Willie moved across the cell and squatted close to them.

"We're off," he breathed. "Quinn, you'll 'ave to carry Janet till we get outside. Keep a few steps be'ind me and tread soft." Quinn nodded and stood up, turning. Willie took Janet under the arms, lifted her, kissed her quickly on the cheek, and put her on Quinn's back.

The passage was dimly lit by a single bulb at the far end. Halfway along, the walls fell back for a short distance to form a square chamber four times the width of the passage. Willie glanced back, received a nod from Quinn, and moved silently on. He had taken only two steps across the chamber when a brighter light blazed suddenly from a centre bulb. The Japanese called Ito, dressed in slacks and a sweater, was rising from a camp-bed against the wall, his hand on a dangling cord-switch. He was on his feet instantly, dropping into a defensive crouch, eyes fixed on Willie, his hand leaving the switch to seek a large round bell-push screwed to the wall. And in that moment Willie drew himself loosely to attention and bowed from the waist.

The hand reaching for the bell-push was still. Ito cocked his head curiously. His eyes flickered past Willie to where Quinn stood just within the passage, Janet on his back. Then he looked at Willie again, and grinned, shuffling forward with spread legs bent slightly, perfectly balanced.

In the split seconds of the confrontation, of sighting the Japanese, of knowing there was no time to reach and silence him, and of seizing the one hope that remained, Willie Garvin had at the same time made an instant appraisal. This was the man who had favoured aikido rather than karate or one of the other systems in the demonstration with Sexton. He would go for disabling throws and holds rather than blows.

Willie said softly, "Stand still, Quinn."

Quinn obeyed, leaning against the corner of the wall to ease the weight of his burden a little. He felt weak with shock, and could feel the trembling in Janet's arms clasped across his chest. He understood vaguely that Willie had contrived to silence the Japanese by a challenge, and that some peculiar notion of pride had made the man accept.

Willie's left arm dangled uselessly. He turned his right side to Ito and inched forward. The Japanese seemed to flow at him with a smooth, undulating movement. Willie struck for the throat, lunging with stiff fingers. It seemed incredibly fast to Quinn, but the blow missed by a fraction and Ito's hands caught the arm at wrist and elbow. A foot swung to Willie's armpit, then Ito fell sideways with a rolling motion and Willie was flung up and over as if he weighed no more than a sack of hay.

Quinn heard Janet draw a sobbing breath, saw Willie arch his back to take the impact of the fall with his feet before hitting the flags with his back. Ito still held the arm. He rolled, locking the arm with his leg, hands flashing out for a neck-lock with Willie beneath him.

Willie's legs lifted, bent, then snapped out and down. His body lifted six inches in an abortive shoulder-spring, taking the weight of the Japanese with him. And then, as he fell back, Willie's head flashed forward in a butt which cracked home savagely on the bridge of Ito's nose.

The neck-lock broke. Ito rolled and came to his feet like a cat, blood pouring down over his mouth. Willie rolled sideways and rose more slowly, left arm still dangling. To Quinn's horror he seemed dazed from the butt, for his back was towards the Japanese as he straightened. Ito sprang, one arm snaking about Willie's neck from behind, the other hand clamping on his own wrist in a curious way, with the thumb extended and probing into the neck.

It was then, as he stood half-crouched with Ito clamped against his back, that Willie's left arm came to life. It curved up and back, reaching over to catch Ito with hooked fingers under the base of the skull, and in the same instant Willie flexed his legs and somersaulted forward.

It was not a complete somersault, it could not be with the weight of another man to carry. For one fearful moment Quinn and Janet saw the two locked bodies seeming to hang in the air, heads down, bent in a kind of jack-knife position. Then they fell, and as they fell Willie straightened his legs and brought head and shoulders forward.

Alone, he would have hit the floor with his shoulders. As it was, Ito's head struck the stone with Willie's full weight on top of him. There came a dull, ugly impact. Willie gave a hiss of pain. For a moment all was still, then Willie rolled painfully away from the man beneath him and rose slowly to his feet, working his shoulders. One of Ito's legs twitched, and then he was still again.

Janet whispered, "Is he . . . dead?"

Willie bent and felt for the throb of the carotid artery in the neck. "It's a good description," he said a little breathlessly. "That's what 'appens when you're too academic. I tried 'im bar-room style, and 'e couldn't adjust quick enough."

He moved to Quinn, put a hand on his shoulder, the other hand to Janet's cheek. "You two all right?"

A ghost of a smile twitched Quinn's pallid lips. "We feel a bloody sight better than we did half a minute ago. I just wish it had been Sexton."

Willie said soberly, "I'm glad it wasn't. Come on."

Janet stopped him with a quick gesture. "Just a minute, Willie. There's a key hanging on the wall there. It might save time."

He looked, then smiled. "Good for you, love."

*   *   *

Tarrant lay on his bunk exhausted. His body felt as if it had been broken in bits and put clumsily together again. It was the worst session he had experienced with Sexton, and once again he had been taken by surprise, unready for it. He wondered if he would ever again be able to get up and walk. It was hard enough to breathe. His chest felt as if it were in clamps.

Modesty was bent above him, her hands firmly massaging his diaphragm. He croaked, "Please, my dear. It doesn't matter. You must rest. You've got to rest . . ."

She smiled briefly. "I'm all right. And you'll feel better soon. He's been at your nerve-centres, but I'm using *katsu*. It's a restorative technique——" She broke off and her head came up sharply, listening. The key was turning in the lock. Somebody tapped very softly and in rhythm. Two taps, three taps, one tap. Her eyes widened, and as she heard the small sound of the drop-bar being lifted she whispered, "My God, it's Willie."

The door swung open with a faint creak. Willie stood there. Beyond him, Quinn was supporting Janet as she stood on her one good leg, leaning back against the wall, the trouser of her other leg hanging empty.

Modesty stared, then looked at Willie. "The leg," she said softly, and shook her head. "I'd better take up ludo. Why in God's name didn't I think of it?"

Willie rolled up his eyes in sympathy. "I know 'ow you feel," he whispered. "Which way do we play it, Princess? They 'ad a Jap on guard but I've done 'im. Reckon we can clean 'em up while they're all in bed?"

"Did he have a gun?"

"No."

She stared blankly through him for long seconds, then said, "We won't try cleaning them up. It's tempting, but there's an internal alarm on the main stairs somewhere, and probably others. We don't know the layout upstairs. And if it came to a fight through the chateau ..."

Willie nodded. As a group they would have no mobility. Tarrant, Quinn and Janet would be passengers in a running battle. He said, "The kitchen window, then?"

She mentally re-ran their long study of the chateau from outside. "Yes. It's ground level and they keep the cars in the courtyard there. No gates. Go and kill the alarm on that window, Willie, then check the cars. I'll follow with Quinn and Janet. You and I can come back for Sir Gerald."

Willie moved off quickly. Modesty turned back to Tarrant. "Just lie quietly. We'll be back soon." He nodded weakly, and she went out to Quinn and Janet. "Time to go home. What's the easiest way for you, Janet? Piggy-back, or holding you up between us?"

"I'll ride Quinn if he doesn't mind." She managed a smile. "Sorry to be a drag."

Quinn whispered fiercely, "Don't ever bloody well say that again! *Ever.* Give a hand to get her up, Modesty."

They made their way along the passage, through the door and up a flight of steps, then turned left to enter the big kitchen. The window which looked out on to the courtyard stood ajar. Thin wires, bare ends twisted together, hung from the lintel. Quinn, panting now, was about to lower Janet to a chair, but Modesty said, "No, we'll get you both outside. You first Quinn. I'll pass Janet to you."

Quinn stood Janet down and Modesty supported her while he climbed out through the window. The cill was six feet from the ground below. Janet said, "Oh Christ, I feel so helpless. I hate myself."

Modesty pressed her arm gently. "Stop feeling like that. You upset Quinn badly just now. Come on, he's ready." She put an arm round Janet's waist, hooked the other arm under her good knee, and with astonishing strength lifted her and slid her through the window. Quinn made a step for her with one hand, then caught her round the loins and let her slither down until she was able to stand with her back to the wall.

Modesty stood at the window, staring into the darkness. It was an almost moonless night. Willie would be working by touch alone. Once she heard the muffled sound of a bonnet being lifted. Five minutes passed, then Willie loomed out of the darkness and looked up at her with bleak eyes.

"There's only the van and the Simca," he whispered. "Both immobilised. No distributor arms. No sign of the Safari."

She had half expected the cars to be immobilised, and shrugged in the darkness. "You'll have to do it on foot, Willie love. Can you carry Janet with that shoulder?"

"Sure."

Quinn said, "I can carry her."

Modesty glanced down at him. "You'd be knocked out after a couple of hundred yards," she said gently. "You can't use the road. It'll be light in an hour, and they could be scouring the area for you ten minutes later. You have to go across country, and that's hell. But Willie can make better than a mile an hour even with Janet on his back."

She looked a question at Willie, her face just visible in the light that filtered into the kitchen from the passage.

Willie thought for a moment, then nodded. "Quinn leads. I tell 'im which way to go. He clobbers 'imself on any rocks, or trips in any ruts. I can't risk a fall with Janet."

"Right. Which way will you head?"

"North. The other way's too steep. Besides, we can make for where we 'id the car if we go north."

"All right." She visualised the terrain. "You'll have three valleys to cross. Then you hit the stretch of road with a long drop on the far side. You'll have to move half a mile along it before you can get down into the last valley and swing east for the car. That road's going to be the danger if they come after you on wheels, so watch it, Willie."

Quinn whispered, "What the hell's all this 'you' stuff? Why don't we get going?"

Willie said in a flat voice, "She's got to 'ang on for Tarrant."

"Hang on?"

"He's just had a twenty-minute session with Sexton," Modesty said, and though she whispered her voice held the edge of Toledo steel. "Ask Janet what one minute's like. He can't move."

Quinn sagged against the wall, pushing back the hair from his sweating forehead. Willie said, "How long before you can get 'im mobile, Princess?"

"An hour. Not less. Then he'll only be able to creep."

"It'll be getting on for sun-up by then."

"I know. Probably safer to take him out through the cave. I'll see." She reached down and touched Janet's shoulder. "You'll be all right with Willie. Just do whatever he says. You too, Quinn."

Then she was gone. Willie turned his back, crouched and picked up Janet. "I'll lead till we turn off the track," he whispered. "That'll be when we come to a gully after about a minute. Then you take over as front legs, Quinn. It's going to be rough, so go careful. I don't want to end up carrying you as well."

"All right," Quinn said in a low, tired voice. "All right." He did not speak again until they had passed through the open gates and were moving down the track. Then, "You know she's going to get killed, don't you? She'll never try to take Tarrant through that cave, she knows the cold will kill him in his condition."

"Not if she gets 'im through pretty quick. Tarrant's a gutsy old bugger. And anyway, 'e won't dare die on 'er, not the mood she's in now."

"Oh, for God's sake," Quinn muttered bitterly.

As they moved on into the blackness, Willie felt something warm splash on his neck. He whispered very softly, "Don't cry, love. Last lap now."

He could barely hear her voice as she said. "That poor old man, Willie . . . and Modesty. It's awful leaving them. Awful."

"Try not to worry, Jan. We won a break and she's got the bit between 'er teeth. I've seen 'er like that before." Willie nodded to himself, remembering. "She'll bring 'im out. And Christ 'elp anyone who gets in 'er way now. Anyone."

CHAPTER THIRTEEN

Fraser said humbly, "Forgive me for telephoning you at this hour, m'sieu, but I felt I should inform you without delay."

Réné Vaubois, sitting up in bed with the telephone to his ear, said frostily, "Let me understand you clearly, Mr. Fraser. You suspected that she was on Tarrant's trail. You decided to question her house-boy, and learned that she and Willie Garvin left with two others for Chateau Lancieux three nights ago."

"Exactly so, M'sieu Vaubois. Weng says that he expected them to have telephoned at least twenty-four hours ago. I very much fear that something has gone amiss."

"You knew nothing until you questioned the house-boy, presumably at about five o'clock this morning, Mr. Fraser?"

"Nothing, m'sieu. Of course." Fraser sounded hurt.

Vaubois thought, "Liar." He knew something of the man's record. Aloud he said, "A curious hour to decide upon questioning him."

"I am on night duty, m'sieu."

"I see. The Chateau Lancieux, you say?"

"Yes."

"Very well. You realise that I consider such unauthorised activity on French soil to be gross interference?"

"You are right to be angry, M'sieu Vaubois," Fraser said virtuously. "And I hope very much you will have the opportunity to take action against Miss Blaise and Mr. Garvin. It's not the first time they have offended in this way. You may recall that occasion in Montmartre when—oh, but you were there yourself, of course. It was you the assassins were trying to kill."

Vaubois sighed and said, "I take your point, Mr. Fraser. Thank you for calling me. Goodbye for the present." He put down the telephone and picked up a green one beside it.

In an office in Whitehall, Fraser sat back and began to clean his spectacles gloomily. He hoped he hadn't jumped the gun. Vaubois sending his men in might be the worst thing that could happen. But it looked bad. The silence had gone on too long now. It was the old story of agonising alternatives. You could only make a choice and hope to God it was the right one.

* * *

Colonel Jim looked down at the map and rolled an unlit cigar between his fingers. Grey bristle covered his unshaven jowls. It was six-thirty, and fifteen minutes since Muro had gone to relieve Ito and found him dead.

Mr. Sexton, Clare and Angel were in the study with Colonel Jim. Mr. Sexton said, "They got out of the kitchen window. I'd say they headed across country."

Colonel Jim nodded ponderously. If he was shaken by the escape he showed no sign of it. "That figures. But Tarrant and that gimpy Mrs. Gillam are going to slow 'em down. They can't take 'em south. That's for goats. So they go north, this-away. If they don't hole up somewhere, we'll get 'em on this stretch of road. And we got plenty of time. So you strike direct after 'em on foot, Mr. Sexton." His hand moved on the map. "The rest of us 'll cover the roads way out to here and here, closing in."

Mellish came into the study, sweating. He said, "The only car left is the Citroen. That was parked at the back. They tore the high tension leads out of the other two."

Colonel Jim stared at him unmoved and said, "Right. You and da Cruz start getting everything packed up. Could be we gotta make an emergency move." He waited till Mellish had left, then turned to survey Sexton and the two women. "Could be they split up," he said. "Blaise or Garvin going solo to get to a phone fast. You follow me? So organisation-wise we have to figure on temporary suspension of operations, and dispersal of executives with a view to reconstruction later. Right?"

Clare said, "Whatever you think best, Colonel Jim."

"We got contingency plans for dispersal. Passports. Identities. The full works. But from a corporate point of view you just can't avoid the redundancy element in this kinda situation."

Colonel Jim rolled the cigar back and forth, and shook his head. "What I gotta say now is sad. Very sad. I want you all to know I feel it real deep. But you can't run a business on sentiment, so here it is. Momma's gotta go redundant. She's been a great kid and I'm crazy about her, but she's gonna be bad medicine on the run. Unacceptable risk. She's dumb, and she's gonna be complaining all the time, and she'll talk out of turn. That could blow us all. You understand?"

Clare said, "Of *course* we understand, Colonel Jim. And I'd like to offer you my very sincere sympathy."

"You're a real person, Clare. I appreciate that." Colonel Jim turned his head to look at Angel. "Go fix her, Angel. Make it nice and quick, honey."

Angel smiled, and ran her tongue round her lips. "It won't take a jiffy," she said.

The door closed behind her. Mr. Sexton said slowly, "Are

you quite sure one redundancy is sufficient, Colonel Jim? Clare here is sound as a bell. We need Mellish and da Cruz, and they'll follow the contingency arrangements anyway, for their own sakes. But Angel has . . . a rebellious streak. There's a touch of spite——"

Colonel Jim waved a hand. "I'm ahead of you, Mr. Sexton. Angel needs good supervision, and that's out, once we scatter." He tapped a finger to his temple solemnly. "She's kinda kinky up here. I sometimes wonder if that kid knows right from wrong. So she's gotta go. I hate firing folks, but it's just part of the job and I'm not gonna duck it."

He paused and blinked wrinkled eyelids. "I just do the best I can for the whole team. That's how come I chose Angel to fix Momma. It'll give the kid a little kick before she goes." He glanced at the door. "She'll be pretty well through with it by the time you get upstairs, Mr. Sexton, so you better run along and sign her off. Make it fast." He returned to the map. "I want both them stiffs down the chute in five minutes."

Mr. Sexton smiled and moved briskly to the door.

A stone's-throw away, Tarrant lay on his belly, clinging to the rope that hung down the water-slide. In the moving beam of Modesty's helmet lamp he could see the stream to his right, racing down the trough to the depths below. His feet rested on her shoulders, and she was taking most of the weight from his chilled and feeble hands as she moved steadily down.

It was over an hour since she had returned to the cell and told him that the cars were immobilised. Willie was on his way with Janet and Quinn. On foot, but they would be all right. Now she was going to give him some more restorative *katsu*, and in a little while he'd be able to move. She just wanted him to relax, close his eyes and imagine himself floating weightless, in darkness, not seeing, hearing or feeling. Not even thinking. Nothing.

He looked up at her and said, "Modesty, it's no use. I beg you to go now."

The midnight-blue eyes became black and cold as she said, "Don't you dare. Don't you *dare* let me down. Just stop talking and turn over so I can get at your spine."

She whispered to him as she worked, gently compelling him into a quiet dark void. Gradually pain ebbed from his joints and muscles. Gradually the numbed nerve-centres began to re-establish communication with the areas of the body they controlled. It could not be said that he fell asleep, or woke up, but he lost all sense of time, and it was as if he had slept soundly when she said, "That's all there's time for. We have to go now."

To his astonishment he could stand. His body still knew pain, but it was distant. His muscles were still slow and feeble, but they obeyed him, and he was able to follow her out of the cell and along the passage.

They reached the cellar on the far side of the kitchen only three minutes before the alarm was raised. Tarrant felt sick with shock as the distant clamour reached them, but she said quietly, "We were just in time. They're not going to look in here. I left the kitchen window open." She had been into the depths of the cellar seeking old sacks, cardboard, newspapers, anything to pad out the garment he wore, but without result. Now she was on one knee by the bench, peering at the cans, bottles and containers there, and said, "What are you wearing under that track suit?"

"They gave me somebody's underwear when they took me out of the stink-hole."

"All right." She stood up with an open can of car-grease and set it down on the bench where one of the caving helmets lay. The other had disappeared. "Strip off and smother yourself in grease, then dress again. It's cold down there." She moved to the chute and reached inside. Her rope was still looped over the stub of iron, as she had left it. Not trusting the rusted iron to hold against the double weight when they went down, she drew the rope across the cellar to the bench, secured the end round the big vice, and hauled with her full weight. The bench did not move.

She unclipped the lamp from the helmet. It was the larger helmet, Willie's. Tarrant could wear that. She would carry the lamp, in her teeth if need be—no, she could make a headband with a strip torn from her shirt-tail. Two minutes later it was done. She turned to Tarrant. His movements were laboured but controlled, and he seemed very calm. His body was thickly greased from head to foot, and he was just tucking the vest into some coloured shorts.

She whispered, "You're not claustrophobic?" He shook his head. "That's good. But a cave can be a little scary, first time. Especially the squeezes. Try not to waste energy on what you can see coming next. Try not to think about time, or cold, or anything except whatever we're doing at that moment."

"I once climbed a few mountains. I think I know what you mean."

"Fine." She gave him a quick smile as he finished buttoning his track suit. "Sorry to act the bossy bitch. I only do it because I'm the bossy-bitch type."

"You inspire confidence. What next?"

"I'll help you through the slot, then I'll pass you and go down first. It's a forty-degree slope, and slippery, but you can use my shoulders for foot-rests." She picked up the can of grease, eased the hook of the wire handle out of the hole on one side, and attached it to the back of her belt. "We'll take the grease along. You won't be feeling too flex-

219

ible just now, and it might help when we reach the tight squeeze. Ready?"

The descent of the slide took little more than four minutes. As they went down Tarrant became increasingly aware of the penetrating cold on his hands and face, but it was not yet chilling his body. He tried to shut his mind to hope and fear, to anxiety and speculation, focusing entirely on her whispered instructions and hoarding the remnants of his mental and physical energy. He was in her hands, and his greatest fear was that he might fail her.

When they reached level rock she said, "Wait. Don't move. He saw the beam of her lamp swing away and down, saw her dim shape crouch, and heard a faint sound. A match flared, a light flickered. Rapidly the light became a brilliant incandescent glow which threw back the blackness, and he saw that she had lit a pressure lamp.

"That's better," she whispered. "I was hoping Sexton hadn't found it. He's taken our gear from the end of the rope, but that doesn't matter now." She turned. "Follow me over this stretch, and keep close. It's fairly easy, but watch where you step. We can do without a sprained ankle."

Tarrant began to follow slowly at her heels, watching the rocky floor in the light of the pressure-lamp which she held to one side as she moved.

*   *   *

Lucy Straik was sitting at her dressing table when Angel tapped on the door and entered. Angel's hands were behind her back. Lucy glared at her sulkily in the mirror.

"So what's he want *now*?" She said irritably. "First he says we can sleep late, then he's awake early with the hots, knocking for me to spread, and *then* there's all this ruckus about goddam Tarrant and the others."

"Well, it's serious, Mrs. Straik," Angel said apologetically, moving forward to stand behind her. "Ever so serious. We've got to be ready to move out fast, Colonel Jim says."

"Fast? When do I get to *eat*? When do I get to *pack*?"

"Oh, you needn't worry, Mrs. Straik." Angel giggled suddenly. "You'll be staying."

Lucky Straik stared at the girl's reflection. "Staying? What the hell's that supposed to mean?"

"What it bleeding well means is this, ducky." Angel's right hand came out from behind her back. The thin glistening wire whirled through the air, coiling about the white neck. Her left hand caught the flying toggle. There was a choking gasp and a thump as Lucy Straik was dragged backwards off the dressing-table stool.

A minute later Angel took her knee from the back of the dead woman and stood up, releasing the toggles. "Soppy fat bitch," she said contentedly, and turned Lucy Straik over with her foot. A sound made her glance round. Mr. Sexton stood in the doorway.

Angel sniggered, and jerked her head at the body. "Popeye the Sailorwoman, eh?"

"A nice job, Angel," Mr. Sexton said approvingly. He moved forward and smiled into her eyes. "It's rather a pity, but Colonel Jim told me to make this quick, so——" His arm flashed up, scythed down. The edge of his hand hit her skull like an axe. She was dead before the knowledge that she was about to die could register.

Mr. Sexton left the bedroom walking briskly, carrying a body over each shoulder.

Three minutes later, in the study, Clare was saying diffidently, "You didn't mention it, Colonel Jim, but I was wondering if you wished to look upon Mrs. Straik for the last time before . . ." She gestured delicately.

Colonel Jim looked up from the map and said, "Who?"

"Mrs. Straik. I wondered——"

"No, Clare. I guess not." Colonel Jim shook his head and sighed. "I want to remember Momma just the way she was."

"I think you're wise, Colonel Jim. I feel the same about Angel. A dear girl, but——"

She broke off as Mr. Sexton came in quickly. There was a taut eagerness in his manner but his voice was cool as he said, "It wasn't quite the way we thought, Colonel Jim."

"How's that?"

"I've just taken the late Mrs. Straik and Angel down to the cellar. The light was on and the rope from the chute had been fixed to the bench. Some of them went out that way."

Colonel Jim said slowly, "Some of them?"

"It's not the best way to go, except for anyone too crippled to walk far—or who couldn't get out before sunrise, like the rest."

Colonel Jim flapped a hand. "Hold it. Let me figure this."

After a little silence the big head nodded. "Yeah. Ito must've been dead a good hour before first light, Mellish reckoned. Could Tarrant make it with 'em then?"

"No. I'd just been treating him. I'm surprised he's been able to move at all."

"He couldn't take the cave on his own?"

"Not a chance. Somebody stayed with him until he could make a move, and that can't have been long ago."

"Blaise. She took him down."

"I have the same feeling, but I'm not sure why."

"The Scotch woman, Mrs. Gillam, she can't walk. That thing you found in the cell was a false leg, or what was left of it. Right? So Garvin carries her. Blaise waits with Tarrant. Quinn could have gone with either of 'em."

Colonel Jim blinked at the ceiling. "Right. We got only

the one car, and we need that for Garvin's party, so we can't cover where the cave comes out. Hell, we don't *know* where it comes out. How long you reckon Blaise and Tarrant been gone, Mr. Sexton?"

"I think they were in the cellar when Muro raised the alarm," Mr. Sexton said softly. "She couldn't have got him mobile any earlier. I think they've been gone no more than ten or fifteen minutes."

"You can catch, 'em?"

"Oh, yes." Mr. Sexton smiled. "They'll have to move at Tarrant's pace. I can catch them all right."

"Do it. I'll take care of Garvin's party." Colonel Jim glanced out of the window, looked at his watch, then tapped the map. "We'll catch 'em on this piece of road." He rubbed his chin with a thumb. "It's looking good. If we can pick 'em all up we're in the clear."

He shook his head, frowning. "Maybe I acted a little hasty over Momma."

*　　*　　*

The sobbing, rasping sound of his own breathing beat at Tarrant's ears, magnified in this tiny capillary of the earth's skin along which he crawled. There seemed to be no oxygen in the air, and his heart was thudding in an effort to compensate.

The ten-foot pitch had taxed his strength, even with Modesty's help. The long squeeze through the bedding plane had taxed his nerves. He had claimed not to be claustrophobic, but this was something new. He had felt that the great mass of rock was moving, pressing down upon him.

The narrow triangular passage in which he crawled widened a little, and the silhouette of Modesty ahead of him stood up. His effort to copy her failed, and he crept on. Then the walls fell away and he stared drunkenly about him. They were in the great cathedral of the stalactite chamber, a crystal hall with the light darting and winking flamboyantly from the long, fairy-like needles which clothed the roof. She turned to help him to his feet, but his legs would not respond. He shook his head, clutching her arms, and wheezed, "A moment, my dear . . . please, just a few moments . . . I'm trying, but my wretched body won't obey."

She crouched, holding him, and said, "We'll take two minutes. Just breathe deeply and——" Her voice snapped off and she drew back a little, head tilted, staring at the rift from which they had just emerged. He saw her mouth go hard, her nostrils flare.

She moved away and into the mouth of the fissure, then crouched with a hand cupped to her ear. There it was again. As if in a whispering gallery the faraway sound was brought to her along the labyrinth, the faint rustling scrabble of a shoe on rock. She could pin-point it, a sole-edge scraping as someone inched through the bedding plane.

She turned away from the fissure and said in a flat voice, "Somebody's coming after us." A pause. "It's Sexton." She knew with utter certainty that it would be Sexton. Vaguely she heard Tarrant croak, "Oh dear God . . ."

Before his voice faded to silence she had made a dozen calculations and knew what lay inescapably ahead for her to do. There was the lake and the hidden boat. They would have time to cross, but Sexton would not be stopped by the water. He would swim. The best place to deal with him would be on the far side, as he tried to climb out. But if he had a gun he could shoot them both down as she waited for him across that thirty-foot stretch. And if they went on he would surely catch them long before they reached the cave's end where the rifles lay.

She said quietly, "We've got about four minutes. You have to make one big effort. Come on, hang on to me."

Together they stumbled down the step-like ridges of rock, her arm about his waist, his arm across her shoulders. Then came the flat stretch and the brink of the small lake. She let Tarrant sink to his knees, ran to fetch the little dinghy from behind the outcrop, stood the pressure lamp on the flat surface of a hummock of rock, returned with the dinghy, set it down on the water, and took off her headlamp. Tarrant watched her without a shred of hope. Sexton was coming, and that must be the end. He wished she would leave him and go on alone, but knew it was a waste of breath to urge her.

What was she doing now? He blinked at her bemusedly, and wondered if she had gone mad. Fingers flying, she had whipped off her shirt and the string vest beneath. Now the plain black bra. The boots came off. She was unbuckling her belt, setting down the can of grease in front of him. She hooked thumbs in the long woollen tights and the nylon briefs beneath, and stripped them off together with her slacks in one bundle.

She stood up naked, holding her shirt and wrapping it about both her hands, then said sharply. "Grease me. I can't do it myself, I've got to keep my hands dry. Grease me all over. Hurry."

He pulled himself together, scooped two handfuls of grease from the can, stood up, and began to smear her neck and shoulders. In a shaking whisper he said, "But you can't . . . you can't *fight* him."

"Oh yes." Her eyes were huge, and ebony. "This is the place. Not his gym. No smooth mat for fancy footwork. Hard stone, and uneven. He's a warm-weather man. Didn't want to swim that pool unless he had to. Likes a warm-up. I start better than most from cold, so he's lost his edge on speed down here." She moved her arm. "No—leave a strip clear round that right elbow."

While she spoke, Tarrant had greased the front of her body from brow to groin, and her arms. She half turned for him to grease her back, and after a few seconds said, "Now the legs. All the way. This isn't a surface for fancy kicks and chops, so he'll want to get hold of me, and I need an edge there. He's too strong."

Tarrant knelt and obeyed. Buttocks, thighs, calves, ankles—his hands moved over her firm flesh, and he was dimly surprised at its warmth. No other emotion moved in him, no embarrassment or sensual stirring. There was only sadness. He felt like some ancient priest of Egypt performing a funeral-rite, oiling a beautiful young body too soon, before death had finally struck.

A gleam of bright light showed at the point where the rift entered the chamber. Modesty said, "All right. Get in the boat, quickly. Face this way, paddle with your hands, and be careful climbing out, you mustn't get wet." She crouched and held the dinghy steady while he obeyed, then threw in the tow-rope, her bundle of clothes and the head-lamp.

Tarrant looked into her face from only a few feet away, and scarcely recognised her. The features might have been cast in bronze, and in the eyes there was a dark intensity. Cold, brooding, primordial.

She said, "As soon as you're across, take the headlamp and go on. You can't miss the way from here. There's a pot to climb, but it's not high and you'll find a rope-ladder there ready. I'll catch you up."

She gave the boat a gentle push, and in the same moment her expression changed. She smiled, the corners of her eyes

crinkling in the way he knew so well, and gave a little reassuring nod. "Don't worry, old love," she said gently.
"We're going to win this one now."

Then she stood up, turned her back on him, moved away
to the centre of the flat stretch of rock, and stood waiting,
her arms hanging by her sides. As he began to paddle, Tarrant knew that from this moment she had forgotten him
completely.

CHAPTER FOURTEEN

Sexton was coming. He moved steadily down the stepped
ramp from the rift, emerging into the great sphere of light
thrown by the pressure lamp. In his hands were a large
flash-lamp and a machine-pistol. Tarrant dragged himself
out on to the pool's edge, head twisted to look back, unable
to tear his eyes from the scene. It was like looking upon a
well-lit stage.

She had moved across a little and turned, so that she was
in semi-profile to him, watching Sexton as he moved at an
angle down the slope, the light catching his golden hair
and beard. She stood with feet apart, her head thrown
slightly back. By some trick of the reflected light which
shone down from the glittering mass of needles in the
dome, her body was turned to silver. Her hair, drawn
tightly back, gleamed like a black helm. But for the slow
rise and fall of the breasts under her steady breathing, she
might have been an heraldic figure; woman rampant, silver,
crowned sable.

Blood pounded in Tarrant's brain, and he felt his sense
of reality slipping. Here, in this timeless womb of earth,
the weight of ages bore down upon him, and as he gazed
spellbound across the black lake she seemed a myth made
flesh, a daughter of Mars, supreme mistress of the warrior
arts, carrying an aura taut, lusty, bracing. In his tired
wavering mind he seemed to hear the brassy voice of trum-
pets against a swelling background of martial music. Now

was the moment when all finer shades of choice were wiped away, leaving only a diamond-hard simplicity . . . a time to kill or a time to die. She stood ready for either.

For the space of a few heart-beats Tarrant felt the heady splendour of her challenge so strongly that it swamped the dark ugliness he knew must come. Then he saw Sexton moving down upon the silvery figure, sure-stepping, poised, incomparably skilled, unimaginably strong, unique in his mastery; and the blood chilled in Tarrant's veins as he remembered that she was no indestructible creature of myth, but a young woman of flesh and bone. Flesh to be torn and bone to be broken by the iron lightning of this man's frightful power. Not even the silver mistress could withstand the golden master.

Mr. Sexton stopped, surveyed the situation, then chuckled He was wearing a roll-neck sweater instead of his usual blazer. He bent to put down his pistol and torch in a crevice of rock, then moved on down to the flat stretch of rock.

She had known, Tarrant thought. She had known Sexton would want to do this with his bare hands, given the slightest chance. The man came on and halted six paces from Modesty. "I hope you're not expecting to seduce me," he said. "Aren't you rather cold like that?"

She stood like a statue, not answering. Sexton glided a step nearer, testing the footing carefully. Then suddenly, moving very lightly and with that deceptive fluency which concealed speed, he came at her.

Tarrant could never afterwards remember the sequence of that dreadful battle. He knew after the first few seconds that she was matching Sexton for speed, but even with his analytical fencing brain he could not follow the moves and counter-moves. He remembered only a general impression of the two figures weaving, closing, parting as if in some eerie dance. He saw the flash of striking hands, of lashing feet. Once Sexton tried a leaping karate kick, but almost lost balance on take-off and had to twist cat-like away from a whip-lash counter with the ball of her foot.

Mostly what Tarrant remembered was Modesty's body, silver-gleaming in the light, firm-breasted and long-limbed, always circling back, back, gliding and turning in a darting counterpoint of movement that seemed to unite in a pre-arranged harmony with Sexton's attack. There was blood on her side now, where a glancing kick had torn skin from the ribs, but she seemed unaffected by it. The grease had helped the deflection, and was serving her well. Twice Sexton caught her briefly, once by the forearm and once by the ankle as he evaded a kick. Tarrant's scalp crawled with fear, but each time she twisted the greasy limb free as the awful fingers closed.

They were moving nearer to the lake now. Sexton's back was to Tarrant. He was crouched a little, arms slightly spread, edging towards her. It was then that she moved forward for the first time, suddenly flowing at him with bewildering speed, into the iron arms. The move was so wildly insane that it took Sexton unawares. But it caused him no flicker of concern. Her face was against his chest, her arms round his waist, and she was encircled by his grasp, too close to drive knee into groin. Her greased body would not help her now. With a flicker of surprise Sexton felt her lift his weight, so that his feet came an inch or two clear of the ground.

He laughed, knowing that from this position there was no way she could throw him, no way she could escape. Hooking his hands together behind her back, he prepared to crush her slowly. But she was still moving, carrying him back . . . back. In the instant of shock, when he realised her purpose, it was already too late. They were falling, locked together. He snatched a frantic breath as his back hit the water, then the ferocious cold enfolded him, striking into his bones. He was unready for it, mentally and physically, and there were seconds of almost total paralysis. His grip slackened as they sank down, and then he had lost her, the slippery body writhing from his enfeebled grasp.

Fighting sudden panic, he kicked out hard for the surface, but she was behind him now. A forearm slid under his chin, clamping tightly against his throat as the hand found a grip on her other arm, at the crook of the elbow; and the hand of that other arm was spread against the back of his head in a lock that could have broken his neck but for his abnormal strength. Her legs coiled about his waist, putting pressure on his ribs.

On firm ground he could have dislodged the hold in one of five ways, or by sheer strength alone. But here there was no purchase for his feet, and the paralysis of cold had sapped power from the great muscles. He fought for mental balance, then reached back for her upper arm, seeking a nerve-centre to probe. His fingers slipped over the greasy flesh, and she hammered with her heel at his groin with one foot, using her other leg as a flail-like paddle to turn their locked bodies in a slow backward roll.

Water rushed up Sexton's nose. He snorted it out, losing precious air from his lungs, then suddenly went mad, groping for thigh, arm, shoulder, face, anything he could reach, anything he could savage to make her loose the hold.

Somehow he caught her foot at his waist, and tried to summon strength to snap the ankle. There was thunder in his head, agony in his chest. The grip across his throat slackened. Hope roared in him . . . then vanished utterly, for he knew that even in the easing of the hold she had tricked him. His diaphragm, seeking relief for the tortured lungs, responded before he could control it.

231

He breathed—and breathed water.

Then the neck-lock snapped tight again and his spirit broke. His obsessed mind cried out with bitter agony that he had been tricked, not defeated. The last thing he knew was a surge of corrosive hatred that swamped all else, even the fear of death.

Modesty felt him go limp. It was not enough; not with Sexton. Her own body was clamouring for oxygen now, but she subdued it. Dredging up the last reserves of her strength she poured them all into a sudden leverage against the massive but unresisting neck.

Tarrant knelt by the lake's edge, staring fixedly. The ripples were dying. He had seen one slight upheaval when her leg broke the surface briefly, but that had been a full minute ago. His nerves, flayed with the tension of waiting, became suddenly slack. It was over. A few minutes before, when he had paddled across the pool in the dinghy, he had felt the icy water snap venomously at his hands like a living thing. Such cold was a killer. She had gone, taking Sexton with her. They were both dead.

Something splashed in the water ten feet to the left of the point at which he had been staring. His head snapped round. He saw the gleam of her body against the blackness of the water, heard the great sobbing inhalation as she dragged air into her lungs. Her hair had come loose and covered her face. She threw it back with a jerk of her head, and swam three slow strokes to reach the edge of the lake on Tarrant's side.

By the time he had unlocked his creaking joints and stumbled towards her she had dragged herself out and lay face down on the rock.

"Aaaah-huhh . . . Aaaah-huhh . . . Aaaah-huh." The racking sound of her breathing echoed through the great chamber. He crouched beside her, patting her shoulder futilely, and croaked, "My dear, my dear . . . you must get dressed. The cold . . ."

She lifted her head, looked up at him blankly for long seconds, then panted, "Clothes . . ."

When he brought her the bundle of clothes she was already kneeling up, sitting on her heels. She took the string vest and began to dab herself with it. The water rolled easily away from the grease covering her body, the grease which had saved her from the grip of Sexton's hands, and had given a vital measure of insulation against the numbing iciness of the pool.

She stood up, gave Tarrant the vest and turned. As he dabbed her back he saw that her right arm had been savaged from shoulder to elbow, and was bleeding. She took the vest again, but it was sodden. Throwing it aside she made a bundle of her pants and bra to dry her legs.

Her breathing was steadier now. She pulled on the woollen tights and denim slacks, then put on her shirt. He saw that her hands were shaking and could hear her teeth chattering, but sensed that this was only partly a result of the cold. He had glimpsed something in her eyes, in that first moment when she looked at him, and had recognised it as fear. Fear in retrospect, released within her only when it no longer mattered. She had veiled it instantly, but he knew he had not been mistaken, and in that moment of revelation his respect for her soared to the ultimate plane.

She buckled her belt with trembling hands, looking at him balefully, and said in an uneven voice, "Why the hell are you still *here*? I told you to go on."

"My dear," he said simply, "I couldn't."

"Couldn't?" Her eyes flared, and she stuttered slightly. "Of c-course you could! Christ, you m-men are all the same! It t-took me two *years* to make Willie get on with his own bit and leave me to do mine!"

Tarrant felt a wave of feeble, idiotic laughter rise in him, and held it down. "I'll try to beat Willie's time," he said meekly.

Her anger fell away and she looked at him with something like a smile. "Wait here, I'm just going to get the lamp." She paddled across in the dinghy, secured the pressure-lamp and paddled back. As she climbed out beside him the surface of the pool rippled suddenly, disturbed from below. Something rose slowly from the dark waters, a sweatered arm, then a mop of sopping fair hair. Sexton's sightless white face emerged. His body rolled, and slowly sank again. Before it vanished Tarrant saw that the head lolled at an impossible angle from the great shoulders.

He said shakily, "You made sure."

She nodded, and bent to wring out her hair. "You don't get a second chance with a man like Sexton. He was the best I've ever seen. I could never have taken him on his own ground."

"On his own ground," Tarrant repeated slowly. She was no doubt right about that. But the ground and the situation were all a part of the battle, any battle. A point Sexton had missed and she had not. She had been interested in his aversion to severe cold even in the cell, because she had sought to know her enemy. She had used the grease, the terrain, and the pool.

Tarrant said, "He wasn't the best. He lacked your resource in seizing exterior advantages."

"Maybe. But I wouldn't like it to do over again. How are you feeling?" She straightened up.

"A little tottery." He smiled at her. "But immensely confident now."

"Good. There's only one tough bit left. A fifteen-foot climb. In twenty minutes we'll be home and dry."

In fact it was seventeen minutes later when she picked

up the bed-rolls, haversack and two rifles, and led the way on for another fifty paces to where the cave broke surface in a little hollow set amid bushes on the valley-side. The sun was up and hung in a clear blue sky, shining along the length of the valley. Close to total exhaustion though he was, Tarrant felt his spirit lift as he looked upon the new day.

She made him take off his shoes and get into one of the sleeping-bags, then opened the haversack and fed him chocolate, raisins and glucose tablets, followed by a stiff measure of brandy from a flask.

Pushing back a thick tress of damp hair from her face she said, "I'm sorry I bit your head off back there. I seem to get a bit edgy after something like that."

Tarrant said, "Please." He was too tired to laugh.

"It was stupid. You've been so good. Now lie down and sleep." She patted the rifle she held. "Nothing to worry about any longer. If we haven't seen any signs of life by noon, we'll start moving."

He lay back, the sleeping-bag warm about him, the brandy glowing within him. "We must take turns," he said laboriously. Finding words seemed suddenly a great effort. "You need to rest too, and I can . . ." His words slurred, then faded into silence, and he slept.

*　　*　　*

The ill-kept little road clung to the slope of the winding valley, a rock wall on one side, a fall of fifty or sixty feet on the other, almost vertical. At one point the rising face was pierced by a gully which angled into the road from above. It was one of those rare days of early April, when the air is dry from first light and the sun gives a foretaste of its summer heat.

Willie Garvin stood at the edge of the road where the gully debouched into it, listening. Lady Janet stood on her one leg, Quinn's arm round her waist for support. Her hair was limp and dusty, plastered to her head. Her trousers were black at the thighs from the sweat of Willie's back. Quinn's shoes were scuffed and cut by rock, his trousers torn at both knees. He looked a scarecrow. Distress haunted his eyes as he said through dry lips, "They'll guess. They'll realise we couldn't have carried Tarrant as well. They'll guess she took him down the chute. That American bastard's a maniac, but he's got an instinct."

Willie said absently, "Shut up, I'm listening." There was nothing but the deep silence of the Pyrenean valleys. No sound of a car. He relaxed only a little, not relishing the next fifteen minutes when they would be exposed on the road, moving along it for half a mile before they came to the point where the sharp drop became a slope and they could move down to cross the next valley. Off the road there was at least a certain amount of dead ground to provide cover. Once on it, they were committed to fifteen minutes of exposure.

He turned to Quinn and Janet. "Right. All aboard. We'll make this next bit as quick as we can."

Quinn said with nervous anger, "Don't you bloody well care?"

"Eh? About what?"

"About Modesty, for God's sake. I just said, they'll guess and they'll go after her."

Willie turned his back to Janet so that she could put her arms round his neck, and picked her up. His bruised shoulder was one huge ache, and he was very tired. He said patiently, "You're always aggravating yourself, Quinn old mate. You keep unpacking your troubles from your old kitbag and 'aving a good brood over 'em. I'll start worrying

236

about Modesty when I can *do* something about it. Now belt up."

Lady Janet said wearily, "Don't go on at him, Willie. I keep thinking of her, too. And that poor old man. It . . . it's all right for us now, but——"

"Let's 'ope you're right, love. Off we go."

They moved on to the road and started down it, Willie setting a pace that was almost a lope.

Half a mile away, on a high mound of rock, Tokuda lay with field glasses to his eyes. He lowered them and began to slither down a long slope to where the Citroen stood. Colonel Jim sat at the wheel, Clare beside him, da Cruz and Muro in the back. Clare and da Cruz carried machine-pistols, Colonel Jim a heavy Colt .45 holstered on his hip. Only Mellish had remained at the chateau to watch and wait.

It was Janet who first heard the distant sound. They had just passed a point where the narrow road widened in a bulge to form a lay-by on the open side, so that vehicles could pass. There had once been a barbed wire fence edging the drop here, but this had long since been broken down, and all that remained were half-a-dozen rusting angle-iron supports.

Janet said, "Willie, I heard a car."

They stopped moving and listened. She shook her head. "It's gone now, the valley plays tricks with sound, but I know I heard it. From somewhere behind."

Willie looked about him. He did not doubt her. Colonel Jim or Sexton was coming, probably with company, and there was no way off the road now, no time to go back to the gully.

Despair came very close. He shut his eyes for a moment, then opened them and turned, sweeping the whole scene in search of any factor which could be turned to advantage.

The face of the rising rock was bare of the slightest crevice for concealment. The drop on the other side was sheer, a killer. He heard the distant note of the car's engine himself now, and said hoarsely, "Take 'er, Quinn. Quick. Look, there's a sort of bulge in the rock face about fifty paces on. Tuck in be'ind that."

As Quinn took Janet on his back he said hopelessly, "It won't hide us, Willie——"

"I know." Willie's voice was surprisingly gentle. "Just do what I say though, and make it fast." Then he turned and began to run back up the road, towards the bend they had just passed. The lay-by was sixty paces short of the bend. He gripped one of the tall angle-iron supports and began to work it back and forth in the hard ground, thrusting and pulling with furious strength.

Quinn staggered to the bulge of rock, turned, and set Janet down. She stood leaning against it, her hand gripping his arm, looking back up the road towards Willie. Quinn whispered, "What's he doing?"

"I don't know." Her voice shook. "He's got something in mind."

"They always have. But I don't see . . ." The words trailed away.

They saw Willie crouch, grip the loosened support and drag it slowly from the ground. He stood up holding a seven-foot length of rusted angle-iron, cut obliquely to a point at one end. Then he moved out into the middle of the road, holding the angle-iron across one shoulder in his right hand, hefting it, finding the balance he wanted.

The sound of the car was louder now. It was moving in third gear for the bends, but not slowly. Willie cocked his head, listening, judging. They saw him lift the angle-iron, poising it like a spear. The noise of the high-revving engine warned that the car was on the straight stretch approaching the bend. Five seconds passed, and Willie began to run forward. After a pace or two his gait changed to a curious, stiff-legged sideways run. Quinn recognised it. He had seen it once at an international athletics meeting. It was the run-up of the javelin thrower, though the poise of the iron shaft was not the same, for the vital need was for accuracy rather than distance.

The car whipped round the bend smoothly, and even as it straightened up Willie made his judgment and his throw, putting all the trained co-ordination of nerve and muscle behind it. His skills were wide, but this was his special gift, to throw a missile, any missile, with an instinctive understanding of its properties in flight, and a faculty for judging distance and power to produce superb accuracy. The crude spear flew on a very low trajectory. The car was thirty yards from Willie when the length of angle-iron left his hand, and twenty when the point shivered the windscreen. In that second of time he glimpsed Colonel Jim and Clare in front, others in the back.

Sixteen pounds of hurtling sharp-pointed iron hit Colonel Jim high up in the chest, its speed combining with that of the on-coming car at the moment of impact. It drove through him, through the back of the seat and ended with its point buried under da Cruz's ribs.

The windscreen was opaque, crumbling under the weight of the iron shaft now. The car came straight on. Willie watched it, crouched, waiting for the swerve. It was a gradual swerve, inwards towards the rock face, and the nearside wheel would catch him. He jumped, a diving roll, his body curving over the corner of the front wing. As he came to his feet, gasping with the renewed pain in his shoulder, he heard the crash and the shriek of metal against the wall. The car bounced off, raced for the edge and flew out into space.

The clangour of its fall echoed through the valley. It was still bouncing and rolling when Willie reached the edge. Then it erupted in flame. He stood watching for a few seconds, drained of all emotion. The wreck lay upside-down. Nobody had been thrown clear.

He looked up the road, remembering some flicker of movement his eye had caught as the car raced down upon him. One of the Stechkin machine-pistols lay on the ground. Clare, or somebody, must have been riding with it at the ready, hand resting on the ledge of the open window.

He walked a few paces and picked it up, then began to trudge down the road to where Quinn stood supporting Janet. They had managed to move to the edge now and were looking at the furnace of the blazing car. As he came up their heads turned to look at him, relief mingling with shock in their eyes. Quinn said hoarsely, "Did you see who . . .?"

"Colonel Jim and Clare. Two others in the back, maybe three."

Quinn made a shaky sound that was not very much like a laugh. "You're not bad, Garvin. Not too bloody bad at all. She said we'd be all right with you."

Willie looked at Janet. "You okay, love?"

She looked down at the fiery wreck, eyes hard in the damp, dust-smeared face. "If you mean that, I'll not be sending any flowers, Willie. I just hope Sexton was in it."

Willie grinned tiredly. "You Scotch women are a hard lot, Mrs. Gillam. Come on. Time for piggy-backs again."

Twenty minutes later, when they were halfway across the valley, the clatter of a helicopter broke suddenly upon them as the machine lifted above the ridge ahead. It was an Alouette-3, and passed to their left at three hundred feet before tilting to swing in a tight circle.

Willie looked quickly up and down the valley floor,

spotted the flat area where the helicopter was most likely to land, and nodded to a huddle of boulders a stone's-throw to his right. They reached cover at a stumbling run and he stood Janet down.

Quinn's face was drawn. He said, "Do you think . . . ?"

"No." Willie shook his head and checked the machine-pistol. "I think a bloke called Fraser got windy and started something. But just in case Colonel Jim whistled up reinforcements, we'll be a bit careful. They won't reckon we're armed, and we've got good cover 'ere. I'm not much cop with 'andguns, but once I see the whites of their eyes they'll get a nasty surprise."

The helicopter swayed down, raising a thin cloud of dust. Its skids touched the ground two hundred yards away and the sound dropped to a gentle clatter as the rotor idled. Two men got out. One wore a combat jacket and carried a sub-machine gun slung. The other was in a dark business suit.

As they approached Willie laughed, moved a pace or two out of cover, and waved. "It was Fraser getting windy," he said. "That's René Vaubois."

Janet wiped sweat from her face with a dirty hand. "Is it . . . is it really all over then, Willie?"

"Just got to pick up Modesty and Tarrant."

"I hope it's just that for them." She drew in a long slow breath and went on almost absently, "Well . . . I wanted to know. I wanted to know how it was for you with her. Now I've found out in a big way. And I'll tell you one thing, Willie. God forbid you do anything like this again, but if you do I'll not be jealous. She can have this bit of you and welcome."

Quinn, supporting her with an arm about her waist, said, "That gets my vote too." He put up a hand, turned her face towards him and kissed her briefly on the cheek. "If anyone wants to know, I think you're an extremely smashing lady. So whenever he buggers off with Modesty, you just give a whistle. I'll fill in for him."

She looked at Quinn, smiling with wry affection. "Now if only you were a bit older, Quinn. And if only I were a bit more promiscuous . . ."

Vaubois picked his way over the rough ground and halted facing Willie. His manner was stiff and unfriendly. He said in his excellent English, "You do realise that you are on French soil?"

Willie eyed him with frowning admonition, and turned to Janet. "Lady Janet," he said, "may I present M'sieu Vaubois, a very old friend. M'sieu Vaubois, I present Lady Janet Gillam and Mr. Henry Quinn."

Vaubois gave him a glare, then bowed to Janet and Quinn. "Lady Janet, Mr. Quinn—a great pleasure."

Before he could speak again Willie said aggressively, "We know we're on French soil all right. Is this 'ow you welcome tourists? It's a bloody disgrace. We come 'ere to do a bit of caving and next minute we find ourselves in some chateau being knocked about by a bunch of real frighteners. I nearly 'ad one of my bad turns. Honest, Réné, you ought to——"

"And you happened to find our mutual friend Tarrant in the chateau?"

Willie looked surprised, then nodded with eager innocence. "I can't think 'ow you guessed, but you're right. It was a very rum coincidence, that was."

"All right, Willie. I've already had some of Fraser's double-talk today. But this was *my* job, and I am very angry with you."

Willie grinned. "No you're not. You're steamed up because you're worried about Modesty. That's why."

"Nonsense!"

Lady Janet said politely in an arctic voice, "You seem not unfamiliar with this kind of affair, M'sieu Vaubois. Tell me, if you had been in Sir Gerald Tarrant's position, who would you have wished to come and get you out?"

Vaubois sighed, and met her gaze with a good-humoured smile. "Forgive me if I do not answer you, Lady Janet."

Willie said, "You got men watching the chateau, Réné?"

"Yes. Very discreetly."

"You can tell 'em to move in now." Willie looked along the valley to the pall of smoke rising above the burnt-out car. "I don't reckon they'll find much left there, though."

"I'll get on the radio," Vaubois said. Then, impatiently, "Now, where *is* she? And Tarrant?"

"I'll show you where they ought to be. Can you take the three of us in that chopper?"

*   *   *

Tarrant opened his eyes. The sun had filled the valley with warmth, and the glare had roused him. His body was sore and his joints ached, but his mind was quiet for the first time in many days. He turned his head.

Modesty knelt less than two paces away, gazing out above him at the valley through a gap in the low bushes. The rifle was held loosely in one hand, resting across her knees. She held a stalk of long grass in her teeth, nibbling it absently. The freakish heat was such that she had rolled up the sleeves of her shirt. The front hung unbuttoned. He studied her with quiet wonder, for she was not simply keeping watch. Her face held a look of absorbed pleasure, as if she were drinking in all that met her gaze as she slowly turned her head. After a few moments she took the stalk of grass from her lips and touched it to a rock just beside her. Tarrant was able to make out a large beetle on the rock, examining the proffered stem.

He raised himself on an elbow and said, "Good morning."

She looked at him, a little surprised, smiling, making no attempt to hide what the open shirt revealed of her body. He knew she was not deliberately displaying herself. It simply did not occur to her that it mattered, not here and now, after so much.

"Hallo," she said. "You're not supposed to wake up yet. You've only been asleep for an hour."

Her right arm was blue and yellow with the bruises raised by Sexton's probing fingers, and the sight made him wince. He said, "You haven't slept at all, my dear."

"That's all right." She gestured vaguely about her. "I'm enjoying it."

He wriggled stiffly out of the sleeping-bag and stood up, puzzled, rubbing a hand over his bristly chin. As he looked about him, at the valley and the sky, something stirred in the depths of his being, and next moment a great wave of exhilaration surged through him, so sudden and strong that he caught his breath. Then he understood what she had meant, and reached out to take her hand as she stood up beside him.

It was as if his blood had turned to champagne, by no means wiping out the weariness of his aching body, but making it of no importance. The impact of this totally unexpected sensation caused his head to swim, but he heard himself laugh with joy.

It was over. The long agony was behind him, and he lived again. The cell, the drugs, the probing, the filth, the slimy horror of Clare's monologues, the mounting dread of torment under Sexton's pitiless hands . . . all were past.

Bemusedly, he looked upon the outside world once again.

It was not a pretty valley, with its semi-barren slopes falling to a broad, rock-strewn bottom. But spring had begun, new grass was thrusting from the scanty soil and crevices. The scrubby bushes were wearing green again. Insects darted busily in the air. And above the line of the ridge was a canopy of bright blue sky holding a golden sun.

Modesty said, "It's good, isn't it?"

He nodded. She stood gazing out over the valley as if seeing it for the first time, and despite the dark circles under her eyes her face seemed very young. Tarrant knew that in this moment he was at one with her. The moment would pass, but he felt that he had been born anew from the cave's womb and been granted the gift of seeing the world with new eyes. It was a feeling incomparable with any he had ever experienced, and he knew that he would never be quite the same man again.

With extraordinary happiness singing in his blood he said, "Yes. It's very very good."

The sudden sound of the helicopter as it appeared over the ridge did not startle him. When Modesty touched his arm and dropped to one knee he followed suit. She reached for the haversack and changed the magazine of the M16, watching the helicopter as it tilted and swung along the slope of the valley below them at little more than a hundred feet.

She said, "That just could be reinforcements Colonel Jim's called up, but——"

She stopped. The unmistakable figure of Willie Garvin sat in the open doorway of the helicopter, one arm waving slowly back and forth. Tarrant heard the note of relief in her voice as she said, "They made it, then. And there's our Willie making sure we see him. He knows I've got a magazine of incendiaries here." They stood up again and she linked her arm through Tarrant's, waving the rifle above her head. "Good for Willie. After me, there's nobody more cautious."

Tarrant looked at her and saw that she had spoken with sober approval. He took her hand and began to laugh.

CHAPTER FIFTEEN

In a Whitehall office on a morning in early May, a few minutes after five-thirty, Tarrant unplugged the shaver, put it away in his desk, smoothed a hand over his chin, put on his jacket, and straightened his tie.

Ten minutes later his driver dropped him at Curzon Gate and he began to walk briskly through Hyde Park. The sun had not long risen, and the day was crisp but not cold. He was conscious of a sense of well-being, and looked forward to the thirty-minute walk which would bring him to his flat.

A month had passed since the day when Modesty brought him out of Chateau Lancieux. Of that time, he had spent ten days at Dr. Georges Durand's clinic, undergoing a variety of tests and remedial treatment, and two weeks of convalescence at Modesty's house west of Tangier, the house where she had lived in *The Network* days, set on The Mountain and looking out across the straits. There he had been sumptuously cared for by her steward, Moulay.

She had sent flowers to him at the clinic, and flown out once to Tangier to spend a day with him. At first he had thought it strange that she and Willie made no contact with him, but later he understood and was grateful. Reaction had left him less than himself, and he was glad they had not seen him in his weakness, given to inexplicable bouts of shakiness and emotion which brought

247

tears to his eyes for no reason he could recognise. But this was past and done with. He felt now as he had felt that morning outside the cave, seeing the world with new eyes and marvelling at it, but without the pain and exhaustion he had known then.

During his time at the clinic he had three times laboriously composed and then destroyed a letter of thanks to her, finding the written words stilted and inadequate. He wanted her to be with him, so that she would read in his face some small measure of his feeling, and he remembered now his delight at seeing her that day in Tangier, when his weakness had passed.

When the moment came, she did not stop him or brush his thanks aside, but listened with solemn face and a twinkle in her eyes as he spoke the simple words, then said when he had finished, "There. That's got it off your chest. And now I've some messages for you——"

"Please." He lifted a hand, then felt in his pocket. "It's not quite all off my chest yet. I have a small present for you, my dear. It's quite impossible to find anything adequate of course, particularly for a girl who has everything, so this is just a little memento."

In the padded box he handed her was a charm bracelet with a single gold charm on a heavy chain. Moulay had taken him to a goldsmith who had made the charm to order in three days. Modesty lifted it from the box. "Why, this is lovely. It's a tiny drum, isn't it? I don't quite see why . . . no, wait a moment, there's a lid on it and a little handle—oh!" Her face lit up with delight. "It's a can! A can of grease!"

"Not with contents. I trust the need won't arise again."

She stood up and moved to the window, studying the charm in the light. Round the squat cylinder were engraved the words, *With love and gratitude*—G. T. Aglow with

248

almost childish pleasure, she came back to the armchair where he sat, slipped an arm round his neck and bent to kiss him on the cheek. "What a nice man you are, Sir Gerald. Thank you for a lovely present."

"It's just what you've always wanted?"

"But of course."

"Good. Now, you said something about messages?"

"Oh, yes. First, Fraser and Réné Vaubois set their Portuguese colleagues to cleaning up Mr. Wu Smith's end of the blackmail racket we told you about on the way to the clinic." She sat down. "It just means a notice going out to all contributors that no further payments are to be made to that account. Wu Smith protested his shocked horror to learn that his bank had been used in this way, and he's making all speed to co-operate—so that's that bit. Quinn asked me to thank you for the letter you wrote him, and to say he didn't do a damn thing and was more of a hindrance than a help. That's not true, but I'm just passing the message. And Lady Janet sends you her regards."

"Don't tell me there's nothing from Willie?"

"Willie hates you. You saw the bit with Sexton in the cave, and he says it was wasted on you. He can't be consoled for having missed it."

Tarrant fingered his chin. "It's all very well when you know how it came out. But he'd have died a thousand deaths at the time, as I did."

"The funny thing is, Lady Janet and Quinn wish they'd been there too. Not for technical reasons, like Willie. They just wish they'd seen Sexton get his come-uppance. I'd no idea how bloodthirsty nice people can be."

"He was an evil man. But their desire is theoretical, I fancy. There's no pleasure in the reality. Not even satisfaction. Just . . . I don't know. Relief?"

"That's all. Oh, Willie did send a message. He tells me

that for a healthy male in the later stages of convalescence there's nothing to beat a nice enthusiastic hunk of warm woman——"

"Oh, really, Modesty!"

"Yes, he said you'd say that, and I was to tell you not to talk nonsense about 'at my age' and so on. He suggests a mature Frenchwoman in your case, and if you'd like him to arrange it he can recommend the very one."

"He's a blasted pimp."

Remembering as he walked through the empty park, Tarrant chuckled. The odd thing was that Willie's prognosis had been accurate. During the last few days of his convalescence he sometimes wished he had taken the suggestion less lightly.

He walked on, enjoying himself. Tarrant, the new man. There was no doubt he felt ten years younger than he had done six weeks ago, at the Nato Intelligence meeting. By the end of his convalescence he had been itching to get back to work, and had returned to tackle it with a zest which astonished Fraser. There had been a minor crisis in J Section yesterday, and he had remained at the office to deal with it, snatching a few hours sleep on the camp-bed he kept there. But he did not feel jaded.

A bench stood beside the path where it dipped and curved slightly. Tarrant sat down and took out his cigar case. He had not indulged all night, and could not remember when he had last smoked a cigar at six in the morning, but he intended to do so now. He lit the Punch-Punch claro carefully. The fragrance of it blended splendidly with the clear morning air.

From beyond the rising curve of the path came the sound of a voice raised in exhortation. "Come on, Quinn, you can shove 'arder than that. Loosen your truss and get your 'ead down."

Another voice, breathless. "You . . . weigh a bloody ton, Garvin. Either that or she's got a lead backside."

Something appeared at the top of the gentle slope. It consisted of two or three planks set on four wheels, with a rope attached like reins to the axle of the two front wheels for steering. Tarrant had seen children in the slums riding pram-wheel carts of this kind, but not for many years.

Modesty sat in front, Willie close behind her, his legs extended on each side of her so that his feet rested near the front wheels. Her own legs were drawn up, the long white-and-gold dress she wore rucked back to her thighs. A mink cape covered her shoulders. Quinn was pushing. He and Willie wore dinner jackets. As Quinn straightened up and the cart began to roll down the slope, Lady Janet Gillam appeared beside him. She wore an evening trouser-suit in apple-green velvet which set off marvellously her chestnut hair.

Tarrant stood up, raised his hat and saluted with his umbrella as the cart rolled towards him. Willie jammed a foot against one wheel. The cart swerved and slowed to a halt in front of Tarrant.

Modesty looked up at him with pleased surprise and said, "What on earth are you doing here at this hour?"

"Some of us work, my dear. Did you trade in the Rolls for this?"

"No. Weng's waiting with the Rolls at Queen's Gate. We saw a boy with this when we were driving to the Old Vic, and Willie haggled with him."

"I 'ad to go up to two quid," Willie said. "He was a big kid, about eight."

Lady Janet and Quinn came down the slope arm in arm, and Tarrant greeted them, bowing over her hand. "Is this a celebration?" he asked.

"It's the end of one, Sir Gerald." Janet smiled and

251

inclined her head towards Quinn. "He's off to a flying job in the States tomorrow."

Tarrant would scarcely have recognised Quinn as the pallid, red-eyed young man he had seen at Chateau Lancieux. He was very slightly drunk, but looked older and steadier, and was grinning as he said, still rather breathlessly, "How are you, Sir Gerald?"

"Astonishingly fit, thank you. The best of luck in your new venture."

"Give me a couple of years and I'll probably get the American Colonies back. We've been doing the town. First night of the new Stoppard, dinner at Le Gavroche, and a club-crawl. Have you ever been to a casino with those two crooks?" He nodded to Modesty and Willie on the cart.

"Well, I have to be careful of the company I keep. Is that how you wound up the celebration?"

"Quinn's Benefit," they called it. "A going-away present. Started with a tenner and worked the blackjack table as a syndicate." He laughed. "It was an eye-opener, wasn't it, Jan?"

She smiled. "We came away with three hundred and eighty-seven pounds, and Willie says they weren't cheating, you just have to understand about the odds."

"You can't cheat at blackjack, Lady Janet," Tarrant observed, "so we must credit him with telling the truth for once." He turned to look down at Modesty and said severely, "I'm bound to point out to you that you're showing your knickers."

Willie said in a shocked voice, "Language, Sir G! I'm surprised at you."

Modesty shook her head. "He stops at nothing, Willie love. If you knew the scandalous things he gets up to with a handful of grease and a naked girl, you'd blush for him."

There was a time when Tarrant would have coloured

with embarrassment, but no longer. He was another man now. "You missed a rather interesting occasion there, Willie," he said smugly. Reaching out past Modesty with his umbrella he tapped Willie on the shoulder. "All right, get off. It's my turn now."

Willie looked astonished for a moment, then grinned and edged himself off the cart. Tarrant handed him the umbrella, cigar and hat, and took his place.

"Rest your 'eels 'ere, Sir G., ready to brake——"

"Kindly save your breath for pushing us up yonder slope, my good man," Tarrant said briskly. "And the next one. I intend to see this young lady to her carriage."

Quinn gave a crow of triumph. "Loosen your truss, Willie old mate."

The cart began to roll. Tarrant reached past Modesty and gripped the rope, steering carefully, peering forward over her shoulder. Willie trotted behind.

Quinn took Janet's arm again and they walked on companionably down the slope. After a little while Quinn said, "I'm excited and grateful about the job, but I'm sorry to be going."

"I know. But after a year or two you'll be able to pick up again here, if you want to. And anyway . . ." she pressed his arm, "you know you'd never be permanent for her. Only Willie's permanent."

"Yes. I can't help wondering how permanent either of them's going to be."

"Please, Quinn. Don't."

"Sorry, love. It was an idiotic thing to say. No reason why they should get involved in anything like that again."

"No reason at all."

She thought, "Until one comes along." But she did not speak the thought aloud. Perhaps Quinn's hopeful assertion would prove true, and they would not go away again. Or if they did, surely they would come back . . . ? Time enough to be afraid when the moment came. And it might not come.

She said, "Have you had any good nightmares lately?"

He half laughed. "Just one. More of a bad dream, and that was about Sexton."

"Not so bad as the other kind?"

"Nothing like it. I wouldn't say I'm purged of guilt, but I'm purged of wallowing in it, and that's a hell of a big step."

"Good."

"Are you coming to see me off, Jan?"

"Of course. You and I are the sole members of the Chateau Lancieux Old Comrades Association."

"Well, I seem to remember there were others present."

"Oh, we can't accept that lot." She nodded ahead. "They haven't our amateur status."

On the gently rising slope, Willie was using the brolly to pull the cart now, wearing Tarrant's hat and smoking his cigar.

Modesty said, "We're all going to my place to sleep, Sir Gerald. Would you like to join us for an egg-and-bacon breakfast? Weng can run you home afterwards."

"I'd be delighted." Tarrant lifted his voice. "Pull a bit harder, my man. Nearly at the top now."

"Very good, your honour." Willie dragged the cart over the low crest, stood aside and touched his borrowed hat humbly.

The cart rolled on, Tarrant steering happily as it gathered speed. Modesty lifted a hand and waggled it in front of his face. He was absurdly pleased to see that she wore the charm bracelet on her wrist.